WELL DRESSED FOR MURDER

Well Dressed For Murder

Laverne Rice

Coachwhip Publications
Greenville, Ohio

Well Dressed for Murder, by Laverne Rice
© 2019 Coachwhip Publications
Introduction © Curtis Evans

Well Dressed for Murder published 1938
Cover: Russell Patterson, "Where there's smoke, there's fire."
    (192-) via Library of Congress
No claims made on public domain material.
(Other image use per USC Title 17 § 107.)

CoachwhipBooks.com

ISBN 1-61646-476-3
ISBN-13 978-1-61646-476-9

MURDEROUSLY REFINED
Well Dressed for Murder (1938), by Laverne Rice

Curtis Evans

I.

On October 23, 1938, the *New York Times Book Review* published an unqualified rave review of Yonkers, New York, schoolteacher Laverne Rice's debut detective novel, *Well Dressed for Murder*, giving the novel pride of place over four works produced by the most venerable of British males then working in the crime fiction field, one and all of them members of England's august Detection Club: J. J. Connington (*Murder Will Speak*), Christopher Bush (*The Case of the Leaning Man*), E. C. Bentley (*Trent Intervenes*), and John Rhode (*The Tower of Evil*). "Here is a first novel that is both a promise and a fulfillment," lauded *Times* reviewer Isaac Anderson of Laverne Rice's *Well Dressed for Murder*, expounding:

> A promise in that the early chapters engage the reader's attention at once, and

a fulfillment in that there is not a letdown at the end or anywhere along the
way. The author has given us not only
a well-constructed mystery story with
a surprising, yet perfectly logical, solution; she has also contrived to convey
a vivid impression of horror, the suspi-
cions and the suspense among a group
of people, each of whom knows that
some one of the others is a murderer.
. . . The result is a mystery story that
will make far more experienced crafts-
men look to their laurels.

Three days earlier, James Harvey (1877-
1946)—an unmarried retired bank auditor who
lived in the city of Yonkers with his mother and a
sister and was a contributor to the *Bronxville Review*, located just east of Yonkers in the affluent
and "exclusive" (see more on this double-edged
word below) enclave of Bronxville in Westchester
County, where *Well Dressed for Murder* is set—had
sung a similar hymn of praise to Laverne Rice.
Harvey deemed his younger Yonkers neighbor a
most promising novitiate detective novelist:

New detective story writers have a
way of beginning with something brilliant, but then slowly declining in

quality as the years go on. Miss Laverne Rice in her first detective novel,
"Well Dressed for Murder," fully
lives up to [the first half of the] tradition and we can only hope that her
future work will belie the other half.
After all, there are plenty of other
exceptions to it—notably [Arthur]
Conan Doyle—and the firmness of
plotting and care in execution which
her first book reveals bids fair for
the books to come. "Well Dressed for
Murder" reveals what happens when
a wealthy and civilized family suddenly finds that its pride and joy has
married an actress half his age. Nobody gets along with anybody else
after that, and when the objectionable
bride is bumped off on p. 31 nobody is
very much surprised. There is a general
rush for cover on the part of the family and suspicion is directed the wrong
way so skillfully as to keep the reader
palpitating to the very end. A new kind
of clue, a new kind of murder, a new
kind of detective. Don't miss it.

Despite having received such an auspicious
send-off at her maiden mystery voyage, Laverne

Rice, after having enjoyed this one brief season of success, promptly sailed away off the charted courses of detective fiction, leaving behind no further work of hers, as far as is known, that was ever glimpsed by other human eyes. Yet at least the fledgling mystery writer did not suffer the indignity of a slow tapering off from fine quality of early work, as did her aforementioned contemporaries J. J. Connington, Christopher Bush and John Rhode (as well as, say, John Dickson Carr, Agatha Christie, Ellery Queen and Ngaio Marsh, to name some even bigger names in the field). Happily, after a lapse of over eight decades, Laverne Rice's once highly-praised (if now sadly forgotten) lone detective novel, *Well Dressed for Murder*, is back in print in all its criminal finery, all for the delectation of devoted fans of true detection.

Laverne Rice was born on January 12, 1890, in the Catskills Mountains hamlet of Parksville, Liberty Township, Sullivan County, New York, a stop on a recently completed section of the Ontario and Western Railroad and a future jewel in the so-called Borscht Belt, a region of sparkling summer entertainment resorts that for many decades of the twentieth century catered annually to thousands of native East European Jews, pleasure trippers from New York City. Laverne was one of four children of George Eugene Rice, a

prominent Sullivan County realtor and land sur-
veyor who played a notable role in Parksville's
development as a seasonal tourist magnet, and his
wife, Jenny (Lord) Rice. During the years between
her birth and the First World War, when Laverne
lived in Parksville with her family, the community
changed from a quiet little village to a bustling
rural retreat for big city sojourners, with dozens
of hotels, inns and guest houses springing up in
its vicinity. Reflecting the rapidly altering ethnic
composition of Parksville, a synagogue was erect-
ed in the village in 1907, joining the nineteenth
century Baptist and Methodist churches. Within
a few years, according to Federal and New York
State census records, the majority of the Rices'
neighboring households were headed by Jews, such
as Rabbi Isaac Siegel, merchants Joseph Siegel and
Isadore Greenbaum, boarding house keeper Isaac
Myerson, grocer Rebecca Orseck, bookkeeper
Julius Goldberg, carpenter Barney Smitovsky,
tailor Samuel Backman, butchers Nathan Fradin
and Harry Gross, and bakers Nathan Waskowitz
and Samuel Grossman. (Try as I might, I could
not locate a candlestick maker.)

All three of the Rice girls—Laverne, Mabelle,
and Ethel—became schoolteachers, while their lone
brother, William Allen Rice, worked in Washing-
ton, D.C., as a civil engineer with the Public Roads
Administration (today the Federal Highway

Administration). For thirty-seven years, between
1915 and her death at the age of 65 in 1952,
Laverne's elder sister, Mabelle, instructed young-
sters in Manhattan at the Friends Seminary, a
highly-regarded Quaker-run school that is New
York City's oldest continuously coeducational
institution, while Laverne for roughly the same
time taught third grade at Public School No. 8
in the city of Yonkers in Westchester County
(just north of the New York City borough of the
Bronx). During this time the two sisters resided
separately at apartments in the big city, Laverne
alone in Yonkers at 260 Valentine Lane, near the
neighborhood of Park Hill, and Mabelle with her
designated partner, Agnes Spencer Rockwell, a
Board of Education secretary, in Manhattan at 434
West 120th Street (today Morningside Heights,
off-campus housing for Columbia University).
Slightly younger sister Ethel, evidently more of
a home bird, remained in Parksville with her
father and mother for the rest of her parents'
lives (George died in 1931 and Jenny in 1942),
conducting music classes for students locally at
Liberty High School, a large four-story brick
building constructed in 1912.

Neither the Rice girls nor, evidently, their
brother William, seem ever to have married,
though Mabelle evidently lived for some time, as
indicated above, in a relationship with another

woman. Does the maid Ethel in Laverne's *Well Dressed for Murder* constitute a brief, empathetic nod to the author's then forty-six-year-old unmarried sister? "Ridicule. That is where the gravest hurt comes, I believe," sensitively ruminates the early-twentysomething narrator of the novel, Helen Sherwin, after she and her family and friends have been subjected to hostile press scrutiny arising out of their connection to a high society homicide case. "Scorn and censure are not half so devastating to our little prides and self-respect. True enough they may be, as in the case of our own Ethel, loyal and efficient for years, who was described as a gaunt, spinsterish woman of fifty, with sharp, shrewd eyes. But who can come through days of that sort of thing and be quite the same?"

Similarly, could the spinster private secretary Miss Wicke in *Well Dressed for Murder* reflect something of the qualities of the author herself? "Somewhere in her late thirties, probably, she was tall and wore good-looking clothes of the severely tailored type," observes Nancy of Miss Wycke. "She was even rather handsome in a dark, heavy way that belonged somehow to her independence which, I vaguely realized, was defense mechanism of some sort."

Public School No. 8, where Laverne taught for so many years, was housed in an imposing

1893 Second Empire structure located on Bronxville Road off the prosperous Yonkers neighborhood of Armour Villa Park. Today houses there
typically sell for $500,000 to $1,000,000. Blog-
ger Elizabeth Malyon, who attended PS8 in the
1960s, recalls that "[m]any of the kids that went
there were from well to do families that lived in
the area; many of their parents were high pow-
ered professionals who worked in NYC—a thirty
minute commute by train. There were also a few
UN Ambassador's kids too."[1] At PS8 Laverne took
particular interest in helping her third graders
compose poetry and put on plays. During a 1930
parent-teacher conference held at the school,
at which the case was made for raising the pay
of Yonkers elementary schoolteachers to a level
comparable with that of middle school teachers,
Laverne carefully explained how a myriad of skill
sets had been drawn upon to put into production
"The Little Bedouins," the play her young charges
had performed for the parents that afternoon:

> In the writing of the play, which the
> children did themselves, they got their
> written English, their writing and their
> spelling; in assembling the material,
> they read; in measuring for their cos-
> tumes and scenery, they learned arith-
> metic; in speaking their parts, they

were trained in oral English; in making the scenery, in drawing the pictures
and making the model boats exhibit-
ed to the audience, the children were
trained in manual arts; and in reading
source books, they learned geography.
. . . They also have fine problem work
in planning their play, and, in choosing their committees, qualities of judgment and leadership are developed. . . .
And the children not only enjoy the work,
but they learn from practical experience.

Laverne's interest in the rewards of literary
labor clearly manifested itself when at the age
of forty she enrolled in a creative writing class
at Columbia University in Manhattan. (Among
her classmates were future noirish crime writers
Benjamin Appel and Dorothy B. Hughes.) Two of
Laverne's short stories, "Wings for Janie" and
"Haze," were anthologized in *New Copy,* Columbia University's annual collection of student
stories and sketches. "Wings for Janie" (1931),
an ironic tale about the trial of a husband for
the "mercy killing" of his bedridden wife, was
later included in *O. Henry Memorial Award Prize
Stories of 1931,* appearing with short fiction by
William Faulkner, Wilbur Daniel Steele, and
Booth Tarkington. "Haze" (1932), although not

remotely criminous in its subject matter, is also of interest for its elegantly-composed depiction of the impact of a visit to the stolid Midwest by a young, modern-living New York matron. Possibly it reflects the author's own attitude at the time, when she contrasted life in the Parksville of her youth with that of the New York City of the Roaring Twenties.

The one-shot detective novelist retired from school teaching in 1953 and passed away thirteen years later at the age of 76 on August 11, 1966, at the town of Goshen, Orange County, New York, about fifty miles from Parksville, where she had gone to live with her surviving sister, Ethel, who predeceased her by less than two years in 1964. After a service at the simple white wooden clapboard Parksville Methodist Church—for the construction of which nearly seven decades earlier, her father, a longtime church trustee and treasurer, had raised funds—Laverne Rice was laid to rest after a long life of creative labor, joining her sisters Ethel and Mabelle and her parents George and Jenny in the serenely shaded seclusion of the Rice family plot at Liberty township cemetery.

II.

Let me tell you something. I love this country. Because they took in the Jews. They took in the Irish, the Italians and everyone else. . . . Remember this. There's a lot of Germans in this country fighting for America, but there are no Americans over there fighting for Germany.

> —Eddie Kurnitz in Neil Simon's *Lost in Yonkers* (1990)

I had realized a little amusedly that Ham, without being aware of it himself, was thinking of the procession of clever investigators who marched through the pages of mystery fiction: those brilliant and erudite men, so faultlessly dressed and superbly nonchalant; the disarming unassuming ones who insinuate their subtle deductions with slyly gentle astuteness; the dashing, forthright young chaps—all of whom solve their baffling and intricate problems in such satisfactory ways.

> —Narrator Nancy Sherwin in Laverne Rice's *Well Dressed for Murder* (1938)

On November 14, 1963, one month after the
infamous Sixteenth Street Baptist Church bomb-
ing in Birmingham that claimed the lives of four
young black Sunday School students and just eight
days before the assassination of President John F.
Kennedy in his motorcade at Dallas, Texas, 185
residents of Bronxville, New York, a wealthy enclave located just east of the city of Yonkers and
ten miles north of the Bronx, the northernmost
borough in New York City, formed a Committee
on Human Rights to fight against Bronxville's
notorious exclusion of blacks and Jews from its
community. Bronxville's deliberate exclusion
of Jews, at least, had been the subject of criti-
cal reportage in recent years. Four years earlier
Bronxville's genteel bigotry had been piercingly
anatomized by Harry Gersh in the consensus lib-
eral Jewish magazine *Commentary*, in an elegantly
scathing piece entitled "Gentleman's Agreement
in Bronxville: The 'Holy Square Mile'." Bronxville, New York, wrote Gersh sardonically,

> is a pleasant, handsome suburban vil-
> lage in lower Westchester County, fif-
> teen miles north of New York City. In
> most respects it differs little from other
> fashionable metropolitan suburbs, al-
> though the average income seems higher,
> the residents more homogenous, the

schools superior. . . . Bronxville, however, is unique in one respect. It doesn't
like Jews and won't admit them as residents.[2]

The same year the Anti-Defamation League
wrote more clinically and no less bluntly than
Gersh concerning the troubling prejudice that
characterized that "holy square-mile" of Westchester County:

> The incorporated village of Bronxville
> in Westchester County has earned a
> reputation for admitting to its precincts
> as home-owners or -renters only those
> who profess to be Christians. Accord-
> ing to informed observers, this mile-
> square village, with a population of
> 6500, does not have any known Jewish
> families residing within its boundaries.
> Even in the apartment buildings locat-
> ed in Bronxville there are no known
> Jewish tenants.[3]

Perhaps it is telling that when Laverne Rice
left her family nest at the village of Parksville in
the Borscht Belt's Sullivan County, New York, to
take a bite from the Big Apple and lesser adjacent
fruits, she came not to Bronxville, but to nearby

Yonkers, a diverse city which in contrast with the literally exclusive Bronxville had, as even a casual Neil Simon fan will know, an actual Jewish population. However, Yonkers presented its own issues of ethnic chauvinism. In Yonkers both Jewish children and Christian children from Bronxville attended Public School No. 8, where Laverne Rice taught for over three decades, but David Cohen, a co-op resident in the Bronxville-Yonkers-Tuckahoe borderland, conceded regretfully in a 1959 letter to *Commentary* that the school's "traditions are difficult for the Jewish students. Christmas pageants along religious lines are strongly entrenched; and, despite an increasing number of Jewish students, some teachers insist that the Jewish students participate."[4] It was, after all, just the way things had always been done, so the thinking of these teachers likely ran; what harm could come from simply following a pleasant institutional tradition?

In a bow to the already waning tradition of the classical Golden Age country house detective fiction that was published in both the United Kingdom and the United States between the First and Second World Wars, in which so very little of social reality was allowed to intrude on its deliberately artificial stages, there are no Jewish characters to be found within the murderously refined pages of Laverne Rice's austerely classical 1938

detective novel, *Well Dressed for* Murder, nor for
that matter any non-WASP ethnicities or nation-
alities (with one apparent exception, the presumably Irish Catholic Frank O'Meara) or non-white
races. In peopling her novel Laverne chose to
draw upon her knowledge, however tangentially
derived from her experience teaching in Westchester County's public school system, of the county's
upper crust, its social register set. One finds a
couple named Paul and Ruth Schwaggerman, to be
sure, but there is no indication discernible to me
that the Schwaggermans are of Jewish, rather than
German Christian, derivation. Perhaps Laverne
derived the bulky surname from a non-Jewish
friend, Agnes Schwagerman (1910-1988), a Yonkers resident and schoolteacher at Public School
No. 24.[5]

The fatal events in *Well Dressed for Murder* occur very much in the starchy bosom of a WASP-ish
"old money" Westchester family, the Shephards,
who live in regal isolation outside an unnamed
village in a monumental Federal-style mansion,
with deceptive humility named simply Shephard
House. With both its first and second floor plans
provided in the book (we find a great hall, drawing room, dining room, terrace room, library,
study, sun porch, kitchen, pantry, servants' dining
room, servants' porch, upstairs sitting room, ten
bedrooms, and nine bathrooms), it seems clear

that Laverne Rice modeled Shephard House after graceful and imposing white-columned Hudson River valley mansions like Edgewater, a house originally built by the "aristocratic" Livingston family in the early nineteenth century that today remains situated in rural splendor only fifteen miles north of Yonkers. The late author Gore Vidal, one-half authentic patrician and the other half outrageous pretension, owned Edgewater between 1950 and 1969, during his dominion there composing, in the mansion's elegant octagonal library wing (designed by Alexander Jackson Davis), his cynical trio of semi-hard-boiled "Edgar Box" mysteries, randy quickies that were, to be sure, rather less refined than Laverne Rice's earnest detective novel, a conscious homage to the pristine Anglo-American country house puzzlers of the 1920s.

Trouble begins in *Well Dressed for Murder* when the scion of Shephard House, longtime fifty-something bachelor Hamilton "Ham" Shephard, a sober and respected author of lengthy historical novels, shockingly brings home a showy wife not quite half his age, Jocelyn "Joss" King, a star of popular revues in New York City with a controversy in her recent past. (It seems that Jocelyn, like Agatha Christie a dozen years earlier, mysteriously "disappeared" for a short time.) Sparks only really start to fly, however, after the brazen and brittle Jocelyn cavalierly remodels Shephard

LELONG

Author Laverne Rice attires Jocelyn King in fashionable dresses similar to this Lelong gown, from a 1934 Parisian sketch collection curated by Julia Coburn.

House's renowned Georgian paneled drawing room in flagrant Art Deco style while Ham's brusquely formal sister, Marian, is away on a recreational trip in Europe. A great respecter of family traditions, Marian naturally is furious with Jocelyn's effrontery, as are, in their more understated way, the two other denizens of Shephard House, Marian's and Ham's dependent relations Helen Sherwin and her daughter Nancy, a debutante of five years vintage and heir presumptive to the Shephard fortune, who narrates the story.

Things come to a head at Marian's weekend house party at the desecrated yet still stately mansion. Poshly on the scene when bloody murder shockingly strikes at Shephard House are the several Shephard friends and neighbors: blithe Brooke Bennett and facetious Frank O'Meara, wealthy middle-aged dilettantes and men-about-town; lovely Katherine Haskell, a longtime "warm admirer" of Ham Shephard; and sardonic scientist Dr. Jarvis. Then there are the unhappily married Larry and Irene McIver, show people whom Jocelyn thoughtlessly invited to Shephard House at the same time as Marian's house party, he boyishly charming, she shrewish and prone to theatrics; Miss Wycke, Ham's intensely devoted spinsterish personal secretary; flighty Mrs. Ruth Schwaggerman, who just happened to drop in for a call; and the various Shephard house servants, the latter of whom presumably are "below suspicion," to borrow a term from John Dickson Carr. (Just for the record, these are eight in number: Thompson, the butler; Annie, the cook; Ethel, the housekeeper; Alma and Mildred, maids; Leo, the chauffeur; McAllister, the gardener; and Eddie, his assistant.) Even excepting from suspicion the servants, however, this makes for no less than a dozen possible suspects when Nancy discovers Jocelyn, clad in a stylish black Lelong frock, quite messily murdered in the upstairs sitting room, gauchely bludgeoned with a workman's wrench. We the readers know that narrator Nancy did not do it—surely a mystery writer would not have dared to pull such a hoary trick as late as 1938—but everyone else, surely, is fair game for our sport.

Two handsome young men seem, in Nancy's eyes, to offer the greatest hope of solving the terrible case: Osgood "Oz" Brown, an insouciant neighbor employed as an electrical engineer with a New York firm of architects, who is thought to be smitten, if perhaps only disconcertingly mildly, with Nancy; and an earnest young policeman named Cooper, about whom Nancy observes (in a comparison that must have come readily to the schoolteacher author): "There was something undeniably schoolmasterish . . . the wide-spaced eyes behind their spectacles, the quick appraisal, a general sizing up of who was there as he came on in. The young instructor taking over his class." Both men, as well as Nancy, have their hands full, however, as more mayhem takes place in and around stately Shephard House, including, in classic style, early morning shenanigans in the library as well as two shootings of ill-fated attendees at the fatal house party. Who will be the next to die before the case is finally concluded?

As reviewers noted at the time, *Well Dressed for Murder* is remarkable for the rigor of its mystery plot at a time when many detective novelists were downplaying formally clued puzzles in their mysteries. With this fine baffler the reader should enjoy matching their wits with the sleuths in the Cluedo-like problem of who killed Jocelyn with the wrench in the sitting room at Shephard House. My only regret after completing *Well Dressed for Murder* was learning that Laverne Rice never wrote, to our knowledge, another detective novel, perhaps one set not in swanky Westchester but rather in the author's native Sullivan County. A book entitled, say, *The Corpse in the Catskills* or *The Body in the Borscht Belt*.

Such a story that would have been!

NOTES:

[1] See "Child's Play: 1960s," 28 February 2014, at *My Artsy Odyssey* by Betty Malyon, https://myartsyodyssey.wordpress.com/tag/armour-villa-park/.

[2] Harry Gersh, "Gentleman's Agreement in Bronxville: The 'Holy Square Mile'," *Commentary* (February 1969), at https://www.commentarymagazine.com/articles/gentlemens-agreement-in-bronxvillethe-holy-square-mile/; "Bronxville Residents Form Group to Fight Ban on Jews in Township," Jewish Telegraphic Agency, 14 November 1963, at https://www.jta.org/1963/11/14/archive/bronxville-residents-form-group-to-fight-ban-on-jews-in-township.

[3] James W. Loewen, *Sundown Towns: A Hidden Dimension of American Racism* (The New Press, 2005), 126.

[4] "Perspective on Bronxville," *Commentary* (April 1958), at https://www.commentarymagazine.com/articles/perspective-on-bronxville/.

[5] Ironically the most famous person with that variously spelled German surname appears to be SS-Haupsturm-fuhrer Gunther Swagermann, an adjutant of Joseph Goebbels who on May 1, 1945, helped dispose of the dead bodies of Goebbels and his family in the Reich Chancellery garden outside Adolf Hitler's bunker complex.

WELL DRESSED
FOR MURDER

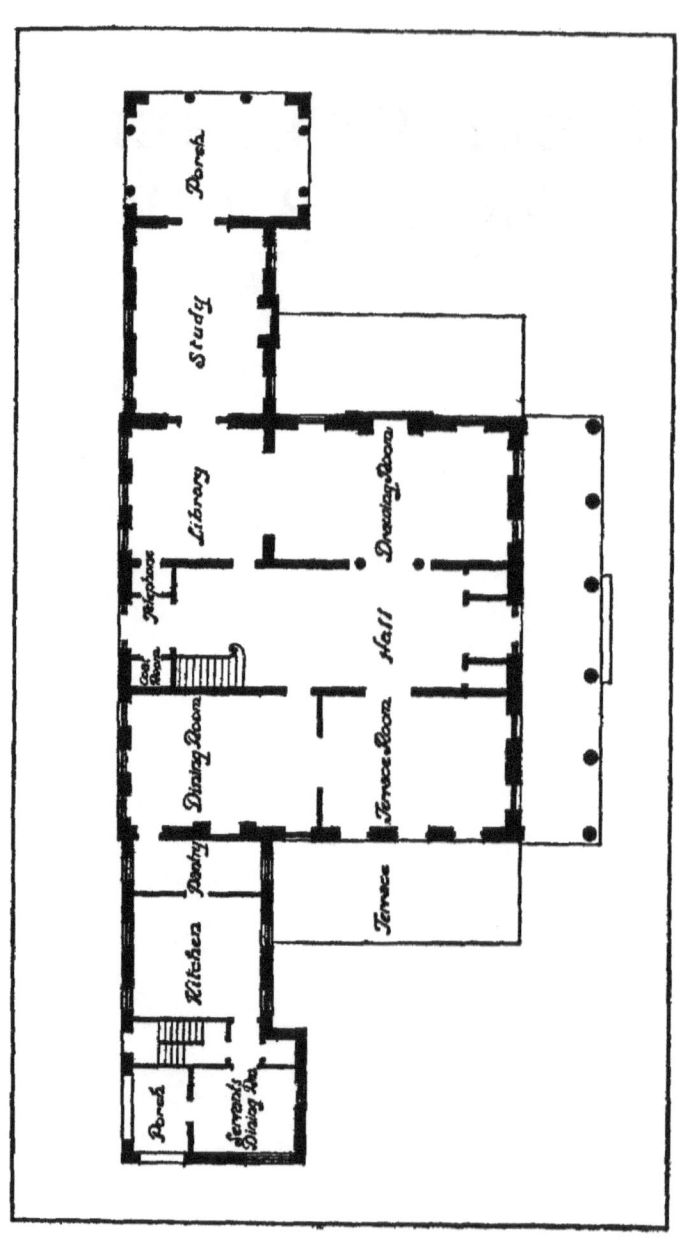

FIRST-FLOOR ARRANGEMENT

1

The house has never possessed a name, has never, so far as I know, borne any of those distinguishing titles of Park or Hall or names derived from great trees around the place. The sort of thing that is usual to similar estates. Known only as the Shephard House, it is so listed and written up in certain of those collections that, variously titled, depict the fine old homes of America. In each of these volumes the photograph which accompanies the section devoted to the Shephard place invariably presents the columned east front. The same view that the photographers chose when they rushed to the scene after that first crime.

Only the central portion with its six tall pillars belongs to the original part. The great wings, north and south, were added later, appendages that have no architectural incongruities so that they seem always to have been there. So it is with the interior. Alterations there have been to be sure, but the final result of many bathrooms, changes

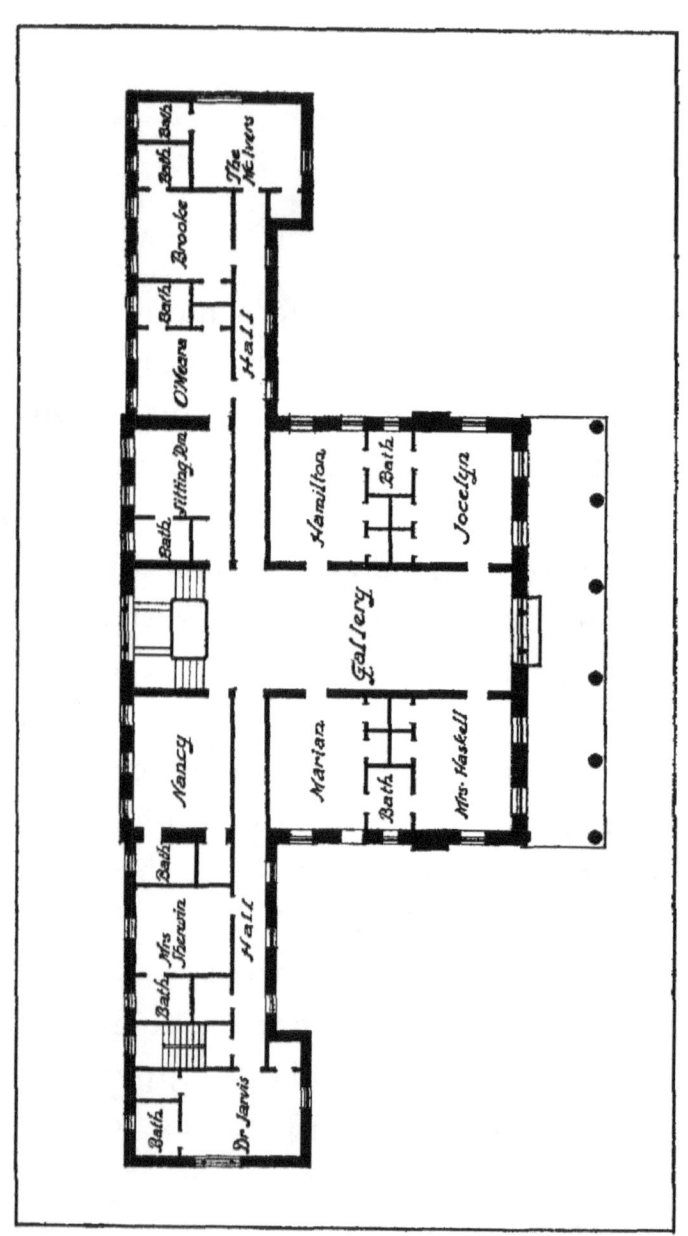

SECOND-FLOOR ARRANGEMENT

in the way of decoration and furnishing, is one of entire harmony.

More of the original grounds remain than are usually left to these places, one-time centers of far-reaching acres. "And round about the house," reads one of those chapters, "were orchards, vine-yards and wellkept borders of flowers." The orchards and vineyards have long since disappeared, but the lawns with great trees and beautifully laid out gar-dens still spread so widely about the house that we have no neighbors in any direction nearer than five hundred feet. The surrounding park has turned gradually into a residential section, a little out-side, but still a part of the rather nice suburban village.

To me there was something wrong and indecent in the way the gracious old house was pictured in the papers of a nation and captioned to match those hideous headlines, so that vast crowds gath-ered beyond the bounds of shrubbery and stared as at something unspeakable.

It was the same with us who dwelt within the house, of course. I have wondered since if it is possible for any group of people to come out un-scathed when crime, spectacular crime, automat-ically makes them subjects for searching investi-gation. Out of a dozen or so people only one is guilty perhaps, but all must be exposed to the same ruthless publicity that puts strange, significant interpretations on ordinary actions, magnifies little oddities, and with blunt descriptive phrases even holds up for ridicule small physical peculiarities.

Ridicule. That is where the gravest hurt comes, I believe. Scorn and censure are not half so devastating to our little prides and self-respect. True enough they may be as in the case of our own Ethel, loyal and efficient for years, who was described as a gaunt, spinsterish woman of fifty, with sharp, shrewd eyes. But who can come through days of that sort of thing and be quite the same?

But so it is. Family, guests, servants—their smallest privacies are invaded with the same relentless thoroughness as the house itself, whose only publicity through several generations of Shephards had been the dignified notice of important events: the marriage of a daughter of the house; a picturesque ball in the wide, portrait-lined gallery on the second floor; dinners in the great dining room.

I love the place. I've loved it since the first time, as a little girl of six or seven, I went there with Mother for my first brief visit, though the newspapers have proclaimed Mother and me as designing interlopers, just waiting for the Shephard fortune to fall into our laps. And since our position in the house figured so prominently in those early accounts of the crime, I would better explain here how we came to be a part of the household.

It is a fact that we are not so closely connected as several others, and I know full well that there are those, nearer in actual relationship to Hamilton and Marian, who speak of our footing there in bitter, even vituperative terms. "Trust Helen Sherwin to worm herself into a soft nest!" Things like that. But they are scarcely fair. True, Mother has a mild, pretty manner, and that, the very quality which makes her adaptable and soothing to have about, they see only as a scheming weapon to defraud them of their natural rights. Human enough, I suppose, and I must admit that Mother in that gentle way of hers seems always to get precisely what she wants.

But after all, it was not design but a chance meeting several years ago that brought it about. Marian ran into Mother at one of the inevitable family gatherings, and on a sudden impulse asked her to stay a little, and then to remain through the winter while she was off for one of her frequent intervals of travel. Mother is the domestic kind who gets actual pleasure out of running a place. The very details which irked and hampered Marian are the natural woman's pastimes to Mother. It left Marian an immense amount of freedom, freedom to come and go, to entertain in the easy, delightful way that is hers, that has always been a tradition of the house.

But when you come right down to it, the thing that really counted was the actual understanding and affection existing between these two so seemingly opposed to each other: Mother, slight and feminine to the point of fragility, and Marian, rather heavily built, with a certain brusqueness about her. And the disgruntled cousins are wrong. Not for a moment did Mother ever put anything over on Marian. "I get somewhat fed up with Ham and me making the whole ménage," she would say. "And besides, I enjoy you, Helen—you're a restful person to have about." And then, with the smile that offset her caustic humor and never failed to charm: "Of course I suspect you of being enormously tactful in handling me, but I find that rather pleasant too."

For the most part ours is a quiet life in the big spreading house, or it was before the coming of Jocelyn. There were numbers of guests. Middle-aged people usually, clever and distinguished in the ways which made them interesting to Hamilton and Marian. But in between these periods of entertaining we were a self-sufficient lot. I don't mean that we were unsocial, but the quiet serenity of our life suited us.

I was not more than eleven when we left the New York apartment that had been ours since my father's death, and went there to live, and with the exception of the years at school, the brief flurry of gaiety when I came out five winters ago, I lived their life. And liked it.

"Possibly we've made you a trifle too serious and bookish," Ham would say. And then: "But you're our kind, Nancy. You have our particular brand of humor, and that makes you belong."

And Ham was right, I think. Resembling Mother more in appearance than my father, who was own cousin to Ham and Marian, I was still their sort. Mother, I know, was faintly disappointed. A varied and continuous round of activities with plenty of young men in the picture—these should be the prized essentials of a young woman of family. But, though Oz was around a good deal, he scarcely constituted a following. And Mother did not quite approve of Oz, who has little in family position as she rates it, and no wealth beyond his own salary as electrical engineer with a New York firm of architects.

But as I said, I liked it. I know now that I enjoyed my position as the only young person in this middle-aged group, only not until Jocelyn came to be a part of our household did I realize this, perhaps. Marian would have her little periodic fits of remorse and join Mother's more continuous proddings. "Heavens, this child should have some young parties!" So now and again there would be a dance given for me in the wide upper gallery, or more often at a hotel in town.

This, then, was our way of life until a scarce six months ago when Hamilton suddenly married Jocelyn King. We were startled, certainly, when the cable came, announcing it. A principal in a recent musical show and not quite half Ham's age—it was amazing, of course. But we were not stunned or dismayed, as the papers have hammered so continuously during all the recent horrible events.

They met on a trip to Europe. Jocelyn had just finished her run in one of those popular revues, and Ham, his newest book complete and ready for publication, was off for one of his frequent stretches of travel.

I don't know, I never could decide, if she cared for him just there at the beginning. Mother was certain that it was the prominence of the Shephard name, the social position. Or standing really, for neither Ham nor Marian troubled to keep up with any regulation social pastimes. But Jocelyn, in her complete absorption of herself, was never aware of any differences in background or education. Perhaps it was just that he was new and different. Certainly he was unlike the men she had known, the ones who later on in noisy crowds of mingled men and girls seemed always to be overrunning our house.

Or his bit of literary prestige might have had something to do with it. Ham writes those long historical novels—they're fictionized biography really—that take a tremendous amount of research. They are vastly accurate and well done and, when they appear at long intervals, are reviewed prominently. But it is fortunate that the Shephard income is ample, for, while the notices bring prestige, Ham's books have a limited sale.

I never thought much about it before Jocelyn's coming, with all the subsequent happenings, but I think he would have loved a wide recognition just as in a vague, unconscious way he must have craved the easy casualness which always characterized his own heroes. For good-looking as Ham is in a quiet, distinguished way, he is just above middle height, stockily built, and looks rather more than the forty-nine he is.

But that Jocelyn was not one of us socially made little difference. Marian, particularly, always adored people who were interesting and different. Never any fussy arbiter of social standards, she took people for what they really were. Much more so than Mother when it came to that.

We had thought to welcome her and make her one of us. But she had no idea of being one of us; she had not the faintest desire or inclination that way. She didn't like us nor did she dislike us exactly. We were never as important as that. For all but Ham there was that faintly amused, faintly contemptuous air. And after that one brief interval following their arrival home it was there for Ham, too, more often than not.

Almost from the beginning she brought her own friends, and all but ignored the family. Everyone, with the possible exception of Ham, might have been just so much background. She was herself and pursued her way as undisturbed and unconscious as if we didn't exist, and for her I scarcely think we did. She went, she came, and, alone or with her accompanying crowds, there was always that ferment of excitement which she seemed to create. She appropriated the whole place, made it hers immediately. And this is important in understanding Jocelyn, I think. It was her own personality more than her position as Ham's wife that accomplished it.

There was nothing you could do about it particularly. Marian cleared out for one of her intervals of travel. That was after Jocelyn had been there for three months or a little more.

"She can't last," Marian assured Mother and me. "She'll demand a place in town in no time. These eighteenth-century rooms are not for her. And for that matter, I don't think Ham is either," she added with her sudden smile. And so, uneasy and disturbed about Ham, of course, but confident that the invasion of the house must be a short one, she had gone for a prolonged stay in France.

But when she returned some weeks later, Jocelyn, far from retreating to an environment more suited to her, had already taken a big step toward creating the kind of thing she fancied; right there in the old Shephard house itself. That changed and mutilated drawing room was a blow to Marian, and, shocked and infuriated as she was, it made her home-coming a tempestuous one.

It was toward the end of her stay in France that the small week-end house party which followed soon on her arrival was planned. A thousand times since I have wished that there had not been the chance meeting with Brooke Bennett in Cannes a day or two before his own sailing, when they arranged this get-together. And then I follow it through and see that it would have made little difference. It could only have delayed what happened.

But planned it had been; otherwise it is doubtful if she would have considered any sort of party at that time, coming as it did right after the upheaval of her return and the unforgettable scene in Ham's study. For, though we had managed to go on so that things seemed natural enough on the surface, still there was a feeling of unease, undercurrents that were disquieting.

Once the plans were irrevocable, however, we looked forward to it, I think. These were friends of long standing, and it was as if in gathering them around us we were making all normal again, asserting in the face of disturbance and change that things were the same.

Brooke was one of those satisfactory guests who radiate a feeling of being where they most want to be that is so gratifying to a host. There was a certain versatility about his liking for people. His friendship for Marian was one thing. Those two could sit for endless stretches and have the best gabs. Just such a one doubtless conceived this very party. His faintly romantic interest in Katherine Haskell was something quite different. And again, there was his pretense of enrapturement for me since I was eleven. And in each relationship he was delightful. A warm admirer of Hamilton and his steady industry, he deplored his own way of life. But even while regretting what he called his indolence and sloth, you knew that he was living in precisely the way that pleased him most: the comfortable ease of his really beautiful New York apartment, travel with indefinite stays where place and people interested him. While his words proclaimed his a wastrel's life, his voice spoke a deep content. I can hear him now, the clear, rather exceptional tone, a quality of depth that was pleasant and oddly arresting at the same time: "A crime the way I'm frittering my life away."

Besides Brooke, there was Katherine Haskell. A friend of Marian's, she too was a frequent guest here. Somewhat younger than Marian, probably in her late thirties, she's attractive in a quiet way. Quiet isn't just the word either. But with no apparent effort she seems always to have attention focused on herself. There's an awareness of her, no matter how many other people are about. To gain all this she seemingly makes no effort, nor is there any effort at response. And yet, indolent as she appears, with her soft voice and slow smiles, she gives somehow the impression of a tremendous energy.

Then there were Dr. Jarvis and Frank O'Meara. I have an idea that Dr. Jarvis was asked with some thought of bringing him and Katherine together. The title is not for medicine. Science, I believe. Anyway, he is with some business organization which occasions a good deal of travel on his part, and Ham met him returning from a West Indies trip two or three years ago. They struck up one of those friendships surprising between people utterly different, and he has been an occasional guest ever since. He seems to have unlimited means and more command over his time than most business people. A bachelor, he lives in an apartment hotel, and I have the feeling, I scarcely know why, that he knows a great many women intimately and is rather proud of it.

O'Meara along with Brooke has been coming here for years. Married, but divorced a number

of years ago, he lives alone, dividing his time between a New York hotel and his own suburban
place which is not more than an hour's drive from
our own. With his shock of prematurely white hair,
he is a striking figure if not good-looking. Heavily built, almost cumbersome, O'Meara refuses to
indulge in the various sports that ordinarily claim
any guest of Marian's. Indeed, he boasts that he
has not walked farther than the curb in years. He
used to conduct a column of comment in a daily
paper, but now what writing he does runs to certain subtly clever sketches that appear intermit-
tently.

Jocelyn was indifferent to the week-end plans
until Mother deliberately brought the subject up.
"Jocelyn, the guest rooms will be filled for three
or four nights. Some people Marian is having. I
thought I'd just mention it." Mother smiled with
what she meant to be good-humored tolerance for
Jocelyn's numbers of impromptu guests.

Jocelyn wasn't entirely attentive; she seemed always to see Mother even less clearly than the rest
of us.

"The McIvers are coming," she said vaguely.

The McIvers, Larry and Irene, had been there a
number of times in the last weeks, usually in the
groups that drove out from New York for a lively
cocktail hour. A novel variation from their regular
haunts, I imagine. These crowds of Jocelyn's were

sure to include Larry. That was obvious even to us who, outside of mealtime, saw them only remote-ly. "They'll stay, I think," she added. "There may be more."

Mother continued, smiling but decided. No, that would hardly do. She made it very clear. Mr. Bennett was to have the Greuze room, so called be-cause of a Greuze portrait over the mantel which Brooke likes, and Mrs. Haskell would have the blue damask room. She went on with her portion-ing out, carefully making no mention of Marian's upstairs sitting room, which has often done duty as a guest room. There would be room for the McIvers in the north wing. (She couldn't quite keep the regret out of her voice. It was plain she had hoped there would be only our own friends with no intruders.) "But that is all there will be room for," she finished.

It came with an ease which was surprising, that scene of Jocelyn's. Mother's smug gentleness called it forth, of course. It was the first open antago-nism; everything else had come under the head of indifference.

"Good heavens," she said, "in all this great sprawling place we can only put up six people!" She said a good deal on just that, worked it up to a real tirade. This was her place, she told us, she was Ham's wife, and she'd ask as many people as she chose. Moreover, she was fed up, completely

fed up with a lot of hangers-on about the place.
No wonder there wasn't room for anyone if all
Ham's relatives were going to camp there perma-
nently. It might have been all right before Ham
was married, but it certainly wasn't now.

It meant little more to Jocelyn, I think, than
any passing fit of deep irritation, the sort of thing
she was accustomed to indulge in if the mood was
on her. And she was not particularly observant
when Mother walked out of the room, her face
white and shocked. Mother could not brook a bad
taste that would give vent to such an outburst.
And doing it before servants—that went beyond
her comprehension.

But at luncheon Jocelyn, characteristically,
seemed to have all but forgotten the incident.
Mother's spent look, Marian's expression of unutterable disgust, my own studied withdrawal—she
was impervious to them all. Toward the close of
the meal she was summoned to the telephone.

"Tell Leo I'll want him to drive me to the station for that two-something train," she said to
Thompson on her return to the table.

"Why not have Leo drive you right in?" Ham
asked her.

She glanced at him briefly. "I'm going on the
train," she told him.

I am not sure she was being deliberately short.
This was so much her habitual manner that it was

difficult to tell. There had never been much more than her flashes of amorous possessiveness, infrequent and fleeting, and Ham, grasping too eagerly at these, was more distressing than when openly flouted. But for a matter of weeks there had quite obviously been something wrong between them. It was Ham who gave the more evidence of it. The fatuous adulation had given place to something like indifference. No, not indifference. Withdrawal describes it better. The only suggestion of a possible cause had been Jocelyn's voice one night, raised to a strident pitch which carried beyond her door. "Keep it? Of course I'm going to keep it!"

But that had happened within the week and did not explain his changed attitude of the time before. Whatever had been the cause, it was a relief to watch Ham's emergence from his hypnotic state.

Miss Wycke, Ham's secretary, rose to leave. On days when there are no guests she has luncheon with the family.

"Leo will drive you to the station," Ham told her. She was off to New York for one of her afternoons of research in the library. Jocelyn watched her go with an expression of utter distaste. On that particular day Miss Wycke was an added exasperation.

"Why don't you get someone else for your secretary, Ham?" she inquired petulantly. "A man. This place is full of women."

A few weeks before Ham would have caught at
this bit of notice directed at him, accepted it as
something amusingly clever. Now he said merely,
"Miss Wycke is an excellent secretary."

"If the McIvers show up before I get back, tell
them I'll be here for dinner." This to Mother with
the same lack of self-consciousness she would have
had for a maid or a stagehand after a burst of tem-
perament.

When she came down she paused in the hall for
a moment. I was taking my riding crop from the
closet and came full on her as I turned. Several
months as it was now since Ham brought her here,
certain of her appearances could still make me
gasp. I know gardenias have done more than their
duty in this respect, but nothing else quite describes the cool smoothness of Jocelyn's skin that,
with cloudy dark hair and black-fringed gray eyes,
gave her a kind of startling loveliness. She stood
glancing into her handbag, that final checkup of
small contents. She didn't go into Ham's study to
say good-by, and again, it was probably no purposeful slight. Intent on something else, it didn't
occur to her.

"Stunning dress, Jocelyn," I said.

"Lelong," she answered briefly without looking
up. Neither was this a snub except in so far as
indifference is always slightly insulting. Satisfied
with her bag, she closed it and went out to the car.

2

It was like our old-time comfortable ease, having tea in the library that Thursday. Despite its size the library is a cozy room with its pine paneling and pink-coated hunting portrait over the fireplace. The recessed arched bookshelves fill all four sides of the room, and the warm red hangings, the soft colors of the deep chairs and divans as the fire caught them, made it extraordinarily pleasant that afternoon.

Jocelyn had not returned, and just the McIvers were there as her guests. The McIvers have a dancing act which had been part of a floor show at one or two night clubs, but they seemed to have had nothing recently. Larry, quite obviously the younger, is good-looking. Tall, lightish and entirely likable, he is a good deal on Oz's type. I don't know why this should have been surprising, but somehow I still expect a professional dancer to be sleekly theatrical. They were a pleasant enough pair, particularly with Jocelyn absent, for it was

Jocelyn that Irene watched with all the awareness of the jealous woman.

Marian's laugh sounded out over and over as she sat listening to one of O'Meara's tales. It was a pleasant sound and somehow reassuring after the tension of the days since her return.

It was a pleasantly relaxed interval, more so than any since Jocelyn's coming months before had created an atmosphere of unrest, an excitement more tempestuous than stimulating. Mother presided over the silver tea service instead of Marian, and Larry McIver was standing near, running on in his cheerfully ingenuous way to her, and to Katherine Haskell, too, when she turned toward him. Larry was enjoying himself, but Irene was ill at ease without Jocelyn there. She disliked and distrusted Jocelyn; still, she was her kind as these people with their talk of a recent horse show were not.

It was the first time any of the three men, Brooke, O'Meara and Jarvis, had been there since Ham's marriage, and I think they were all mildly curious in a half-humorous way about Ham's girl bride, as O'Meara had already dubbed her just after his arrival, when with Marian he surveyed the wrecked drawing room. "Well, well! Where is the girl bride that wrought the changes?" he wanted to know.

It was the first time for Katherine Haskell, too, for that matter. She sat now talking to Dr. Jarvis, her own responses scarcely more than monosyllables and slow smiles. She was lovely today, her dark hair that always has a shine to it parted sleekly in the middle and done in smooth coils over her ears. A creamy, light beige cloth dress with only a wide black belt to relieve its smart severity. Gradually, in the three years following Stacy Haskell's death, the idea that she and Ham would one day marry had grown to a more or less settled conclusion. Then had come the cable announcing his sudden marriage to Jocelyn.

I stopped beside Marian and O'Meara with a tray of cakes.

"You've had enough, Frank," Marian told him.

He helped himself before he turned to her, reproachful and accusing. "Is this, then, the fine old Shephard hospitality famed through the years?" he asked. "The groaning board, the cellar aflow, the guests warmed and cosseted? Sit down, Nancy." He moved his heavy frame over to make room for me beside them. "In you, at least, are the gracious old traditions perpetuated and carried on. How's the new sister-in-law?" he inquired affably of Marian.

"Frank, I feel like the Victorian maiden aunt: tolerated, allowed about, because I must have a home, poor old thing. She's as bad mannered as she is beautiful—to reverse the fairy-tale lingo. And she is beautiful. I'm a just woman and I admit she's extraordinary as far as looks go."

"I know that," he told her. "It's those other little touches that you do with the gentle hand that interest me. I know about the beauty. I saw her show—the important one. I even wrote quite a good piece about it. And I've seen her testimonial photographs on the back covers of our best periodicals. The Shephard background shows up nicely." He grinned at her with cheerful malice. "And last year, when she did her disappearance act, I saw her pictures in all the papers. Very pretty pictures they were, too," he said and took another cake.

"A play for publicity like everything else." There was contempt in Marian's voice, and by "everything else" it was patent that she meant her marriage to Ham.

"Ah"—O'Meara grinned again at her virulence—"now those are the pungent, revealing bits I like to get my nose into. Well, she had her publicity and plenty out of that. Ran the show an extra six weeks, I'd say." With their voices slightly lowered because of the McIvers, I left them to what would have been a good gossip had not Ruth Schwaggerman dropped in for a call at that moment.

She was all gay apology as she made her way across to Marian.

"I didn't know I was barging in on a party. I saw you were back—saw it in the papers—and I just suddenly decided to drive around and have a look at you." Her smile took in the room; she knew everyone there except Dr. Jarvis and the McIvers.

I was a little surprised, amused too. Marian and Mrs. Schwaggerman were scarcely on a solid enough footing to bring Ruth over in this rush of welcome. Theirs was a casual friendship, brought about through Brooke or O'Meara, probably, both of whom know the Schwaggermans rather well.

She finally settled between Marian and Frank with an allusion to a cocktail meeting of the day before, a casual encounter, apparently, on which she now rallied Frank.

"I rescued him," she told Marian. "If I hadn't happened along he would have been taken up by the wrong people."

"So now you follow me right down here. Brazen hussy!"

She laughed, no embarrassment that his words suggested a mention of the house party, a knowledge she had just blithely disclaimed. She plunged at once into a continuous chatter of bright comment that reached out and drew in the others, a brisk sparring back and forth, with her little exclamatory cries and shrieks directed at Brooke, who played up to her in a lazily amused way.

"Nancy"—she had worked her way around to where I sat with Brooke and now dropped down beside me—"what are you up to these days? You young things amaze and astound me."

This was consummate flattery, and I laughed in frank derision to hear her impinging on me a social round that exceeded, or even matched, her own whirling pace.

"They're terrible, aren't they?" She appealed to Brooke, persisting in her portraiture of me as a fast-stepping young thing. "It's a sign of the times or something."

It was Brooke who engaged her attention now; she hadn't maneuvered herself into this position to talk to me. Rich, good-looking and unattached, Brooke was attractive to women, but he was adroit and clever, never allowing himself to become involved. This was something I knew instinctively, rather than from any firsthand observation, for on his appearances at our house he was the person whom Marian found so eminently satisfactory, traveled and intelligent, with a ready wit that matched her own. In another environment, in the young married set of Mrs. Schwaggerman, for instance, he probably became a somewhat different person, interested in women as women, instead of the pleasant relation of give and take that he bore to Marian.

Something of all this, I was thinking, had changed the quality of the afternoon since Ruth's arrival. It was gayer, certainly, noisy with a rush of talk and continuous gusts of laughter, but something that was infinitely satisfactory had been dispelled. This sounds farfetched, even priggish, for there was nothing of importance. It was in the glances that Ruth bent on the men, her quick sizing up of Irene McIver—to Ruth all other attractive women are potential enemies, I fancy—her practiced eye registering the subtle details of Katherine's dress. Too intangible to be pinned down with these minor bits, it was there nonetheless. Into Marian's atmosphere of easy comfort and a deep content, which I have come to see is rather rare, Ruth's invasion had brought the more usual one of strife; strife for notice and place, strife for men. No, she would never become one of Marian's intimates. But the withdrawal would be unconscious on Marian's part; she just didn't run to the kind of thing that passes for amusement with so many women these days, a constant rushing about, an anxiety to be seen at the right places, and the excitement of new men and the competition of their appropriation.

"Do you know what I'd like?" Ruth was saying to Brooke now. "I'd like to go through that lovely old gallery. I'm always enchanted with it," she averred to me, though she had been there only once to my recollection.

Brooke's laugh derided her desire to stare at old portraits, and he made no move to carry out the suggestion.

She was not discouraged. "Marian," she called out above the clatter of voices, "I'm trying to make Brooke take me for a walk through the gallery. I feel such a nice person when I get in a setting like that—stately and grand."

"Brooke"—Marian swung around promptly—"if a lady wants to feel stately and grand it's your business to see that she does." He flashed her a smile, got what he wanted in her answering glance and rose, pulling me up with him. "Come on, Nancy, we'll take the lady on the grand tour."

Did I imagine it, I wondered, or was I now witnessing an example of his discretion? An affair that had progressed far enough was finished as far as he was concerned, and she had missed the signals or refused to see them. But I had no idea of trailing along and left them in the hall; I must see Annie a moment, I said and went toward the kitchen, leaving Ruth unhampered. They were gone only a short time, however, and on their return to the library, Brooke steered Ruth around to Marian and O'Meara and then drifted back to his place beside me.

It was right after this that Jocelyn came. Through the windows I had seen her drive to the rear entrance. I didn't recognize the man, just noticed that he was large and middle-aged and seemed to belong to the opulence of the long, light-colored car. She didn't get out for several minutes while they sat talking earnestly. Then abruptly, angrily, she opened the door, slammed it and left without any further farewell. Another moment and she was standing in the library door, smiling, lips slightly parted in that eager breathless look she could turn on with such tremendous effect. Not a hint of the recent flare-up outside. She was very beautiful in that instant of pausing. Beautiful—and there was something appealingly young about the black dress with the broad, oddly cut white collar, her hat in the hand that hung at her side.

Hamilton had not returned from his walk—he had left just before the arrival of the first guest—so it was Marian who rose and managed the necessary introductions.

Jocelyn's entrance had interrupted the talk here and there, and for a minute the room seemed suddenly quiet.

"How's Oz?" Brooke was asking me. "If I'm to tolerate all these rivals I'm entitled to the privilege of catechizing you. The Brown boy will do to start with." Close to thirty now, Oz is still the Brown boy.

Then Marian was there and he had Jocelyn by the hand. She was looking at him in a sort of startled surprise that was effective and vastly different

from the careless notice she usually accorded the
old family friends. His tall good looks, perhaps,
his air of finished distinction.

I felt an absurd jealousy. For so long I had held
my position as the only youthful member in this
middle-aged household, with Brooke and O'Meara
my special devotees.

"Sit down, Jocelyn," he said when Marian had
moved on to rejoin O'Meara, and she took the
place on the divan that Irene had just left. But after that first flash of interest she was remote and
withdrawn. It occurred to me that something in
the exchange of words outside had given her this
distrait and oddly quiet attitude. Her eyes watched
Brooke as he talked, but her own responses were
vague, as if she scarcely heard what he said.

I was piqued. Brooke was alert and interested, a
quick shift from the pleasant raillery he had been
carrying on with me a moment before. It was plain
that Ruth was not pleased either; she called out
to him once above a burst of animated talk in her
own group, but though he turned a quick smile on
her and on the others, he made no polite effort to
break away and go to them. And when Ruth was
leaving a few moments later, he called a good-by
across the room and stayed where he was. It was
Jocelyn who stood abruptly.

"Is Ham here?" she asked, her eyes turned toward the study. Her tone struck a curiously urgent
note in all the mild chatter.

"He hasn't come in from his walk," Mother told her.

"Ham trudges out a certain number of miles, guests or no guests." O'Meara's tone was gay, but even he seemed to feel the currents of unrest that Jocelyn always managed to stir up.

With great abruptness she turned and went over to Marian, who had just come back from seeing Mrs. Schwaggerman off. She spoke softly, hurriedly. Marian looked astonished and then seemed almost to recoil from her.

Thompson appeared at that moment and called Jocelyn to the telephone. She stood an instant longer, looking intently at Marian, before she wheeled about and went swiftly to the telephone room which opens from the library. Her words were clearly audible through the open door.

"Why?" she said briefly in answer to something, and added, "I see. . . . All right." Then quickly, as if she interrupted, "Ham, when you do come, stop in my room first. Right away. No"—with the irritation more pronounced—"I can't tell you now.

"Ham says he'll be late," she said when she came back, and without troubling to explain, turned as if to go.

"Not walking out on us, Joss?" Larry went to her quickly and, talking, moving aimlessly, it seemed, they went into the hall. They were still there, near the east door where they had progressed when, shortly after, the others began drifting out and up the stairs.

3

Tea is tea at the Shephard house, but before dinner there is one excellent cocktail, two for those that wish. I was down early, expecting to see Mother, who was already gone when I stepped into her room after dressing.

Marian was in the terrace room giving deft, rearranging touches to a great bowl of zinnias. I suspected that she was designedly there to steer the party away from Jocelyn's piece of flagrant modernism across the hall. Marian was looking particularly well tonight. She had no flair for clothes really. Her good, expensively conservative things all had a certain sameness as she wore them. But tonight there was a glow and excitement about her that made the dark blue lace with the silver touches vastly becoming.

"This about ends the garden flowers," she said as she turned. "After this rain they're due for a freeze, I'm afraid."

"You look all lit up," I told her. "Nice."

She smiled. "Did Hamilton come in?" she wanted to know. Thompson came through the door for a look at the fire, and she repeated the question.

"Why, yes," he told her. Mr. Shephard had come in and gone right up without any stop in his study. It was shortly after he had finished in the library.

"I might run up," she said without explaining, seemed to consider it briefly and then abandon it in forgetfulness as Mother came in.

And after all, Hamilton was dressed and down in good time, ahead of some of the others, though everyone was there when Thompson appeared with the tray. Except Jocelyn. I was not surprised particularly. Jocelyn would never be cheated of an entrance, and tonight would be a fairly good one, though the audience was made up largely of these middle-aged friends.

Still nagged by the small torment of Brooke's immediate engrossment, I waited her impending appearance, timed to a moment. White gown and the emerald bracelets which had belonged to Ham's mother. And from that instant on everyone else would seem more or less shadowy background, the way an artist creates one figure in a picture of more vitally vivid stuff.

But glasses were being refilled here and there, and still she did not come. She was not there when Thompson announced dinner.

"Ham, what's keeping Jocelyn?"

Hamilton looked embarrassed at Marian's question. It was not so much embarrassment at her tardiness as at a casualness that never troubled to consult him.

"I didn't see her," he said. And then in some confusion, realizing that this was odd in itself, "I came in late and just made tracks in an effort to be on time." He managed a laugh, but it was not greatly amused. "I'll go up and see. She may be asleep." And he dashed off in the new, overlively manner.

"She may have decided on a small nap and not wakened yet." Mother was still upset at the morning's experience, but she kept up her pretense of nothing wrong. This seemed possible. In fact, Jocelyn had done just that on at least one other occasion.

Hamilton came back and his annoyance was obvious now, though his eyes behind their glasses were determinedly humorous.

"She's not there," he said and glanced at Marian. "And I don't think she's been there—not to dress."

Marian's face showed no surprise. It was as if she said, "Well, that's to be expected along with everything else." But it was a fleeting look, and she asked with just the right shade of concern, "Thompson, did Mrs. Shephard go out after tea?"

But Thompson disclaimed any knowledge of her going, and no, Mrs. Shephard had left no word, no message. He would ask the maids, but he was quite certain.

"Curious," Hamilton said. But he was aware, as was every one of us, that this careless indifference was neither unusual nor extraordinary. "Some appointment or other doubtless came to mind." Ham attempted to carry it off as something of a joke, a vagary of the temperamental woman of the stage. But he was uncomfortable. His face, for all its tolerantly amused smile, was displeased. It struck me favorably at the time, another sign that the groveling devotion might be a thing of the past.

Marian alone suggested no explanation. Neither did her silence conceal her contempt for such impossible behavior. I don't believe anyone was really disturbed. O'Meara, Brooke, the others who had had no previous experience, seemed to take their cue from the rest of us, were a little amused, I think, at this swift initiation into the pyrotechnic antics of Ham's wife. Even as they contributed their own polite suggestions of something important and urgent, the conclusion was that she had just walked out to some more enticing engagement, forgetting to leave any word or, what was just as possible, deliberately omitting it. Jocelyn took delight in doing the bizarre and unexpected.

But it was difficult for Ham. "She may have meant to return," I said. "I did notice when we were having tea that she seemed in a hurry to get away." I looked at Brooke and Irene, who had been of our group.

"You know, I believe she was." But Brooke's very promptness made it almost amusingly obvious that he had noticed nothing of the kind.

"That's very likely it," Mother said smoothly. "I think we'll not wait any longer." She glanced at Marian, still silent and disdainful. "We'll leave her place. Then if she does hurry in later . . ." The most plausible of the offerings was accepted and we went in to dinner.

It was back in the terrace room that we returned for coffee. I was sitting between Brooke and Larry on the Immense Chippendale sofa, the low table in front separating us a little from the others. Larry was silent and morose. Though there had been no mention of Jocelyn through dinner, he turned suddenly and said, "Well, isn't he going to do something about it? Telephone or something?" He looked at Ham with open annoyance.

As dinner had passed without word from Jocelyn, Ham's discomfiture had grown. It was the more discomposing, of course, that he had no means of trying to locate her, no way of knowing with whom she might be, so little was he in her confidence.

"I don't think she intended to be away." Larry's insistence had something unpleasant about it.

I started to speak, to reiterate, I suppose, the sort of inane thing we had said before dinner.

"Oh, I know," he said quickly, "with Jocelyn it's first, last and always a grandstand play for attention. I thought myself she'd come in when we finished the soup."

I nodded. "Contritely lovely, a little mysterious about what delayed her."

He grinned briefly. "Sure, I know. Her bag of tricks is not large, but it's a good act and the spot stays focused on Jocelyn."

"And one finished performance is better than any amount of variety," Brooke supplied smoothly.

"She intended to be here," Larry said doggedly.

"What makes you so sure?" I asked, a little curious.

"Why"—he was suddenly confused, reached for a cigarette and lit it—"just something she said." And he was frankly relieved when Mother came in and called from across the room, "Nancy, Osgood is on the phone." And then to Marian as she caught her expectant look: "I forgot them, Marian. I'll go back—"

"Don't be foolish," Marian told her. "It makes no difference. I just thought as long as you were going up . . ."

"A folder of photographs," Mother explained as I stopped inquiringly. "A blue folder. On the desk in Marian's sitting room."

"I'll bring it, Marian," I called back on my way to the telephone. "I'll be going on up for a wrap."

"Don't bother, Nancy!" Marian's voice sounded after me, and later that night I was to recall that cry, and wonder if there was some sudden sharp anxiety in it.

And so it was I who discovered Jocelyn's body on the floor in Marian's sitting room, lying just inside, and out of the path of the door so that once in the room and the switch at the left pressed, I was standing almost beside it.

I cried out, I know, and the sound of my own voice was frightening. Alma, who had been doing the rooms for the night, rushed in from O'Meara's room which is next, and after one terrified look with her fist pressed into her cheek began running and screaming toward the stairs.

I didn't run after her. Jocelyn was dead. I knew that. And yet it seemed that someone should stay with her until help arrived. I was still there when Brooke and Dr. Jarvis came, the others following close but staying just beyond the door.

She had fallen so that her head touched one of the feet of a small tiptop table, and the table was pushed a little out of place. She was lying face down. My eyes stared in horror at the mutilated back of her head and the part of her face that was visible. She was still in the black Lelong frock, the wide white collar crumpled and stained. There was an ugly irregular stain on the burgundy carpet, too. Almost at my feet and within reach of her hand lay her bag and gloves, but the small black hat had been flung wide and now stood tilted against the valance of a chintz-covered chair.

It was Dr. Jarvis who bent over her completely. Brooke, beside him, sent his quick glance in turn to each of those scattered possessions on the floor.

"You haven't touched anything, Nancy?" he asked softly.

I shook my head. Touched anything! I was still standing in that one spot, frozen, unable to move.

Dr. Jarvis straightened. "Jesus!" It came out in a hissing whisper. The two men looked at each other, and then for the first time Jarvis seemed to be aware of me standing there beside them. They both made those involuntary motions, but it was Brooke who took my arm and propelled me out of the room.

Jarvis closed the door. I have a confused recollection of exclamations, white, shocked faces, of hearing Dr. Jarvis explain, and his words passed on to those farther down the hall. But I have no clear picture of those moments. And while my eyes had seen it, I entirely missed the significance of the large wrench lying on the floor near Jocelyn's body. I had not seen at all the small statue flung into an armchair, one of a pair of bronze figures which have stood for years on a narrow console table beneath a wide mirror in the gallery outside.

There was talk while we got ourselves downstairs, the partly hushed talk that death produces, the shocked horror of a death by violence.

"Then she must have been there right along—she didn't go out after all," someone said.

Jarvis as well as Brooke had observed the small possessions flung about the floor. "She never got past that door." His voice was grim.

A look passed between Mother and Marian. A conscience-stricken look, I thought. They had been so sure she had walked out in her usual indifferent fashion that they had not bothered to be alarmed.

It was then that the great east door swung back and Ham stood there. With his hand on the brass knob, he looked at us surprisedly. Massed at the foot of the stairs, silent and staring, we must have presented a curious sight when but a few minutes before he had left us in that pleasantly relaxed interval between coffee and settling down for bridge.

He had evidently stepped out for one of his turns on the long porticoed porch. In the excitement I had not missed him or given any thought to his absence. There was an instant when no one spoke or moved. It was Brooke who pushed out from the rest of us and went to him.

"There's been an accident, Ham." Brooke spoke quietly. "It's Jocelyn—"

"Where is she?" Ham kept his eyes fixed on
Brooke. The damp of the cold fall rain was coming in, and Dr. Jarvis went over to shut it out,
Ham's hand on the heavy knob only loosening its
hold as the door was pushed firmly back.

"She's upstairs, Ham." Brooke's voice was still
quiet and controlled, but he watched Hamilton
anxiously, putting out a detaining hand as Ham
made an involuntary move in the direction of the
stairs.

"Wait!" Brooke sent a helpless glance to the rest
of us and tightened his grip on Ham's arm. "Wait,
Ham. There's something else. It's—it's murder,
Ham." He got it out.

"Murder?" There was something dreadful in the
incongruous quiet of the echoed word. His bright,
dark eyes behind their glasses sought out Marian
as they had before dinner at Jocelyn's failure to
put in an appearance, but when he spoke it was to
Brooke.

"When did she come in?"

"She hadn't been away," Brooke told him.

Ham watched Brooke, trying to take it in, slowly
comprehending. His broad shoulders didn't slump,
his square jaw never slackened. It was Brooke
whose hand worked at the handkerchief which
edged the pocket of his dinner jacket, whose face
twitched nervously. Then Ham jerked at his arm

to free it, and together, as at a signal, they started down the hall. We parted to let them through, and they went up the stairs, a heavy, measured tread.

The bell rang, and Jarvis, who had stayed where he was after wresting the knob from Ham's hand, opened the door. I had completely forgotten Oz and the telephone call which had precipitated my finding of Jocelyn's body. He looked a little astonished as he reached forth a hand to greet Dr. Jarvis.

"What's up? What you all playing?" he wanted to know. And then, as Jarvis began explaining in low tones, he stood, an arm held in suspended motion over a Chinese chest, unaware that Thompson had taken the coat from his hand, eyes fixed on Jarvis.

His subdued nods of greeting for O'Meara and the McIvers, as he came across to me, were in odd contrast to his gusty entrance.

"Ham upstairs?" he asked quickly and was off up the steps himself, a little too much the manner of a small boy fearful of losing out on any of the excitement.

Again it was Dr. Jarvis who was first and telephoned for the police in those meticulous tones that even now seemed to hold a conscious precision. The rest of us, curiously still and inactive, stood silent and watched him.

"Who comes?" he said when he turned back to us. "What happens in a place like this? They can't leave it to the village police—"

"The county would come in on it, I'd say," O'Meara answered him.

There was talk in the short wait. The usual thing of recalling the last moments of the person gone.

"She stood right over there with Mr. McIver when I went up. Right over there by the door."

"Jocelyn never went into that sitting room. I don't believe she's been in there a half-dozen times in the months she's been here." That was Mother, and she clung to a chair to steady herself as she spoke.

There was but a short interval to wait, so that Ham and Brooke were still upstairs when the police car arrived. It was Rumsey, the village chief, and another man. Neither was in uniform, though I had expected to see blue-coated figures. In a way their coming brought relief. The quick, clipped questions and sharply penetrating glances were like a dash of something cold and reviving after the inertia of shock. Jarvis led them upstairs, and after they had disappeared those of us left below again took up that vein of futile talk. What had taken her to Marian's sitting room? How had anybody gotten in? There had been a robbery in the park a month or so ago. That sort of thing.

It was not long before Rumsey came back down. He looked around. "Telephone?" he inquired and saw the hall phone as he put the question. He looked us over while he waited an instant for his number and asked for Dr. Stanwix. In a few terse sentences to the medical examiner he gave words to the picture imprinted in my mind. "Done with a wrench," he said. "Yes, Crichton Park. The Shephard place." He gave explicit directions. "You can make it in fifteen minutes," he said and hung up.

"Who's the family here?" he wanted to know as he straightway reached for the telephone again.

"Mr. Shephard is upstairs," Marian said. "She was his wife. I—"

"Send me Cronyn," he was saying, "and Teeple—"

He had been listening to Marian, however, and looked to her to continue as he replaced the telephone and stood.

She explained the relationships, and his eyes rested on each of us in turn, and on our guests, as she mentioned them and their arrival that afternoon. Brooke and Ham, with Oz trailing them, came down while she was talking. He knew Ham, of course, and Oz, the rest of the family too, as police in a small town are more or less familiar with everybody in it.

"Now who was the last one here to see Mrs. Shephard alive?" he demanded.

We looked at each other. Who was? She had
stood by the door talking to Larry when I went up.
Beyond that I did not know. We were still making
efforts to determine who had been with her last
when Cronyn and Teeple, the two patrolmen, arrived. Rumsey stopped to station one outside, and
to the other: "Go on up, Teeple. Slade's up there.
Don't let anyone in that room until Doctor Stanwix gets here," he ordered and was back at the job
of establishing the last to see Jocelyn.

But it didn't turn out to be easy. It narrowed
down finally to Larry's going out on the terrace
and Jocelyn turning back to the room. That was
all Larry knew; he hadn't seen her go toward the
stairs. When he came in she wasn't there, and he
had gone on up to his room in the north wing.

Thompson had not seen Larry come in, but he
supplied the fact that Jocelyn had made a telephone call. She had called from the telephone
room off the library, however, not the hall. He
was setting the library to rights; he'd been in and
out. He didn't know whom she called. He was under the impression that she hadn't gotten her party at first and had tried someone else. The only
thing he had heard her say was, "No, it's not that.
It hasn't anything to do with them." This was just
as he came back from a trip to the pantry, and
the words had carried out as he stepped into the
room.

On being asked if she had sounded excited he hesitated, and Hamilton looked up sharply. "Well—yes. But Mrs. Shephard was always . . ." He paused and it was plain he was feeling for some way to express the fact that Jocelyn always pitched everything high. "She was usually in a great hurry," he finished.

Apparently, then, it was Thompson who had last seen her. But he hadn't observed her going up. He had carried the rest of the tea things to the pantry, and when he came back she had gone.

The bell rang, but Rumsey, not Thompson, opened the door to admit the medical examiner. A youngish man whose bright, dark eyes roved over us impersonally while he listened to Rumsey. He asked no questions nor made any comments beyond a nod as they moved from their detached position by the door, and Rumsey indicated the stairs.

The rest of the servants were rounded up then. "Now let's have what you know," Rumsey said, and his voice was sharply audible to us still lingering in the hall. As it turned out they knew little. It was a time when they were all at work in kitchen, pantry or dining room. No one had been on the second floor with the exception of Alma. She had gone up in answer to a ring from Katherine Haskell, who had asked to have a small bit of pressing done on a dress.

"A great crease right here," she said to Marian, drawing her fingers across the shining smoothness of her skirt.

At this point Rumsey plunged in with his rapid, almost browbeating questions. Flat assertions, too, that he seemed to expect would bring admissions when his questions failed.

Up in Marian's sitting room the medical examiner finished his work and came down to telephone the district attorney in deliberately low tones, his back to the room. Flashlights were taken, the wrench and bronze statue examined. In a confused way I was aware of men striding through our house, of others outside with electric torches, of the group of frightened servants huddled at the rear of the hall before the dining-room door, where Rumsey relentlessly questioned them. Of windows examined and the shrubbery beneath plied with light. Of the district attorney arriving with two men and going directly upstairs.

There was the beginning of that long and baffling search for gloves. For gloves there must have been, they decided. That night, however, in the midst of it as I was, I knew little. It was only afterward, from scattered talk, the newspapers, that I was able to piece it all together. But it was obvious from the first that the bronze statuette had been taken in as the weapon and then discarded for the heavy wrench which lay beneath the radiator.

It was when they reached this point that Eddie was sent for. Curiously I watched him taken through the hall and up the stairs by the uniformed officer. Eddie is a nice youngster who assists McAllister, the gardener, about the place and has a knack for handling all sorts of small mean jobs both inside and out.

"Know this wrench?" he was asked.

"Yes," he told them. He had brought it in from the garage that morning. Something was wrong with the radiator, and Thompson told him to have a look at it. But while he was working Miss Shephard came in and after a minute or two asked him if he could leave the radiator until later. She didn't like the noise, he explained. That was all. He had shoved the wrench underneath the radiator and inquired if it was all right to leave it there. She had glanced up and said, "Certainly, Eddie." Marian corroborated Eddie's story, and he was dismissed for the time.

With Eddie's departure, the servants were inquired about in detail. Marian listed them, giving assurances of their trustworthiness and the unlikelihood of their being implicated in any way: Thompson; Annie, the cook; Ethel; McAllister. All of them had been with us for years, had been well

established when Mother and I went there to live.
In addition to these there are Leo, the chauffeur;
Eddie; Alma; and Mildred. They had been there
for varying lengths of time. Alma was the only
one who could be called a recent addition, and she
had been of the staff for the better part of a year.

In that interval before the district attorney's arrival family and guests had been ordered to check
carefully for robbery. But so far as we could tell,
nothing was disturbed or missing.

"So that's out," Rumsey had remarked succinct-
ly, pushing a hand through his grayish, sandy hair.

When the district attorney came down and established himself in the library I was the first one
sent for. He sat with elbows on the flat top of the
Chippendale desk, hands stretched out over the
red leather covering. A good-looking man with his
gray hair and heavy black brows.

He began at once with my discovery of Jocelyn's body in Marian's upstairs sitting room. The
time, of course, when I had last been in the room
before finding the body, what had taken me in
that evening. He wanted to know why we had not
been alarmed when Jocelyn was missing, and this
point he pressed home insistently. Accustomed as
we ourselves were to Jocelyn and her impromptu
comings and goings, this was difficult to explain
to an outsider.

It was when he began, somewhat as Rumsey had done earlier, his effort to find out when Jocelyn had gone into the room that the need for the others became apparent, and they were summoned.

"Then everyone was here in the library?" he said when they had been herded in and, after a first momentary hesitancy, sat down or stood about with some semblance of naturalness. A single sweeping glance seemed to take us all in and place us accurately as he added, "Everyone except Mr. Shephard?"

"Yes." Marian looked round the group. "All but Osgood," she said, glancing at Oz. "Mr. Brown came just after the—the discovery." His questions on the afternoon had recalled Mrs. Schwaggerman to her mind, and she went on to speak of Ruth's visit. "She went directly after Mrs. Shephard's return," she concluded.

"Then Mrs. Shephard wasn't here?"

"Not until later." Marian explained about Jocelyn's trip to New York. And no, she had no idea just what had taken her in nor where she had spent her time. Leo must have brought her from the train, she said.

I left Oz, whose hand I had been clutching, and went to stand beside Marian. "Someone drove her home," I told him. "I was by the window and noticed when the car came in." I indicated the

windows which give on to the drive. He asked
numbers of questions; he was interested in Jocelyn's abrupt departure. But I had no idea who the
man was, and he gave it up with an air of letting
it drop for the moment, something that he would
come back to later.

He eyed us all thoughtfully. "Now when you
left this room what happened? How did you go?
Not all together?"

"No." Marian considered, glanced around for
assistance. "No—people just drifted up. Just as it
happened."

"I think I was the first to leave," Mother spoke
up. "I wanted to see to the table after I was
dressed—and various little things." Her voice was
steady enough, but her words as she went on were
rambling, even incoherent, and she twisted continuously at her rings.

Mr. Bigelow was patient. Monotonous questioning brought out that we had gone up in about
this order: Mother; Katherine Haskell and Marian
together; Irene McIver, whom I had followed. And
after that, O'Meara, Jarvis, Brooke, Larry, Jocelyn
and, somewhat later, Ham.

He worked with pencil and small notebook. We
watched him, no one speaking except in answer to
his short, quick questions.

"This is rough"—he looked up—"not exact as
to time, but I want to check it." And he read us
his little tabulated list.

Mrs. Sherwin goes up at about	*5:30*
Miss Shephard and Mrs. Haskell	*5:35*
Mrs McIver	*5:37*
Miss Sherwin	*5:42*
Mr. O'Meara	*5:46*
Dr. Jarvis	*5:49*
Mr. Bennett	*5:53*
Mr. McIver	*6:00*
Mrs. Shephard	*6:03*
Mr. Shephard	*6:10*

As nearly as I can piece it out from all the welter of question and answer that helped the district attorney build his little table, the scene after my own departure was something like this. Larry and Jocelyn continued talking there in the hall where we left them, with the three other men making another group nearer the stairs. Then O'Meara went on up, and Dr. Jarvis and Brooke moved down to the door with the idea of going out for some air, saw it was beginning to rain and started back with the intention of following O'Meara. But Brooke, drawn into Larry's and Jocelyn's talk, lingered on a bit, while Jarvis went along up, to be followed by Brooke a few minutes later.

As Brooke and Larry remembered it, the two of them, with Jocelyn, had stayed near the door as they talked. Larry was going out, and Brooke called back from the stairs that it was misting, but Larry had gone on. Thompson had already established that Jocelyn had then made a telephone call, perhaps two; he was not positive about that point.

There were countless questions as to what we had done on going up, and to this the invariable answer from each was that he had gone directly to his room, not leaving it until coming down to gather in the terrace room for a cocktail.

As to seeing and meeting other people in the gallery and halls abovestairs, the district attorney checked on everyone with care, and here his patience wore a little thin at the repeated insistence from each of us that we had seen no one. Except Marian and Katherine, who had gone up together. It was to this that he weariedly came back.

"Now, Miss Shephard and Mrs. Haskell, you left at the same time?" They assented, and he continued, "You both went directly to your rooms?"

Katherine looked hesitantly at Marian, who stopped in her half-finished assertion that she had done just that. "No," she said suddenly, her voice loud in the surprise of recalling it, "I did stop in my sitting room." There was one of those strange little silences, but she seemed not to notice it. "I had left a couple of letters on my desk from the morning mail, one that I wished to go over again. I thought of them as I went by and stopped and took them both to my room."

"The halls and gallery were empty then—when you went on?"

"Yes. But I think someone, Mrs. McIver probably, was coming up the stairs."

Irene couldn't vouch for this, but from low on the stairs she could scarcely have seen anyone in the gallery unless that person was close to the balustrade. The district attorney sent a slim, dark young man, one of the two who had arrived with him, to experiment, and this was found to be so. And the thick-piled carpet of the gallery and halls made steps inaudible. That same carpet, which silenced all steps, was to be a continuous annoyance to the district attorney in his investigation.

"Then you didn't leave your own room until you came down for dinner?" His eyes rested on Marian thoughtfully.

"No, I went through my letter and then dressed. I believe I was the first down."

So on through all the rest of us. Each had gone up, gone directly to his room and heard nothing, seen nothing. But this was not unnatural. Once having reached our rooms, there was nothing to occasion our leaving until, dressing accomplished, we emerged to go downstairs.

Mother and I have connecting rooms, but it is her habit to rest at that time, and I had not disturbed her. Nor had she been there when I opened the door and looked in before coming down. The McIvers shared a room and so could check on each other's presence. Still, as it turned out afterwards, Irene was in Jocelyn's room and did not return to her own until much later.

4

So there it was. No servants had been on that floor in answer to any calls, except Alma in response to the ring from Katherine Haskell's room at about six-fifteen. Bits of pressing, that sort of thing, are ordinarily done downstairs earlier in the day so that the whole staff is free from personal service during their own dinner hour, which is at six. Jocelyn had been the only one to deviate from this, and there had been no calls from Jocelyn that evening. The servants in their testimony spoke of thinking this odd. It was Ethel who remarked when Katherine's ring summoned Alma, "I thought so. We couldn't get through a meal without her wanting something."

"With a six o'clock dinner," Thompson explained, "we have plenty of time to get it cleared and out of the way before the family dinner, which is at seven-thirty." And everyone, he said, had been in the servants' dining room at that time, no one leaving except Alma.

But out of all the endless questioning a few things stood out. There was O'Meara in the room next to Marian's sitting room, who recalled hearing someone call softly, "Joss, Joss!"

Larry was the only one who had that name for Jocelyn, and involuntarily everyone looked at him and then, in swift realization, as quickly away. Larry denied it strenuously, even angrily, tearing a hand through his thick light hair as he talked.

"I didn't see her after I left her there at the door. I was only out a few minutes, long enough to smoke a cigarette. She wasn't there when I came in, and I went upstairs right away."

"Did you see anyone in the hall?"

"No, I didn't." Larry's tone had come down a little, settled into sullenness. "I went straight to my room. I didn't see anyone."

"While you were talking to Mrs. Shephard, did she appear disturbed? Was she quite herself?"

Larry took a minute to think that over. "I don't know." He said it doubtfully. "She had something on her mind—I couldn't make her out." This seemed to have come to him for the first time. The churlish resistance fell away as he considered it. "We'd planned to break away after dinner—it was a settled thing—and when I brought it up, she wasn't so sure. Didn't bother to explain. She wasn't half listening anyway." He stopped, flushing miserably. In the sudden recollection he had been swept into disclosures he had not intended.

Mr. Bigelow continued to regard Larry steadily for another moment, but his next question was for O'Meara.

"What time was it, Mr. O'Meara, when you heard the call?"

But Frank couldn't place it exactly. "It was some little time after I went up, for I had picked up a magazine and read a few minutes." O'Meara's face under the shock of white hair was more florid than usual. "I was just starting for the bath," he added.

"Was it a man or woman who called?"

O'Meara hesitated, and again we all refrained from looking at Larry. "I had taken it for granted that it was a man," he said finally, "but I suppose it might have been a woman. It was soft," he said ruminatively, "rather under the breath—and guarded. I wouldn't have heard it, of course, but for the door between."

The door in question connects the two rooms, but since Marian converted one of them into a sitting room the door has been locked, with no entrance from either side.

Mr. Bigelow made some effort to get the time placed with more exactness, leaving it at length with that same air of not being finished with it.

"Now"—he looked my way, decided that there was no more to be gained from me for the present, and passed on to Marian—"if you'll return to the other room, I'll want statements from each of you.

"Just a minute," he said as we rose to go. He picked up from the desk before him a flat metal case, enameled brightly in red. "Does anyone recognize this?" he asked.

Irene McIver spoke out of the unpleasant silence. "It's mine," she said. Just that and no more. And her tone said, What of it?

"This was found in Mrs. Shephard's room." He waited an instant. "A maid has stated positively that it does not belong to Mrs. Shephard, and she's fairly certain that it was not there when she put the room in order after Mrs. Shephard's departure in the early afternoon."

"I probably left it there sometime," Irene began in the same challenging tone, and then, even in her state of obvious panic which insouciance failed to cover, it must have come to her as it did to all of us, that small incident of the afternoon when O'Meara picked it up and pushed back the lid to discover in growing amazement its varied compartments. Powder, rouge, lipstick, comb and spaces for change and six cigarettes. "What! No stove!" he had demanded of Irene in comic consternation.

The district attorney was waiting.

"I left it there this afternoon." The contentious tone had flattened out. Her face, narrowed to thinness by the smartly drawn back dark hair, looked strained and tense.

He ruffled the pages of a notebook but did not actually look at them. "You told us previously that you went directly to your room in the north wing and did not leave it."

"I know." She spoke hurriedly. "I had forgotten—I went into Jocelyn's room first. I wanted to see her when she came. I thought it would only be a minute or two. So I stayed awhile. Someone did come to the door once. I thought it was Jocelyn, but when I looked around to see why she didn't come in, no one was there."

His interest quickened. "You're sure of that?"

"Yes." She continued to speak in the breathless, hurrying manner. "The door was open a little way. Someone was there. I thought it was Jocelyn, and when she didn't come on in, I looked around to see why."

Further questioning did not change her story. She had not seen who it was. Neither had she heard any sounds of going away.

"How long were you in Mrs. Shephard's room?"

"I don't know—not long. A few minutes."

Well, there were four cigarette stubs, smoked down to their ivory tips, in the tray, and the lid was off the partially filled box that stood beside it.

She thought perhaps some were already there, but on that he pointed out that the room had been put in order after Jocelyn left. Ash trays, as always, had been emptied and washed.

"It didn't seem long," she insisted, making a pathetic attempt at indifference.

"Why did you wish to see Mrs. Shephard?" he asked.

"Why"—her face that had been pale under its rouge flushed violently—"nothing important. Just to talk. She had been away all the afternoon, and there hadn't been a chance with everyone around." Assurance flowed back to her voice as she felt the plausibility of her explanation.

"Was Mr. McIver there when you went to your room?"

She didn't answer for a moment. A quick glance went to Larry, who stared back at her. Though his face changed not a particle, you knew, somehow, that he could have choked her for that desperate look in his direction.

It was embarrassing to watch her painful effort to say the right thing.

"Had he started to dress?"

"No." She answered steadily, no floundering now. "He never starts until the last minute."

Mr. Bigelow went back to her hesitant assertion that Larry had been there, but she was not to be shaken in it, though her nervous alarm returned as he persisted.

It was left there, and once more we turned to leave. In the informality of breaking up I burst out, "Marian, what did Jocelyn say to you this afternoon? Just before she went to the telephone? You remember—you looked so astonished and—" I was going to add "utterly disgusted," but remembering that Jocelyn was now dead, I didn't go on.

The district attorney was taking charge again. "When was this?" he asked.

"While we were having tea," I explained. "Jocelyn was called to the telephone, and a moment before she spoke to Miss Shephard. I just happened to think of it." I was embarrassed. It sounded foolish, inconsequential to anyone who had not observed the incident.

"And what did Mrs. Shephard say to you?" he asked Marian perfunctorily.

She seemed about to answer readily as I expected, and then, for some unaccountable reason, delayed her reply. "Why, it could have been nothing important," she said. "I don't seem to recall—"

Always brusque and direct, Marian couldn't lie well, and those of us who knew her were uncomfortably aware that this was a lie.

Mr. Bigelow prodded her mechanically. "It might have some importance, Miss Shephard."

"I believe there was some remark about the McIvers . . . what time they arrived . . ."

But her effort for something plausible came too late and too clumsily. As I remembered Jocelyn's excitement and Marian's quick recoil of disgust, I was painfully conscious that others were recalling it too. Jocelyn never did anything unobtrusively, and that moment between the two had been there for all to see.

I was relieved when a man, whom the district attorney addressed as Holt, came in and gave a lengthy report about the windows. "We've been over them all, and that's out," he finished in a tone loud enough for us to hear clearly. "If anyone got in from outside he came through the door."

But McAllister and Eddie had both been about the grounds all day. Leo had not been out after taking Jocelyn to the train, and, working in the garage with open doors, he had had a good view of the rear and north end of the house.

It had been Mildred's afternoon off, but the rest had been variously occupied in kitchen or guest rooms, going at odd times to their own quarters on the third floor of the center section of the house. Family and guests had been spread over the place before congregating in the library, so altogether the idea of someone entering and secreting himself in an out-of-the-way corner of the house seemed unlikely. Besides, as Rumsey had remarked earlier, referring to Dan, our English setter, "That dog would have set up a howl if there 'd been any strangers around."

Moreover, Thompson was sure of his doors. No one, he was certain, could have entered without his knowledge. "In pleasant weather," he told them, "the French windows to the terrace might stand open, or the doors to the verandas—but we have it on our minds." He was flushed and tired, overanxious to have the district attorney understand. Even more than the others, he had been endlessly grilled. Older in service than most of them, he was also the last known person to have seen Jocelyn.

He hadn't let Mr. McIver in, he admitted. "He must have pushed the catch as he went out." He glanced at Larry, who nodded an uneasy assent. But that was all, he finished. The door was locked when Miss Wycke came.

Up to that moment, strange as it may seem, I don't think anyone had given a thought to Miss Wycke. It was probably because we were so accustomed to seeing her come in sometime in the late afternoon, brown leather briefcase under her arm, that everyone had failed to recall her passing through the hall to Ham's study.

Now that she was mentioned, those two groups who had lingered on remembered her coming in and, almost directly afterwards, going upstairs.

"It must have been right after Mr. O'Meara went up," Larry said. "Not more than a minute or two anyway."

A little more of this, and the district attorney took his pen and added another name to his neat, tabulated list, crowding it underneath O'Meara's, I gathered.

Thompson went on to explain that Miss Wycke, as she invariably did following an afternoon at the library, had left her notes in Mr. Shephard's study and gone upstairs to the sitting room. There was a bathroom opening from the room, which was formerly used as a bedroom, and it was to this that Miss Wycke always repaired to freshen up for dinner. Thompson had not seen her come down; he hadn't seen her again until she came to the pantry to say that she had decided not to stay for dinner after all.

"Then what time did she leave?"

"It was after six—between six and half-past, I should say."

"Miss Wycke up there! While it was happening!" Hamilton voiced what everyone was thinking in that little gasping silence. He stared at Mr. Bigelow. "Why, that—it's incredible!"

"We'll get her here and see," Mr. Bigelow said curtly. "Where does she live? You have her address, Mr. Shephard?"

Ham's look remained fixed on Mr. Bigelow an instant longer; then he wove his way through the rest of us to his study, which opens into the north wing. I followed after a moment, as much to escape the uneasy silence as to aid Ham, whose helplessness in locating anything is a fixed idea in a household of women.

He stood before his desk, cupped hand pulling at his chin, a mannerism of Ham's when he is thinking.

"Here," he said as he saw me, and half pulled out a drawer, murmuring something about the apartments on Paynter Avenue.

"I don't know," he said slowly, and there was concern, not bewilderment, in his look as he watched me find the number, "I don't know what this may bring about."

In the hurry and excitement I didn't ask what he meant. Mr. Bigelow was out there waiting, and I flew back with house and telephone numbers.

And now we actually accomplished the withdrawal that we had begun twice in the last ten minutes. All but Marian. She was singled out to take the chair which had been mine before they were all brought in to establish the order of our going upstairs before dinner. Sheeplike, we were herded to the drawing room.

"Any objection to our going into this other room?" Brooke demurred at the doorway. There was none, apparently, and we went across the hall into the terrace room opposite.

"This Wycke woman may be able to throw some light on things," O'Meara said as he moved about restlessly.

I wondered about that. What could she know? If she had seen or heard anything she would naturally have made some outcry. And yet, if Thompson were right, she might have been there when Jocelyn entered the sitting room.

We fell into small, quiet groups of two or three that changed and shifted nervously about.

"Sit down. You look like a ghost." Oz put both hands on my shoulders, pushing me down to a divan, and dropped beside me, long legs thrust out before him.

"How anything like that could be pulled with all this crowd around," he said. "I just can't see it." He drew a cigarette from a mangled-looking package and lighted it, his narrowed eyes roving over the people in the room.

"Of course I can think of any number of good reasons for wanting to kill her."

"Oz!" I put a restraining hand on his arm.

"I know, I know." He made impatient acknowledgment of my warning, an instinct to speak only good of the newly dead.

"Well, I mean it. Why Ham—an all-round swell guy—should get roped in by that little faker is beyond me."

"Oz!" I said again, but he went on without heeding me.

"Just no meeting ground. No touching point." He was baffled as well as wrathful. Oz had always hit it off well with both Ham and Marian. Younger by almost twenty years, he never seemed conscious of any age differences. This they found amusing, and in some way it increased their liking for him.

"Refreshing," Marian pronounced it, "in this day and age when youth can be so devastatingly smug." It was this thorough approval which had cowed Mother into an unwilling acceptance of Oz.

"It's the puzzle of the ages." But, though Oz brought a new vehemence to it now, I had heard all this before, and I only half listened, thinking, as I was, of that moment in Ham's study. My eyes went to where he stood with Dr. Jarvis, and my perturbation dimmed to a dull wonder. He was gravely poised, altogether himself. But then, neither Ham nor Marian was the kind to give way emotionally.

Miss Wycke came while Marian was still in the library. Noting the closed door, the man who accompanied her indicated a chair. She went to it at once. A big girl, tall and rather heavy, with too much of the dark hair which she wore massed at her neck. All her motions were quick and energetic.

It was an energy that seemed to be constantly announcing independence, an almost aggressive independence. She didn't need anyone, all that hurry and resolution seemed to say as she made her purposeful passings through the house.

She looked alone and isolated now. I thought of asking her into the terrace room with the rest of us, wondered if she would be permitted to talk to anyone before she had seen the district attorney, and then, seemingly incapable of doing anything decisive in my present state, I stayed inertly beside Oz.

Marian came shortly. As she stood in the doorway she was unlike herself in her white exhaustion. Oz rose the instant he spotted her. Standing still beside me, he gave somehow the effect of rushing forward to gather her in. She smiled as she caught his look, moving across the room with her own brisk stride. Brooke wandered our way and was there when she reached us. He patted her knee as he sat beside her.

"Buck up, Marian. It's bad, of course, but don't let it get you."

"Bigelow seems a good sort," Oz said by way of diverting her. He stood before her, elbows dug into the piano top.

"I suppose it's the usual thing in the way of investigation," she said, "but they almost made me feel that I had committed the crime myself.

Oh well—it doesn't sound much." She smiled at Oz, who glared indignantly and brought out something about their damned routine. "I fancy it was the repetition that got me." But she looked both angry and disturbed as she absently accepted a cigarette from the case Brooke held out.

Thompson came in through the dining room and stopped beside Marian. Tapping her cigarette, she looked around at him inquiringly.

"Are Mr. and Mrs. McIver leaving this evening?" he wanted to know.

"Why, no," she said, her tone mildly puzzled, and then with a faint smile: "I doubt if they could if they wished to, Thompson. Or anyone else," she added quickly.

"I just wanted to be sure. Alma said that Mrs. McIver's bag was packed." He murmured something about Leo, the car and trains.

"Oh, some mistake," Marian said in her crisp, assured way. "Irene!"

Irene drew herself around slowly. Huddled in a corner of a sofa, the deflated air called forth by Mr. Bigelow's questioning still enveloped her.

"Irene, you weren't planning on going back to-night?" Marian asked. "Thompson says your bags were packed." A mistake, the tone suggested.

Irene shifted farther around, nervous and ill at ease. "No," she said. "That is—I wasn't sure. I thought I might be going after dinner. Then this all happened . . ." Her voice trailed off, and she sat fussing with one of the clips which finished the square-cut neck of her scarlet dress.

Seemingly no one was giving the incident more than passing attention, but everyone in the room waited for her explanation.

She felt this and made another fumbling effort. "I had things to do. In town, I mean," she added and slumped back into her corner.

She must have packed before coming down to dinner. Some sort of run-in with Jocelyn might have accounted for her sudden urge to leave. But there had been little more than an exchange of greetings between them. Had she quarreled with Larry, perhaps, over his after-dinner engagement with Jocelyn? His quick look of exasperated surprise had betrayed an unawareness of her intentions.

It was right after this that I saw Hamilton taken across the hall. I remember thinking as I watched him go that those statements of ours must be monotonous repetition. For, with the exception of Ham, we had all been together in the afternoon, we had withdrawn at about the same hour to dress, returning to the lower floor for dinner with little difference as to time. And finally, we were still one group when I made that terrifying discovery in Marian's sitting room. Only Ham's afternoon walk made any variation.

Ham had been gone only a few minutes when I was sent for. They were trying to determine how Jocelyn had spent her afternoon. But Ham had not the slightest idea where she had gone or with whom she had been.

Again I described the car which had brought Jocelyn home. The man? Further than the fact that he was large and wore a light-colored polo coat I could tell them nothing. With that meager amount someone would be detailed to find him.

The matter of Ham's own afternoon was taken up next. But as it turned out, Ham had not gone for his customary walk that day.

"I intended to when I set out," he told them, "and then I suddenly decided on a trip to New York."

"What changed your mind, Mr. Shephard?"

The fraction of a minute that Ham hesitated was imperceptible unless you knew him well. "Why, nothing. Nothing in particular. I had meant to go in one day this week, had been putting it off, and—well, it just came to mind. I saw that I could easily make the three-five so I went right to the station."

"You didn't come back to the house first?" A question, but they already knew the answer. Thompson, Ethel too, had already mentioned that return.

"Yes. Yes, I had forgotten that." He stood sharply, as if the effort of sitting quiescent were almost too much for him. Once on his feet, however, the situation precluded the pacing about that is instinctive with him, and almost as abruptly he sat down again.

"Yes, I came back to leave Dan—our setter. I made some slight changes then and went. I still had time to walk it."

His train had arrived in the Grand Central at about a quarter of four, and he had taken a taxi to his publishers' on Thirty-third Street. He hadn't stayed long. "The man I wanted to see was out," he explained.

"So when I came out I decided to walk the dozen or so blocks to use the time. I telephoned before I left town," he added.

"Why did you do that?"

"Well, I had missed the four fifty-three after all, the train I intended to take. We had guests—I was expected earlier, of course."

Mr. Bigelow looked thoughtful and then asked about a bracelet that had been taken from a pocket of a tweed topcoat which Ham had worn that afternoon.

I watched surprisedly as it was lifted from the white jeweler's box. I had never seen it before, and suddenly, as it dangled in the district attorney's long thin fingers—a band of small diamonds with eight square-cut sapphires—I recalled Jocelyn's voice pitched unpleasantly high. "Keep it? Of course I'm going to keep it!"

For a long instant the two men looked directly at each other. There was something of challenge in the look that I found vaguely disquieting.

"I had forgotten that," Ham said. Then slowly, as if feeling his way: "As long as I was going in I decided to take it. A matter of a loose stone or two."

"Then you went to the store." Mr. Bigelow glanced at the name on the jeweler's box and began again. "You went to this store on Fifth Avenue before or after going to Thirty-third Street?"

"Neither," Ham answered promptly. "I forgot it completely."

I sighed in relief. Ham's floundering uncertainty had filled me with a sense of uneasiness.

That was all of his trip to New York. It was of the time afterwards that he was questioned searchingly and at length.

"Now when you spoke to Mrs. Shephard on the phone, you told her that you would be late. That was all?"

"Yes," Ham began, and then quickly: "No—I had forgotten." He jerked himself forward, a stricken look on his face. "Jocelyn did say there was something she wished to tell me, said to come to her room as soon as I came in."

"But you didn't do that?"

"No. As a matter of fact, I had forgotten it. Not exactly forgotten," he amended slowly. "I hadn't taken it as anything important or serious. Jocelyn—Mrs. Shephard . . ." He hesitated—over the tense probably. "She was extravagant in her speech, the way young people are these days."

Mr. Bigelow nodded in doubtful agreement. "Have you any idea what Mrs. Shephard wanted to speak to you about?"

Again Hamilton groped for what he would say. I felt a queer nameless dread creep over me. Ham, of all people, to tell this faltering, uncertain story.

"I haven't, no," he said at last, but the words carried no conviction.

"Would you say she was excited?" Mr. Bigelow's look included me this time.

I tried to make clear what Thompson, and now Hamilton's fumbling attempts, had failed to give. "Jocelyn was always keyed up. No, I didn't think about her sounding any different than usual."

"You have separate rooms?" He turned to Ham. "Yes, the bath between."

"And you didn't make any attempt at all to speak to your wife?"

"No, the bath was empty, and I was late. I just went ahead and got dressed."

"That wasn't unusual?"

Ham considered uncomfortably, and this time I was in full accord. That casual indifference, a deliberate coolness between them these last weeks, could not be explained to an outsider.

"Wouldn't you ordinarily have heard her moving about?" Mr. Bigelow prodded him.

"Yes, I usually do, I think. But I wasn't listening for it. I just didn't notice." Hamilton's assurance here only pointed up for me the hesitancy of his replies concerning the trip into town. Mr. Bigelow didn't go back to those hours in New York, however. Instead he questioned Ham closely as to whom he had seen on coming in and going up to his room. But Ham had seen only Thompson. "I was late. The others were all upstairs getting dressed when I came in."

"Your wife had no enemies—there hadn't been any recent trouble? Anything at all that you can recall?" The flat, almost weary tone with which he brought this out suggested a following out of a routine procedure, a regulation inquiry in murder cases, perhaps.

Probably because of the talk between Marian and O'Meara that afternoon I jumped in at this point and brought up the matter of Jocelyn's disappearance. "Mrs. Shephard disappeared several months ago," I told him. "We didn't know her then, and weren't interested at the time, but it was in the papers." Publicity stunt, Marian had termed it. Had that been only this afternoon? I seemed to have lived years since then.

Mr. Bigelow received this with a show of interest. A moment of thoughtful silence while two fingers tapped on the leather covering of the desk, and he had recalled the case. From Hamilton he got the date, but little else. Ham hadn't known Jocelyn at the time, of course, no more than had we, and his answers to the questions which followed showed that he knew next to nothing about it. His lack of knowledge concerning Jocelyn's background, her friends, her many engagements, had already been a cause for increasing wonder on Mr. Bigelow's part, and now, just as we were about to be dismissed, I had crashed in with this, a topic that pointed up more completely Ham's embarrassing ignorance of Jocelyn's affairs.

"She never discussed it," Ham said. "I did ask about it once—that was shortly after we were married. But I saw it was an unpleasant subject and dropped the matter. We never referred to it again. I rather thought—I had the impression, that is— that it was something in the nature of a—well, a theatrical play for attention." It was out, finally.

Poor Ham; I could understand that it would be a distasteful subject, something that he would let rest along with countless other details of Jocelyn's past.

To my relief, the interview ended here. It was only too plain that there was nothing more to be gained from Hamilton. But the disappearance would be methodically checked, I realized as Ham and I left the room. Now that it was over, I was pleased, on the whole, that I had mentioned the affair of the kidnaping. For the moment, at least, Mr. Bigelow's attention had been turned away from Ham's trip to New York that afternoon.

5

When I came out of the library I saw Miss Wycke, who had returned to her place in the hall after her examination, which had followed Marian's. It was Brooke who roused me to enough energy to ask her in.

"That secretary of Ham's is still here. Why not bring her in, see what she has to offer?"

She sat in the same chair, the high carved back rising above her brown felt hat. Never in all the years she has been with Ham had I seen her look anything but tirelessly energetic. There was a sense of shock now as I went over to her. Her face was gray and drained of all its life, and later, when I heard her speak of a headache as her reason for going before dinner, I believed her. I don't know, but I think perhaps in the light of what happened later that they were holding her there while her tiny kitchenette apartment was searched. It was searched, and searched diligently, that I know.

When I suggested that she join the rest of us, we both glanced at the patrolman at the door, but he offered no objection as she rose and came with me in that same purposefully independent way.

Drawn out to talk, her story, though startling, didn't add as much as we had anticipated. She had seen no one in the gallery or halls either in going up or coming down. But she had heard someone in the sitting room. She had heard that call of "Joss, Joss!" which O'Meara had already mentioned.

She told about it without any probing on our part. Indeed, she seemed eager to have us hear it. If the men, with their air of calm detachment, didn't have quite the avid look of the women, they listened none the less intently.

"I thought I heard someone, and a little later I could hear him call, 'Joss, Joss!' Like that—in a sort of whispering way." She was flushed and excited in her telling; her hands kept twisting and turning the brown leather bag in her lap. "I turned on the water full force to let them know I was there, and that was all I heard really."

O'Meara, who had been interrogated on the point, inquired if she was sure it was a man.

She turned toward him, and he watched her fixedly. "I don't know." Her eyes, under their heavy black brows, narrowed. "It could have been a woman, I suppose. It was more of a whispered call. I didn't hear anything clearly—I just knew they were out there. Whoever it was, I thought they wouldn't be staying long at that time of day, and I would just wait until they'd gone."

It was easy to imagine Miss Wycke penned in and waiting discreetly until she was sure the sitting room was empty.

"I didn't hear anyone fall either. Mr. . . . ." She paused, and Brooke supplied the name for her.

"Bigelow—he's the district attorney," he hurried her on.

"Mr. Bigelow kept asking about that, but I didn't hear anything definite." Her enjoyment of her brief prominence was over, and she was nervously hurried as she went on. "I could just tell there was someone out there. And when it was still for quite a minute I decided they'd gone. So I unlocked the door and turned out the lights." Her words came faster now, leaving no pause or opening for questions. "The sitting room was dark, but there's no switch by the bathroom door, and I just crossed the room and went out without turning on any lights at all. The door was closed—I noticed that because it isn't ordinarily—but I left it that way, just pulled to without latching."

She must have been questioned strenuously at this point, because her voice, more than her rushing words, strove so hard to convince us.

That was all. Did someone there, I wondered later, feel a sense of heavy relief as she finished her astonishing story?

It sounded awfully improbable, and still, I had to admit that she could have done just that. Jocelyn, as I knew, lay out of her path, and with the room in darkness it was possible.

"Thompson says you left without dinner." Marian was only sympathetically concerned, but Miss Wycke's quick glance carried something of withdrawal.

"I was going to stay the evening and get my notes in order," she said. "But I had a bad headache. I didn't really want dinner, and I knew my tray wouldn't be brought in for another hour, so I decided not to wait."

It was Brooke who interposed. "She's all shot to pieces," he said under his breath to me. "I'm going to have Leo bring my car around—I'll drive her home."

I was surprised. Brooke is grand company and all that, but I'd never say that thoughtful consideration for the Miss Wyckes of the world was one of his characteristics. Women in distress, unless they possess something in the way of beauty or position, are apt to be out of Brooke's line. But he did make the effort, approaching one of Mr. Bigelow's assistants, who told him that a police car would take her home. It came with a little shock, that first hint that we were not free to come and go at will.

While we were huddled, first in the hall and later in the terrace room, the whole place was gone over and systematically searched. Clothing in closets and even the contents of laundry receptacles were examined, and the result was nothing. Nothing that could in any way be connected with the crime.

"It looks like the work of a sneak thief, someone who got in with the idea of rifling the place while we were at dinner, and somehow or other Jocelyn goes in and surprises him, hears something perhaps." O'Meara was striving to make of it something less horrible and sinister.

Jarvis shook his head. "That won't work. What about that call of 'Joss'? That's no outsider. And the police—this district attorney—they don't think it's any prowler."

"You're probably right, but shut up," Brooke said half under his breath to Jarvis. "Everyone is pretty well shot as it is."

Jarvis, I think, was angry, an anger that was embarrassment at his own momentary lack of perception.

In that instant I had the feeling that Brooke irritated him intensely.

"Now I'm going to take charge here," he said suddenly, his voice loud, "and everyone is going to

have a stiffish drink. May I?" He turned to Marian
and reached for the bell to summon Thompson.

"Of course," she said. "I think I prefer coffee
myself. We'll have both," she decided.

It was Ethel, however, who came in answer to
the ring. Thompson, she said, was in the servants'
dining room with Rumsey and another man. Before she went out she said hurriedly in passing,
"Miss Nancy, could I speak to you a minute?"

I found her waiting in the hall near the dining-
room door. "Alma's doing a lot of talking," she
whispered. "She's going on all about that day when
Miss Shephard came back. That day in the study,"
she added pointedly.

Up until that moment I had given no thought
to our servants or the importance of what they
would have to say. It came to me now as I listened to Ethel's account of Alma's unrestrained
outburst.

Sitting uneasily on the edge of her chair, she
had answered their questions in a sullen, half-de-
fiant manner that was probably extreme nervousness. It was her journey to the upper hall in answer
to Katherine's ring which they were centering on,
and the constant repetition, the going back and
covering the same ground, over and over, she read
as suspicion of herself, I suppose. For in the midst
of it she flung out, "I didn't have anything to do

with it! There were people in this house that hated her. Miss Shephard hated her because she changed the drawing room. They all hated her." And then she burst into uncontrollable tears and was of no further use for the time.

I was distressed and disturbed. To ask her to keep still was plainly impossible. Moreover, it was too late for that. There was nothing to do but calm Ethel and go back to the others.

Katherine said an odd thing that night as she sat sipping her drink. I found it coming back to me in all the ensuing days, long after I fancied I had dismissed it.

"Something was bound to happen," she said. "Things had reached a pass where it was indicated. And this, I suppose, is it." She was speaking to Brooke at the time and probably failed to realize that her voice carried from their detached position before one of the recessed windows.

"It's a bad mess," he answered her. "Still, as you seem to suggest, it has brought that situation to a head."

The district attorney and his staff had gone to exhaustive lengths. It was as if they were determined not to leave without something conclusive in the way of success. They had proceeded after their usual method of weeding out, with the expectation of coming on something definite in the way of a lead. But though certain eliminations had been made, they were as far from a solution of the crime as on their arrival several hours before.

What puzzled and baffled them from the first was the apparent possibility that almost anyone in the house might have committed the murder. That and the evident lack of preparation.

"It was pulled in a hurry, that's sure," Rumsey said, "with everyone, including the secretary, right on the same floor."

That was the situation when, a little before three, they withdrew, having decided to hold no one as a material witness. But though no one was held, Mr. Bigelow made it clear that he expected guests as well as members of the household to remain.

"I understand you came prepared to spend some little time here. We'll make further examinations, of course, and it will be of considerable assistance if you stay for the next several hours at least."

He seemed to accept the various inarticulate murmurs as assent, and followed the others, stopping for a word or two with the man left stationed in the hall.

"And now they'll spend the rest of the night ferreting out our dark and shady pasts," O'Meara said to Jarvis as the cars sounded in the drive.

"Why should they?" Jarvis asked. "We didn't even know the girl."

"Routine, just routine," O'Meara returned. "No stone unturned, and all that."

The presence of the police had held us there together; with their going we were suddenly stranded and at a loss. To go up to bed, to do any of the normal, usual things, was impossible, and we lingered on in the same dazed, low-talking groups.

It was Oz's going which provided the necessary break. After he had left, a reluctant departure with many proffers to stay the night, Dr. Jarvis took things in hand. "Now I think we'd better get some rest. You should, you know," he urged. "There'll be a lot more of this tomorrow. They aren't through by any means." This wasn't exactly conducive to sleep, but we did get ourselves upstairs, leaving the lower floor to the patrolman in charge.

6

Once more we were behind the same closed doors where we had been when Jocelyn was killed. Was Dr. Jarvis right? Was the murderer behind one of those doors? An hour ago in the terrace room the idea had been grotesque. There had been little pricks of apprehension through the strange, unnatural night, but, fleeting and undefined, they had not really disturbed a hazy theory of some marauder, bent on robbery.

But Dr. Jarvis' calm suggestion, the questioning that was so pointed at various ones in turn, had done their work. I recalled Irene's perturbation on being confronted with the red case and the tray of stubs which indicated a long stay in Jocelyn's room; Larry's anger at the unvoiced implication that the call which must have summoned Jocelyn to the sitting room had been his; Miss Wycke's astonishing story that she could pass through that room and see nothing.

Ham's confusion as he gave his statement to Mr.
Bigelow—that, at least, was understandable. Or
was it? Shocked he had been, of course, but that
didn't altogether explain the pauses, the careful
replies. Ham had been trying to think and weigh
when the questions demanded only simple answers
concerning a trip but a few hours past.

But—I could no longer put it off—the implacable questioning had seemed to center on Marian. Over and over it went through my mind, cul-
minating in that violent explosion of Alma's.

That was unfortunate. How had Alma overheard the scene in Ham's study? For overheard
it she had. Would the district attorney put some
wrong and horrible interpretation on it? The longer I dwelt on it the more restless I became. Those
final words of Marian's on leaving the study last
Wednesday could be made to sound like a threat,
a threat because Ham had not prevented the vandalism in the drawing room.

But when the desecration began, Hamilton,
still under Jocelyn's hypnotic spell, was making
his painful efforts to get started on a new book,
and, feeble as those attempts must have been in
his disturbed relations with Jocelyn, he did spend
the usual hours in the study with Miss Wycke,
and so in all justice to him I doubt if he realized what Jocelyn was doing until the destruction
was well along. Had Marian been there she would

most certainly have prevented it. Mother could only protest, and Jocelyn heard her not at all.

The big drawing room was the loveliest place in the old house. "Like being in another era," Brooke had said. "A finer and more gracious era, with leisure and good conversation and real people. It's had time to become mellowed."

Its ruin was a crime, surely, but I don't think Hamilton had the faintest idea of what Jocelyn had in mind when she announced, "I'm going to do this room over, Ham." As casually as that. And it simply meant to him that the paneled walls would be the same paneled walls with a new finish. The draperies and matching cushions of the recessed windows would be renewed with little change as to color, and against this background would be as always the gleaming, polished furniture, priceless pieces which had stood there for generations, mingling comfortably with deep chairs and divans. No, I am sure that first mention of decoration meant no more than that to Ham.

But when workmen began tearing out the old paneling, the pilasters and cornices, the carved mantel, the built-in glass-doored cupboards, he had not stopped it. Nothing could have been more revealing of what Ham's infatuation for this girl, who all but flouted him, had done to his easy humor, his steady common sense, his keen insight into people. And, of course, his work. For though

he made his valiant effort to settle to his routine,
it needed only Miss Wycke's distress and unease to
tell of its failure.

If only Marian had not looked into that modernistic drawing room without warning, I thought
as I stood in my room that night. The oyster-white
walls, the white leather davenports and flatly low
armchairs with the curious drumlike tables beside
them. The small scattered furniture, lacquered
in black and white, the canary hangings and
white-shaded lamps. Even when you had watched
the growth of the incongruous room in the lovely
old house, its hard whiteness shocked anew each
time it flashed upon you.

But Marian had come upon it suddenly and unaware. We had deliberately refrained from writing.
That was a mistake, but Mother had meant well.
The damage was done so why not let her finish her
stay in peace? had been her thought.

It was unfortunate, too, that she arrived ahead
of schedule and came by taxi to the east entrance,
where Thompson let her in. I can still see her in
her green tweed coat, heavy to the point of dump-
iness were it not for her height, and yet distinguished in her alert carriage and the bold model-
ing of her face.

She stood in the great hall which runs the depth
of the house, the broad stairway with its intricately
carved white balustrade and mahogany handrail

and treads winding up from the rear. From this she gazed into that white-and-chromium room. I was halfway down the stairs, with Mother close behind, but she still stood, immovable, staring. Her embraces and answering words of greeting were all accomplished while her eyes continued to look dazedly into the drawing room. Even here her sharp wit did not desert her. "The windows," she mused, "how did she come to overlook the windows?"

Mother took it seriously and tried to explain. "The window cushions gave her more room for the canary coloring," she said.

As chance would have it, Jocelyn arrived at that moment with a number of people. They came in, laughing and a little noisy, so that Mother's small cries of commiseration were left hanging in the air. Jocelyn's greeting to Marian was made brief by all the bright chatter mingled with careless introductions, and, insensible to any constraint, she followed her guests into the drawing room.

Mother hovered over Marian. Her voice soothed even while it censured and assailed the changes. "I had everything put in storage except certain pieces—"

Marian did not listen. An abrupt turn shook off Mother's hand, and she went down the hall to the library, Mother following and persisting in her little heartening bits.

"The paneling is stored too. It's damaged, of course. . . ."

But Marian, still moving in that swift, decisive way, went straight through the library to Ham's study. She responded to his prompt hurrying forward, but mechanically. She listened to his surprised rush of inquiry, an odd look of curious wonder on her face, even a trace of an incredulous sort of amusement. She withdrew her hand and stretched it back toward the library and the room that lay beyond.

"Ham—that hideous room . . ." She stopped: it was all she could manage.

Hamilton, in his discomfort, took refuge in a humor that was false. He smiled. "It does strike an odd note—"

Instantly she loathed the smile, the words, the supine infatuation which had permitted the destruction of the room.

"An odd note," she said, and her tone was quiet. Too quiet. "That's what you call it—an odd note." Suddenly her voice lost its calm. "You let her do that. To this place that means something to us. Wrecking that room meant no more to her than having a hotel apartment done over. But you stood by and let it go on."

He moved back so that he leaned against his desk. "It was rather far along before I sensed there was to be any great change." He watched her face, concerned at her overwrought excitement. "That is, so much of a change." In the pause I think he sought for a way to tell her of his own regret, to try, perhaps, to explain the aberration which had allowed this to happen.

But she gave him no chance. "You fool!" she said. And again: "You fool!"

It had all been like something unreal, these two pleasant, well-poised people whose slight differences had always been taken out in a good-natured raillery of each other. He didn't remind her that this was his place. It was Marian herself who did that.

"This is not my house but it is my home, and I intend to see that there is no more ignorant vandalism. And since you do nothing to prevent it I shall!" And, unheeding the things he strove to say, she went out of the room.

As Marian had said that afternoon, the house belonged to Hamilton. Instead of being willed to them jointly it was left to Ham with the provision that it should be Marian's home as long as she so desired. But further than the adjustments natural at their father's and mother's passing, the change in ownership had made not the slightest difference. Since neither was married it was to succeed to me. Jocelyn's coming changed that. But so little actual realization did I have of all this that I quite missed the significance of a newspaper heading, "Sherwins Due to Be Ousted."

There had been something stupefying about it all. And for Marian, who had had no opportunity of observing those signs of returning reason, it had not only been stupefying: it had been frightening in what it promised for the future.

Through the partially opened door I could hear Mother stirring about in her preparations for bed. For the first time in all my frightened turning over of the evening's events I remembered Mother's evasive answers when Rumsey asked about our various movements before and after dinner. With Mother it had seemed to come to some sort of an impasse when he sought to discover what she had done with her time after that one brief visit to the dining room on first coming down. And Mother, in her charming, indefinite way, had determinedly resisted all efforts to be pinned down to anything exact. Had she been the same when the district attorney took her statement?

Suddenly curious, I went through into her room. I interrupted her surprised exclamation that I was still dressed.

"Mother, where were you before dinner?" I asked her.

Some of the same confusion was there but she answered, "I was in the library, Nancy."

"Well, why didn't you say so, Mother—when they were asking?"

She hesitated. "I was writing to Uncle Hal. You had seen to the flowers—everything was all right—and there was a good hour almost. So—I had this letter started . . ."

Mother writes all letters, other than the merest notes, in piecemeal fashion. Sometimes they extend over a week or more before she finally finishes and mails them.

"But"—I went carefully; I didn't want to alarm her now that she was settled for what was left of the night—"why didn't you say so? They're so exact about time and things like that."

In spite of my efforts to be careful she was wrought up and excited. "I thought they might ask for it. As proof perhaps. And I shouldn't have liked showing it. A personal letter." Her gentle dignity broke through her nervousness.

"Still—it would have been better," I began and stopped. In a flash I knew what was in the letter almost as well as if I had written it myself. "You were writing about Jocelyn?" I said. A question, but I had no doubts.

Her nervous fluttering came back. "Well, of course that is natural, Nancy," she said defensively. "Uncle Hal is interested—"

I wasn't listening. All that mess at breakfast that morning. I was more disturbed than I wanted her to see.

"I'd written how Marian took the changes in the drawing room," she was saying.

"And what else, Mother?" I hurried her on. I had to know the worst.

"I hadn't finished," she said a little haltingly, "but I was saying what a difference Ham's marriage had made with us. With you, Nancy. I was saying that I wouldn't care if I thought Hamilton was happy, and she the right kind of woman for him. But for this person—a girl like Jocelyn King, a cheap little creature—to come in here and take the place that rightfully belongs to you—"

I was astonished at her vehemence. It was even worse than I had thought. "Mother, where is the letter?" I broke in. Though I knew without asking. "In the little desk?"

The little desk is a small, beautiful affair of satinwood with tiny slippered feet. It used to stand in the drawing room, but in the rearrangement after Jocelyn's changes it had been placed in the library. From the first Mother has used it for her personal correspondence. I think she likes the small daintiness of it, which is somehow suited to her, and the romantic appeal of the secret drawer. One of those secret drawers that everyone knows about. And I knew before she told me that the voluminous pages of the letter to Uncle Hal lay there, if they had not already been discovered. With the search centered on the sitting room and

Jocelyn's bedroom, there was a chance that they had not been noticed.

I made an effort to conceal my worry. "I doubt if they find it, and tomorrow there may be a chance to go in and get it," I told her as I opened the windows and went out, closing the door after me.

Back in my own room, my uneasiness grew. If Mr. Bigelow or his men came upon that letter, wouldn't they read all sorts of meanings into the little thrusts and barbs which stuck out all through Mother's rambling pages? If it were only the usual denunciation of Jocelyn and the impossibility of making anything of that kind of person. But there in great detail, as I well knew, was the altercation of the morning with the threat—for so I suppose it was—to eject us. And, most damning of all, the allusion to my being the heir to all this previous to Ham's marriage.

The more I thought of it the more necessary it seemed that I get my hands on the letter and destroy it. Could I go down to the library? I knew there was an officer in the house, and there was at least one stationed outside. I had seen them as being placed there for our safety. Now I saw them for what they doubtless were—guards to watch our movements and see that no one left the place.

I opened the door and looked cautiously into the hall. Connolly stood far down the gallery. He was either gazing at his reflection in a wide mirror

or studying the features of one of the early Shephards. On the thick carpet I could make the service stairs unobserved if he stayed where he was.
And even if I ran into him, there would be no real
harm. I would merely say that I couldn't sleep and
wanted something to read.

At the rear stairs, which is uncarpeted, I pulled
off my pumps. I passed through kitchen and pantry into the dining room. The whole place was
lighted, not brilliantly, but there was enough
illumination to give the expedition a semblance
of naturalness. In the hall Dan rose and stretched,
but a quiet word sent him back to his place as I
crossed to the library.

The door was closed. There was nothing alarming in this—Connolly had probably left it that
way—but I found myself standing there, held
back by some nameless fear. Only the thought of
Connolly and his imminent return to the lower
floor drove me on. I turned the knob noiselessly
and opened the door a cautious inch or two. The
room was lighted, and I wondered about the man
outside. How much could he see through the cur-
tained windows? Then, pushing the door wide, I
stood gaping into the room. I don't know what
I had expected to find, but so keyed was I for
violence that Dr. Jarvis standing there in pajamas
and a dark silk lounging robe was more startling
than some strange figure skulking in the shadows.

He stood leaning over the large table, turning the pages of a magazine. I began to draw the door to as quietly as I had opened it, when he glanced up.

"Well, Nancy!" He gave the magazine a little shove and straightened, not greatly startled. "I thought you'd been put to bed."

"I wanted a book," I began and stopped. The speech that had been planned for Connolly fell flat with Dr. Jarvis. He was smiling slightly, his eyes on the blue slippers under my arm.

"I thought there was no use running into that policeman," I began.

"No. No, of course not," he agreed quickly. He was too casually matter of fact for the watchful scrutiny of his eyes.

The telephone rang—a strangely ominous sound, coming just then.

"That's my call," he said with perfect nonchalance and went into the telephone room, which has an entrance from both hall and library.

The interruption came as a relief. Why he was telephoning at half-past three in the morning I didn't know or care greatly. It was my own errand which concerned me. The small desk was not visible to Jarvis at the telephone, but once there, with my hand on the key, I looked round as guardedly as any criminal. And then I saw the door which I had closed after me a few moments before opening slowly. With my eyes glued on it fascinatedly, the

crack widened. When Larry McIver slid in and
cautiously drew the door after him I again had
that odd sense of letdown that it should be Larry
instead of some sinister, crouching figure. There
was just an instant while I watched him, unobserved. Then his eyes, narrowed as they made their
wary survey of the room, fell on me, and we stood
motionless, my fingers still closed over the little
key, his hand gripping the heavy brass knob.

It was only when Dr. Jarvis opened the door and
stepped briskly out that we moved. Larry darted a
single swift, calculating glance at Jarvis and came
on in, carelessly offhand. Like Jarvis, he was in
pajamas and robe, his a bright striped affair.

"Looking for something to read," he said airily.
"I'm awake as an owl." He unknotted the sash at
his waist, jerked it tighter and retied it. "God!
How anyone can sleep!" He regarded the book-
lined walls uncertainly.

"Nancy's looking for a book too," Jarvis said casually, too casually. He looked from one to the other
of us with a kind of thoughtful amusement in his
eyes—curious eyes, hazel, flecked with yellow.

"Oh yes?" Larry shot a look my way and went
over to the long carved table. There was almost a
swagger to his purposeful decisiveness. He grabbed
a book, flung it around and flipped it open. In
the silence the savagely turned pages made a hard
tearing sound.

The stillness, the inactivity—it was unbearable. Why hadn't I said at once that Mother had remembered a letter, and then just taken it as a matter of course? I forced myself to action, and with Jarvis' faintly amused eyes following me moved toward the windows and the small desk.

As if in some way my own motion had freed him from his furious turning of pages, Larry left the table and made for the shelves that edge the door to Ham's study. His fingers slid over the rows easiest of reach.

"Doubt if Spenser is what you want for tonight," Jarvis said smoothly.

"What!" Larry snatched his hand from the book and strode back to the table.

"How about a magazine?" Dr. Jarvis offered. His eyes included me in their coolly speculative regard. "Get your book, Nancy?"

Where Larry was violently energetic in his dive at the canterbury which held the magazines, I was determinedly deliberate as I went back to the table and picked up a new fall novel.

How long we might have kept this sort of thing up I can't say, but once more the door began to open, slowly, noiselessly. We stood there—Jarvis poised and alert, Larry stiffly immovable, head thrust forward and eyes narrowed, I with the book in its orange-and-black jacket clutched tightly against my blue dinner frock, all staring at the slowly widening space.

And then from the three of us escaped a single hard gasp as Connolly stood in the doorway. We were absurd in the anticlimax of it. Connolly's eyes, astonished and suspicious, took in our solid line-up.

"Just restless," Dr. Jarvis said easily enough, and stepped out of the tight little row.

"It's pretty late." Connolly's body relaxed, but he continued to eye us suspiciously.

"No one seemed to feel like sleeping," Jarvis told him. "We were just going though. Get what you wanted, McIver?"

Larry looked at him, a swift, sidewise glance of open exasperation, and grabbed up a leather-covered volume from the table nearest him.

"That ought to be soothing," Jarvis said.

I looked. Larry had a worn French dictionary clutched in one hand.

"Not too exciting—for a wakeful night," Jarvis further approved.

"That's what I thought," Larry snapped.

"Well then, if we all have our reading matter . . . Good night, Officer." Jarvis stood aside for me, and we filed out. Connolly followed to the stairs, where he stood watching us, a nonplused, half-angry look on his broad face.

After Larry had turned and gone down the hall to his room in the extreme end of the north wing,

Jarvis dropped his smooth mockery. "I'm sorry, Nancy," he said softly. "I didn't think about that cop coming in." He stood, his compact body alert in the shadowy silence. "What did you want? If I can do anything about it . . ."

"No, there's nothing," I whispered back.

Once inside my room, however, I was decided. The fiasco of my attempt with its comedy touch had erased all sense of fear. To return to the library now required no effort at all. I unfastened the small string of pearls at my neck. Here was an alibi for Connolly if I needed it. I had missed the pearls and simply gone back to look for them.

There was not a sign of anyone as I made for the main stairway. No furtiveness this time. The library was lighted as we had left it, the door standing wide.

Mindful of Connolly's possible observance, I closed it after me and made for the desk. With the same lack of fear or need for stealth I pressed the spring and drew out the sheets of Mother's spidery writing. Another instant and they were tucked securely in the front of my dress.

As I reached out a hand to push the drawer into place I heard a sound behind me, a sound so slight that only the expectancy of interruption made me aware of it. Without a glance around I bent over a chair, ready to be discovered groping between the padded arm and deep cushion. My quick swing about and glib explanation waited only for Connolly's voice.

But there was no astonished exclamation. Instead the switch by the door clicked and the room was plunged into darkness. In the moment while I crouched over the chair in the window I saw something which started a cold perspiration over my body. Connolly, with the outside man, was standing far out on the grounds at the north, so far that a street light brought them into sharp view.

I straightened slowly, fearfully. Standing there motionless, gripped in such fright as I had never before experienced, I heard another sound in that silent blackness, so faint as to be all but inaudible. I could feel rather than hear the steps on the deep-piled carpet. Cautiously, threateningly, they came toward me. I stood rooted, fixed in terror, unable to move or cry out as those menacing steps drew nearer—all but reached me.

What released me I don't know, but suddenly I was moving in a backward retreat as noiseless as that approaching danger. Touching chairs, window draperies, solid rows of books, I half circled the room, followed always by the slow, dreadful steps. My heart beat so loudly that it was a sound I could hear. Whoever was there in the darkness with me could hear it too. I passed the fireplace, the door to Ham's study. With the action my brain

had begun to think and reason. If I could reach
the telephone room I might make a dash through
the other door to the hall. That was my goal, and
like a trapped animal I worked toward it.

And then, stealth abandoned, the steps quickened and rushed on me. I cried out, I know, and
a hand was clapped to my mouth, held there, as
I was pushed into the very haven I had been trying to gain. I heard a key turn—another. Fainting
had been unknown to me, but I lost consciousness
then. Terror and the shock of the sudden seizure.
But screaming could have availed me little, with
everyone on the upper floors and Connolly out on
the grounds finishing his cigar.

When I came to, it all rushed over me in an
overwhelming wave of horror. Sprawled uncomfortably on the floor, I heard a distant door shut-
ting—Connolly coming in through the kitchen
perhaps. The sound of that door, closed without
creeping stealth, had a steadying effect, and I got
to my feet. My hand groped for the knob, turned
it automatically. The door was no longer locked.
The stairs lay just ahead of me, but advance, any
motion, was impossible. I heard Connolly coming
through the pantry, the dining room. It seemed
an endless time until he appeared in the doorway.

For the second time that night I saw his face
change from stunned astonishment to baffled annoyance.

"Just what are you doing back here?" he demanded.

I got myself to the hall and dropped into the nearest chair, my head reeling. "Someone was here! I was locked in!" I cried wildly and burst into an incoherent account. Even then I remembered my excuse for being there and thrust it in, garbling still further the story of the man who had shoved me into the telephone room.

"How do you know it was a man?"

But I was beyond explaining, and without waiting he jerked open the library door, giving the room a quick survey before he went in. With Dan at my heels I went after him; I couldn't be left alone after what had happened. He went over the windows, but mechanically, as if he expected to find them secure as they were. He passed on to Ham's study, continuing his routine examination of each window. At the third one he let out a sharp clicking sound.

"Look at that!" He swung around and showed me the small square pane, loosened of the putty which had held it for years. "Neat," he said and set it carefully back in place.

His next move was outside, where the other man joined us as soon as he saw the flash. But there was nothing. Shrubbery and ground showed no marks of any kind. Besides, Krug had patrolled the grounds throughout the evening, and this

window would have been well within their view
when I saw the two men from the library window. Again, there was Dan; any outside intrusion
would have set him barking wildly.

Back inside, Connolly went rapidly through the
rest of the lower floor. I followed from room to
room and was still close behind when he started up
the stairs. Waiting a few steps below, I watched as
he stood looking down the gallery and both halls.
It was eerie—the dead silence, the closed doors,
the dim light of the wide gallery. He turned finally, and I moved down the stairs ahead of him.

In the lower hall he again said, "How do you
know it was a man?"

"I don't," I answered him. "I couldn't see, but
someone was there, and I thought it was a man."
I talked on, repeating myself, adding nothing to
my story. I wanted to talk; I needed to explain the
horror of those moments.

He listened, staring warily around. "Well, maybe someone else wanted a book," he said jocularly
as I came to a stop. But his eyes were uneasy and
disturbed as he took me upstairs. "I'd stay there
now," he offered when he left me at the door.

The time with Connolly had settled me in a mea-
sure, and I set about undressing calmly enough. As
I pulled my dress over my head the letter dropped
to the floor with a little thud. Dully I looked at
the tight, folded wad; the reason for leaving the

safety of my room had been entirely forgotten. Driving myself to a last spurt of energy, I spread the sheets out, tore them to bits and flushed them down the sewer.

At the sound Mother called out. She exclaimed on seeing me partially dressed and then forgot it as I told of my excursion downstairs, omitting everything but the facts of securing her letter. Relief was in her face as she followed every word of my telling, but somehow not the complete relief I had expected.

I went to bed then and slept soundly, though sleep had seemed impossible when Connolly brought me up.

7

The dining room was deserted when I went down at ten the next morning.

"They're all finished," Mildred told me. "Except Mrs. Haskell. She isn't down yet."

There was a half-sullen unease about her. I speculated on it, linking it with the strenuous questioning the servants had all been put through. As I had before, on hearing of Alma's outbreak, I wondered about our servants and their reactions to all this.

Thompson, I knew, had resented Jocelyn with as much fervor as the family, perhaps more. Annie and Ethel, too, had thoroughly disapproved of her. But it came to me that Alma and Mildred were distinctly on the other side. Each possessed a certain prettiness, and Jocelyn in her relationship with them had alternated between an impatient arrogance and a sort of familiarity. Alma, particularly, had presumed on this favor. It was nothing that you could definitely see and correct; it was

as if she had absorbed Jocelyn's faint scorn for us.
Mildred, who seldom had anything to do on the
second floor, had had less opportunity, but she
too, I realized, had been fascinated by Jocelyn and
her stage connection. Yes, now that I thought of
it, their devotion was as marked as the disdainful
disapproval of Thompson and Ethel.

Brooke came in while Mildred was serving me.
Though he had breakfasted earlier, he had coffee
now to keep me company. Lighting a cigarette, he
looked me over.

"Sleep any?" he asked.

"Not much," I confessed. I said nothing about
my frightening experience; a kind of exhausted
reluctance to go into it this morning made me
shun the subject.

"Nor I." He sat down next to me, and now that
I noticed, he did look worn and harassed despite
his usual careful dress. Probably my own washed-
out appearance caused him to leave it at that. He
commented on the glimpse of garden visible from
the windows, and went on easily without touching
on the murder.

Not until I was all but finished did he ask
abruptly, "Have you seen Marian?"

I told him what Mildred had said.

"I know." He nodded absently. And then: "Nancy,
have you any idea what Jocelyn said to Marian

yesterday afternoon? Did she tell you—or your mother?"

I was right, then. I had not been the only one to observe the oddness of Marian's manner on that point the evening before.

"You noticed it—you brought it up. What did you think at the time?"

I brought it up! He was right about that. How many hundred times since have I wished that I had held my tongue! Would it have made any difference? Or would it have been the same eventually?

"Why, I scarcely know. She looked as if Jocelyn were poison to her," I finally got out, and he nodded thoughtfully, as if he had noticed just that, and now found it disturbing to recall.

Mother came in and we dropped the discussion. This was the first time I had seen her since she had gone down without waking me. The strained whiteness of her face was to be expected, I suppose, but I felt a sudden sense of shock as she stood there twisting her fingers in little spasms of despair. Brooke pulled out a chair, and she sat down limply, staring in a dazed wretchedness as he made an attempt to go back to his casual commonplaces. Almost immediately she shoved back her chair and stood. Something of the same despair was in the gesture as one hand pushed the soft hair from her forehead. With her hand still pressed to her head she started uncertainly toward the pantry and kitchen.

Brooke's eyes followed her with concern. "She's unstrung—all to pieces. I'd get her to bed, Nancy. If you can.

"Bigelow is back this morning, and they've had Marian in there for some time. He's taken over the library again."

I was startled, dismayed for the instant. And then I told myself, as Brooke sat looking troubled, that there was nothing extraordinary in that. It was natural enough that a member of the family should be asked to supply information.

Not until later did I know what took place in the library that morning when Marian, confronted by the district attorney and the same two men who had accompanied him the evening before, gave her crisp, decisive answers.

Alma's outpouring of the scene with Ham had done its work. That, coupled with the fact that the sitting room was a part of Marian's special domain, had caused Mr. Bigelow to request her appearance for further questioning. She alone was known to have entered the room before dinner, and, unfortunately, no one had seen her come out and go on almost directly as she had stated.

They failed, however, to touch on that curious bit of conversation with Jocelyn which had disturbed Brooke as well as me. This was not surprising, since they had not witnessed the incident, and it was easy to see that my allusion to it in the midst of everything else had not been noted as anything important.

Over and over, carefully deferential, but with obvious intent to trip and catch her off guard, they asked about her entering the sitting room and her furious anger of a few days previous, connecting the two with veiled but none the less clear implication.

"Did you know that your sister-in-law yesterday morning made what amounted to a threat to oust Mrs. Sherwin and her daughter from the house?"

"Yes, but it was ridiculous, of course."

"Did you talk it over—take any plan of action?"

After that she abandoned all pretense of amicable helpfulness. Her growing brusqueness worked against her so that they were less cautiously urbane as they proceeded. Finally they inquired about the various sports which engaged her: riding, golf and other physical activities.

"You're a sportswoman—and strong." This was Holt, one of the investigators from the sheriff's office who assisted the district attorney, a short, compactly built man with brisk movements and a voice that irritated in its positive certainty.

The direction toward which they were aiming was so obvious that she said, "I thought you asked me in here to assist with any information I could supply. If I am under suspicion, why, naturally, I shall want my lawyer here. I don't know a great deal about such matters, but I believe that is usual."

She ignored Mr. Bigelow's hurried protestations, and stood as she went on. "It is quite true that I was distressed and angry when I found the drawing room turned into something which belongs in a modernistic penthouse. Neither did I care for Jocelyn. She was distinctly antagonistic to us all. But"—a slight smile expressed her deep contempt for the insinuations of the examination—"I didn't murder her."

With this final audacity she was allowed to go, after a further protest from Mr. Bigelow that she had missed their intent somewhat, that in a case of this kind it was necessary to follow up every lead.

It was after this that Holt urged an arrest. The district attorney pointed out an improbability. If she were going to do it, why would she choose a time when the place was full of people, and an hour when practically everyone was on that floor?

Holt brushed that aside. "It's my idea that she seized on this house party as the best time to do it—made it that much more confusing and herself that much safer. She was in that room. The Haskell woman saw her go in, and no one saw her come out. She resented this new wife of her brother's." He warmed to his argument. "She went away because she couldn't stand her in the house.

Isn't that right?" he demanded. "And we have it on her own admission just what tearing up that big front room did to her. And on top of all that is her threat that there wouldn't be any more of it."

Cooper, the other man, agreed with Mr. Bigelow. "That murder was done in a hurry," he said. "When we know why, we'll be a long way toward having this cleared up."

The newspapers that morning had the account of the crime spread over their front pages with the usual startling headlines. The inevitable pictures were there, pictures that had been on file. A cut of Jocelyn—one of her professional photographs—and on an inside page Ham and Jocelyn, snapped at the boat as they returned from abroad. Marian was shown at a horse show last spring, and there was one of my own, labeled "Society Girl—Member of Wealthy Shephard Family."

But it was not until the evening papers came out that the full force of what newspaper notoriety meant came home to us. Those afternoon editions were rather awful in their innuendos. The implication, not in so many words, but clear for anyone of average intelligence to gather, was that a simple child of the people, her parentage humble in the extreme, had not measured up to the standards of the Shephard family. And after going through columns of that sort of thing the reader could manage certain conclusions for himself.

The papers that morning, however, carried only a hint of this. There was one item there, one which had been of my own offering, that loomed into importance as I read it. What about the man who had driven Jocelyn home, the man she had left with a slammed door as her only farewell?

I was thinking of this as I went in search of Mother. She was in the pantry going over the menus with Annie.

"Nancy," she said, "I wish you would just run up and see how Katherine is. She was really ill this morning. Nausea and a bad head." As she went on with details, how she had looked, what she had given her, she was so much herself that I left to go upstairs with no attempt to carry out Brooke's suggestion.

The door to Marian's sitting room, which had been closed when I came down, was now partially open, and voices were clearly audible, though I recognized neither of them.

"The way I have it doped out, the murderer stood by this door. Probably had it open a crack— just enough to know when she came along. Then"— he hesitated, fumbling for his pronoun, deciding against both—"whoever it was gave that little call. That brought her in. I have an idea that she was struck without seeing who it was. He may have held her mouth—those marks that Stanwix found on her face look like it—and then eased her down

on the floor and struck the four blows that finished her off. Though"—he sounded grim—"the
first was enough and plenty from the looks."

I shuddered as I stood there in the gallery. I
had just read much the same thing in the papers,
and I had seen Jocelyn's crumpled body lying on
the floor last night. But this detailed description
in matter-of-fact tones brought it home with a
new hideousness.

"If it was an inside job where are the gloves?"
the other man asked.

And well he might. For gloves there must have
been. The blurred fingerprints on the huge wrench
belonged to Leo, the clearer ones to Eddie. It was
the same with the bronze figure. That had shown
only marks of Alma's handling as she dusted and
replaced.

The house had already been searched from roof
to cellar in likely and unlikely places. The furnace
had been examined, and the fireplaces in both
library and terrace room where there had been
fires. But neither gloves nor charred remains with
their bits of metal fastenings had been found.

I was on my way to Katherine when Marian
came out of her room and turned to Katherine's,
which is at the front of the gallery next her own.
She saw me and smiled, but went in, closing the
door with a little sound of dismissal. I turned back
to the stairs; over the balustrade I saw the library

door open, but it was Cooper, not Mr. Bigelow, who came out. A young man, very thin and very dark. He was aiming for the stairs with the long stride that was swift while it looked leisurely and unhurried.

I stopped him at the last step. "I wanted to ask about the man who brought Mrs. Shephard home yesterday," I began. "She was angry, I could tell that, and upset, not like herself at all." My tone bristled a little. If they would look in the right direction . . .

He shook his head. "We've looked him up," he said in his pleasant, earnest voice. "It was Ganze. The theatrical producer," he explained.

Well. I waited. Did that make him immune from investigation?

"Ganze drove her out," he went on. "She spent a couple of hours with him. They were at the St Regis. Seems she was planning something different in the way of a stage comeback. Ganze wouldn't make any promises for the kind of thing she wanted. Said he thought a lot of Jocelyn King, and she had a future if she wanted to work. She could do a lot on her looks, he told her, but not everything." Cooper shifted his long legs and jammed one hand against his hip.

"Seems she was out for the lead in a regular drama, and he was telling her it would mean work, and besides, he didn't think she'd had the right kind of experience for that sort of thing. That's what they were still talking about when you saw them. She went right up in the air from all accounts."

"But that's it," I persisted. "They were quarreling." I hated to abandon this one idea which seemed to point away from our household.

He smiled at that. "Well, he didn't kill her and carry her in," he reminded me in his mild, even tones. "She went into the house under her own power. No"—he shook his head—"we've checked up on Ganze. He was having dinner in town at six. That checks. And he had to do some driving to make it, if you use your arithmetic."

"What about the telephone call before she went upstairs? What about that?" I asked as he made his tentative moves to go on.

He settled back, considered and then decided, apparently, to let me have it.

"The calls were traced," he said. "She called J. Stanley Parsons. She made two calls, one at his club and one at his house in New York. She got him at the house and talked about four minutes." He went with that—I was too stunned to hold him with further questions—turning to say, "We're following up everything, Miss Sherwin."

I stood staring after him as he went loping up the stairs, and then dazedly I walked the length of the hall and let myself out on the porticoed porch.

I had been astonished when he mentioned J. Stanley Parsons, astonished and faintly uncomfortable. We had ignored it as one of those bits of gossip that seem to go with certain people, particularly women of the theater, but that Jocelyn's name had been connected with that of the wealthy and important Parsons I did know. It had been nothing more than rumor, and vague rumor at that, which had cropped out at the time of her marriage to Ham. One or two of the lesser papers had touched on it, but so lightly, so cautiously, that it had added little to the word-of-mouth innuendo that had previously been all, I imagine.

I knew Parsons only through newspaper mention, pictures labeled "Financier Returns on the Europa." Things like that. But I knew his daughters. Not well, but here and there at occasional dances I had run into one or both of them.

Why had Jocelyn talked to Parsons? I recalled what Thompson had had to say of that conversation. "No, it's not that. It hasn't anything to do with them." And right after that she had walked upstairs to a horrible death.

Realization was difficult this morning. Leaning against a fluted pillar, everything seemed oddly unchanged. Trees and shrubbery shut off the road, which lay beyond the grounds and the curious crowd collected there. But it was not the same. The district attorney was established behind closed doors in the library. Though they were not visible from the porch, police cars were standing in the drive. Ham, instead of being settled to a morning in his study, was over at the mortuary place where they had taken Jocelyn's body last night. The rest of us, after that suave little speech of Mr. Bigelow's, were virtually prisoners in our own house. Even as I stood there, a man came around the south wing with a camera, and I hastily went inside.

O'Meara and Dr. Jarvis were in the terrace room, Jarvis pacing around and smoking, O'Meara, sprawled comfortably in a big chair, still going over the papers.

"Ham's books are due for a wave of popularity." O'Meara dropped his paper to the untidy heap beside him and stretched. "Wouldn't surprise me if that last tome even made the best-seller list." He yawned and stretched again. "If I were the police I'd go after his publishers."

8

While I lingered in the hall Miss Wycke arrived, letting herself in by the west entrance. I thought perhaps she had been sent for again, but apparently she had come from habit; that or a desire to be on the scene.

"I thought I'd come," she said. "I didn't know . . ."

The telephone began ringing, and she went efficiently to answer it. The telephone had been going constantly. People close to us—and those not so close—had begun calling as soon as they saw the papers. Miss Wycke's presence would relieve Thompson at any rate,

She was still talking when I was called to the library. Ever since waking I had expected the summons which Connolly's report would surely demand.

Mr. Bigelow was behind the desk in almost the identical position of the night before. Cooper, the young man I had talked to in the hall, stood leafing the pages of a notebook. His dark eyes, set far apart, had an owlish look behind their spectacles, and his straight black hair was ruffled and disordered. Something of the same carelessness was in the hang of the really well-cut gray suit.

Mr. Bigelow smiled encouragingly as I sat down.

"I understand you had an unpleasant experience down here last night."

"I came down for something to read," I began. I hated repeating that absurdity of the book, but I was committed to it. Once over that, it went easily. But no words could give the full horror of my second return to the library. The plain facts, as I related them, made that dreadful circuit of the room far less terrifying. Unbelievingly my eyes traversed the course I had woven from desk to telephone room, clinging always to the book-lined walls. Here, in the familiar everyday comfort of the room, it seemed unreal.

"And you have no idea who this person was?" Mr. Bigelow, who had listened without interrupting, now leaned forward and looked at me intently.

"No," I said. The question carried a shock, but in the sane calm that morning brought I had thought of the possibility of Larry's coming back.

"Try to think. Certain smells—toilet lotions, tobacco—sometimes they arouse the memory."

I shook my head. There had been nothing. Or if there had my senses had all been given over to terror.

"You didn't at the moment you were seized touch something? Clothing, hair, jewelry, perhaps?" His voice, his searching regard, urged recollection on me.

I shook my head again. There had been no struggle. It had happened too quickly, and I had been insensible to anything but fear.

"You're sure the entrance was from the hall?"

My eyes went to the door, to the small desk in the window. "Yes, that's where I heard something just before the lights went off. I thought it was the door."

I didn't tell him that I had been waiting for that very sound.

"There's the window," I reminded him after a moment's silence.

"It seems hardly likely an entrance was made there," he said as if his mind were still engaged with the problem of finding the identity of my assailant.

I nodded a reluctant agreement, though I had not yet heard the full report on the pane of glass so neatly replaced after its removal.

It was a pane from one of those windows that are never raised. A room with exposure on three sides—certain ones were opened from habit, I suppose. Now that I think of it, it's the same with most of the rooms on the first floor.

"That window hadn't been raised since the place was painted," was Holt's scornful verdict. "And it wasn't that way last night either." In this he was vigorously supported by both Rumsey and Slade. "I don't know what it was done for, but no one came in that window. It wouldn't take five minutes to slide a knife around it and take it out. But raising it—it was stuck so tight I had to use a wedge on it."

"Miss Sherwin"—Mr. Bigelow's voice and attitude changed abruptly—"of course you understand that in a case of this kind it is necessary to check every possible angle." The smile, the tone, a little unctuous, were meant to assure me that whatever was to come was the merest routine.

"Yes?" I waited, confident of some new approach to the affair of the night.

"Were Mr. and Mrs. Shephard quite friendly?" he asked without any further preamble.

I was surprised, then intensely uncomfortable. How could I answer that? Ham and Jocelyn had been different for weeks. I had observed that with an increasing awareness. But they weren't unfriendly in the sense I was sure he meant. There were distinctions that could not be explained to a stranger.

I was decided. "Yes," I said, and it came firmly. "They were entirely friendly."

"Nothing in the way of a disagreement—ah—no recent quarrel that you recall?"

"No," I answered. I would not tell of those angry voices that one night, nor of Ham's change from fatuous adulation to something that was cold indifference.

He looked at me uncertainly; my unqualified denials left no openings.

"Cooper"—Mr. Bigelow turned suddenly—"ask that secretary to come in. She's here?" He looked at me and settled back to wait for her.

"Miss Wycke," he asked as soon as she was seated, "did you have any opportunity to observe Mr. and Mrs. Shephard together?" And without giving her time to reply, "Would you say they were entirely friendly?"

"I saw Mrs. Shephard very seldom," she said to that. "Ordinarily I spend my time in Mr. Shephard's study."

"And Mrs. Shephard never came to the study?"

"Occasionally, yes."

"When was she there last?" A tinge of annoyance at the shortness of her replies, a deliberate shortness meant to convey contempt for these questions.

"Tuesday afternoon," she said after considering a moment with her heavy brows drawn together.

"I see. And were Mr. and Mrs. Shephard quite congenial at that time?"

"Mr. Shephard wasn't there."

For the first time Mr. Bigelow lost his urbanity. His next question sounded genuinely provoked. "Where was Mr. Shephard?"

"He had gone to dress for an engagement in town. So Mrs. Shephard went on upstairs, I suppose." Manner and voice both continued to show disdain for what she chose to see as petty prying into personal affairs.

"Did this engagement include Mrs. Shephard, do you know?"

"No."

"What was the engagement, Miss Wycke?"

"He was having dinner with Mrs. Haskell." The flat statement came with the right promptness. Hesitancy would have given it too much importance.

As it was, his interest quickened. He was assured once more. "You kept track of Mr. Shephard's engagements?" And at her stiff nod of assent: "Bring me the book, please."

I was in thorough accord with Miss Wycke's refusal to produce the book. It was horrible, I thought, the way the smallest incidents were pounced on and made to loom as something portentous, even scandalous.

"The book belongs to Mr. Shephard," she said, and the whole set of her body disdained this intrusion into a privacy that it was her business to protect.

Mr. Bigelow was angry and showed it. "Miss Wycke, a murder has been committed. It happens to be my business to investigate. Bring it, please."

Ungraciously she brought the brown leather-covered book from the study and handed it to Mr. Bigelow.

When I glanced at it later I was surprised at the number of times Katherine's name recurred. Since her early return to town Ham had seen her frequently, and her name in the book implied other meetings of a more casual nature. Probably Mr. Bigelow would construe these harmless dinner engagements into something telling and important.

"Mrs. Haskell is an old friend," I stopped to tell him when Miss Wycke had gone out, disapproval in every line of her tall, heavy figure. "There's really nothing unusual or out of the way about it." Gratefully I reflected that he couldn't know of the generally accepted belief that Ham and Katherine would marry.

When I left the library Hamilton and Brooke were coming in. Marian, who must have observed the car from upstairs, came down directly with the evident intention of a talk with Ham. Since the day of her return things had been difficult between these two who had always genuinely enjoyed each other. She was putting forth every effort now to bridge the gap of those uncomfortable days, but her very struggle for naturalness defeated her purpose, and she was constrained, not herself.

"Are you bringing Jocelyn here, Ham?" she asked.

"No, I won't bring her back. We've arranged for short services in the chapel connected with the place. Tomorrow morning."

The words, the tone, were all right enough; it was the way he regarded her that was strange. An intent, curious look with something of appraisal in it.

Her hand went out, she seemed about to speak, and then, as if held off and repelled by the oddness of his manner, she merely stood watching him as he passed on upstairs.

"I'm worried about Ham," she said to Brooke.

"Well, all this has been a pretty big shock," he reminded her.

"I know. But it isn't that altogether." Her eyes were disturbed.

"He'll come out of it," Brooke told her, admitting that he too had observed something strange in the look Ham had bent on Marian.

She mused on it an instant longer, then with a little straightening of her shoulders walked briskly across the hall. And fifteen minutes later, when I stepped into the terrace room where people seemed to have drifted listlessly, she was sitting at the secretary with all her usual decision of manner, Irene beside her and Larry standing near, making out cards of admission to Jocelyn's funeral, I gathered from inquiries directed at the McIvers.

Dr. Jarvis was still pacing about with halts at first one window and then another.

"Any idea what they're cooking up in there?" He stopped beside me and nodded in the direction of the hall and library. Brooke turned at the question, and we closed in so that with O'Meara, still sprawled in his chair, we made a little group of our own at that end of the room.

"Not much," I said. The questioning about Ham I would keep to myself. I told them about Ganze. They listened speculatively, made a comment or two. "Nothing there, I guess," Dr. Jarvis said. "Not if he was back in town at six." And the other two nodded in mechanical agreement.

Jarvis threw his cigarette into the fire and wheeled about, his manner in sharp contrast to the dull sluggishness which hung over our end of the room.

"Look!" he said abruptly. "We've got to get together on this."

He ignored my bewildered stare and glanced uncertainly at the McIvers where they assisted Marian; they were the unknown quantity, his look said.

"As near as I can make out"—his eyes were on the disorderly pile of papers on the floor beside O'Meara—"they haven't anything. No fingerprints. No clues. No witnesses. Well, have they?" he demanded with a kind of triumph.

"Well then!" His look took us all in. "If we all sit tight—no one gets panicky and goes haywire—"

"You mean . . ." I began. What did he mean? An undefined fear was slowly welling up around me.

"Where's Mrs. Haskell?" he asked suddenly. Apparently this get-together was to become a fact at once.

"Not down yet. She's ill this morning." The cold incisiveness of O'Meara's tone, so alien to his customary sardonic drawl, disapproved this odd suggestion of Jarvis'.

"I think it's a good idea," Jarvis insisted, a hint of irascibility in his voice. "Wouldn't do any harm." Again he eyed the McIvers with a certain distaste; how far would it be safe to go with them? "Emotionally unbalanced, that Irene," he said in annoyed undertone. "She's just the kind—" He stopped abruptly, and I turned to see why. Cooper had come in and was standing just within the door.

"If he calls on me I'm not prepared," O'Meara said to me out of the corner of his mouth.

I followed his look to where Cooper stood, and smiled a little. There was something undeniably schoolmasterish about Cooper: the wide-spaced eyes behind their spectacles, the quick appraisal, a general sizing up of who was there as he came on in. The young instructor taking over his class.

"Connolly reported that some of you people came down to the library at a late hour last night—or early this morning."

Dr. Jarvis blew a column of smoke through his thin lips. "I was down," he said evenly. His tone was contentious in spite of what he had been saying, which meant, I thought—if it meant anything at all—not to let anyone get a rise out of us.

"Yes?" Cooper waited expectantly, the instructor calling out volunteers, though he knew them as well as I did. "Miss Sherwin, of course." His eyes passed over me.

"I was down," Larry said curtly and with one suspicious glance my way deliberately swung back to Marian, who had stopped her work and was watching intently, her keen gray eyes going from Cooper to the huddle on our side of the room.

"Why were you down, Mr. McIver?"

Poor Larry. Already I had cause to know with what foolish improbability that need of a book at three o'clock in the morning rang out. It would never bear repetition.

Larry gave an effect of bracing himself. "I wanted a book."

At the involuntary gasps of amusement Larry flushed angrily. There was something small-boyish about him in spite of his height; probably the full sullen lips, the thick light hair that, brushed straight back, still stood out in crisp waves.

"A book? You're sure it was a book, McIver?" The mild, pleasant voice had taken on an almost imperceptible shade of menace.

"Yes, a book." He said it truculently. And then, at someone's ripple of disbelieving laughter: "That's what I said. A book." He stuck out his jaw and glared at no one in particular. "I'm crazy about reading. A regular bookworm."

"And you, Doctor Jarvis? Did you want a book too?"

There was another laugh, a quick little snort as quickly suppressed. We all smiled, all except Larry, who stood stiffly, glaring straight ahead.

"I came down to make a telephone call," Dr. Jarvis said in the same even voice.

"At three o'clock?" Cooper persistently kept us reminded of the incongruity of the hour.

"It was a Los Angeles call," Dr. Jarvis explained.

Everyone made the three-hour subtraction, saw the plausibility and went right on wondering.

"It was only an hour later than I had intended calling," Jarvis continued easily, the edge quite gone from his voice. "I remembered it after going upstairs and thought I might as well put it through."

"I see." Cooper nodded understandingly. "Who were you calling, Doctor Jarvis?"

Jarvis barely hesitated; he smiled slightly. "I'm afraid I can't tell you that," he said.

Intrigue, a woman that he didn't wish to involve—that was what he managed to convey. In some indistinguishable way he gave the effect of enjoying himself.

"The call will be traced, Doctor Jarvis," Cooper reminded him.

"Yes?" The slight smile again as he lit a fresh cigarette.

Cooper didn't urge him further. From an inner pocket he drew a sheet of folded note paper and turned to Larry.

"You don't want to change your story, Mr. McIver?"

"No," Larry said shortly, "I don't." But his hands trembled as he fumbled at a flattened package of cigarettes.

"As a matter of fact, wasn't this what you were after last night?" With irritating slowness Cooper opened the sheet and held it out to Larry. "This was written to you, wasn't it?"

Larry glanced at it briefly. "Never saw it before," he said and continued to glower at the same spot on the wall opposite.

Cooper's eyes went from Marian to me; I was nearer. "Is this Mrs. Shephard's writing?" he asked.

I read the note as I examined it. A half-dozen lines in Jocelyn's angular backhand, with wide spaces between the words. There was no salutation.

> Darling, here is fifty. And don't be dumb. You'll step into something any day now. Bound to with all the fall openings. Until tomorrow night. All my love.
>
> Joss

"Yes, that's Jocelyn's writing," I told Cooper. And then, as I would have handed it back, Irene leaped forward, snatching the note from my hand.

"Yes, it's Larry's!" she cried out bitterly, her face white with anger. "But if you think that proves anything you're crazy! Fifty dollars! What's that? Why shouldn't she give it to him?" Her voice went higher, she was fairly screaming. "He's spent every cent we had—and a lot more we didn't have. You can't go to all the ritzy clubs in New York on air."

And with one wild look at Larry she flung herself past Cooper and out of the room.

Didn't she know, couldn't she see, that her hysterical defense was drawing a picture which showed a Larry madly, crazily in love with Jocelyn, a picture that was damaging in the extreme?

I remembered Larry's fumbling at the books the night before, and Dr. Jarvis' remarks, which had held no significance at the time. Had Larry, fearing a search when we were all summoned to the library, slipped the note between the books? Could Dr. Jarvis have pointed out the hiding place? That was scarcely in accord with what he had been saying when Cooper came in. Perhaps a book, disturbed and pulled out of place, had betrayed the hidden note; in all probability the room had been gone over after Connolly's report.

Cooper had picked up the sheet of heavy white paper. He stood looking around from face to face, his brown eyes steady and thoughtful. He didn't press the advantage Irene's swift outburst had given him over Larry. That would come later, as his next words indicated.

"Mr. Bigelow will want to see you, McIver," he said. And Larry, the pallor showing beneath his surface bronze, followed Cooper out of the room without glancing at any of us.

For the space of time that it took them to cross the hall to the library everybody in the room

might have been in a state of suspended anima-
tion. With the click of the door Brooke shrugged.
"Vile scene," he said and turned to stare out at the
grounds. Silhouetted against the lacquer yellow of
the window drapery, the lean handsomeness of his
profile stood out sharply.

Vile scene it was, but for the instant I felt the
callousness of that disdainful detachment following Larry's white-faced departure, his legs moving
with the autonomy of a sleepwalker. I disliked less
the slightly misplaced humor of O'Meara's class-
room analogy. "This session isn't going to raise
our grades any," he said as he pulled himself heavily from the deep chair. He turned his bland look
on Jarvis. "I still can't see that they have much.
Checked up on a few of our heavy readers last
night. But reading's no crime—though some of it
ought to be."

9

After lunch, a ghastly meal at which neither of the McIvers appeared, I went up to sit with Katherine awhile. I knew she had been in bed all the morning with a sick headache, but I wasn't prepared for the spent exhaustion which made her seem suddenly old. I had never thought of age in connection with Katherine. Her warm loveliness, indolent grace and stunning clothes didn't belong to the middle age that Marian frankly acknowledged.

But she was better, she insisted she was better and would get up in the late afternoon.

"I had a headache to begin with," she explained with more volubility than she ordinarily displayed, "and then being up all night . . . The shock and all—it's simply raddled me." She smiled faintly. "You're young. A night like that doesn't take its toll on your face."

She leaned languorously back in her pillows; only her gray eyes, almost black now, betrayed her excitement.

"What are they doing? What do they think
now?" she wanted to know.

I tried to sort out the confused mixture of
fact and unsatisfactory speculation that filled my
mind. Beyond the introduction of Parsons' name
I had little that was new. And this I decided not
to mention.

"Then there's nothing," she said when I had
given her a scattered account of the morning.
"They haven't anything." She repeated it: "I can't
see that they have a thing."

Coming as it did in her slow, effortless way, it
was just a passing comment, her end of the conversation, intercepted at the right moment—nothing
more. Then suddenly I was alive to the relief in
her voice, to the words fraught with import and
meaning. This was what Dr. Jarvis had said a few
hours earlier, and his tone had held the same satisfaction.

I sat looking at her unbelievingly. Again that
ominous sense of dread crept over me. I struggled
against it; I was nervous and overwrought. I didn't
ask what she meant. I couldn't. Instead I plunged
into a hurried telling of the episode of Jocelyn's
note and Irene's violent exit.

She listened, her lips contorted into a wry
smile, expressive of what she thought of Irene and
her lack of any decent covering for her emotions.
"The McIvers . . . I hadn't thought . . ." She lay

musing it over, her eyes half closed. "He was mad about her. Jocelyn, I mean. Anyone could tell that, even without Irene's shrieking it all over the place."

I was still with Katherine when Alma came to say that Oz was downstairs. Standing just within the door after her knock, she was entirely the well-trained servant in her starched maroon uniform and white apron, but, though I couldn't for the life of me have said what it was, there was something irritatingly triumphant about her as she made her correct announcement.

Oz was with Brooke and Jarvis when I went down. A certain edginess that he always displayed with Brooke was discernible only to me. It never amounted to much more than a lessening of the bubbling geniality that belongs to Oz, but he had little use for Brooke. It all dated back, I think, to a horse show of a few years ago, though Oz would probably disclaim this as being the sole root of what amounted to a deep dislike. At the time Brooke was showing a hunter, one of Marian's, which made it that much worse in Oz's eyes. The horse refused the jump, not once but three times. Brooke lost his temper and from Oz's account made a bad exhibition of himself. A matter of laying on with crop and spurs, and a general loss of control which disgusted and outraged Oz. Attempts to alter an opinion formed that day had little effect. "Sure, he's a grand guy," he invariably agreed, "but don't cross him."

"I came over to see the D.A.," he said when we had detached ourselves from the others. "Or one of his men. But they've left, it seems. I've got something I think they ought to have." He was excited, almost pleasurably so, despite his efforts for a mien suited to tragedy.

"Listen, let's go out on the sun porch. I'm driving over to Bigelow's office, but another ten minutes won't make any difference."

But the McIvers were in possession of the sun porch, and quarreling vigorously. We could hear their voices as we stepped into Ham's study. Irene was protesting a longer stay in a house which had become a place of terror.

"You can do as you please," she was saying in a swift, furious tone. "I'm getting out this afternoon!"

"All right." Larry's tone was cutting. "But I'm staying with the rest of them. We're Joss' friends— her funeral is tomorrow. It'll look damn funny, but go on! Grab your things and shove right along. If there's a chance to get me in a deeper mess, don't miss it!"

Oz looked at me, one eyebrow lifted. An added buoyancy as he led our retreat gave further evidence of his exhilaration over unwonted happenings.

In the end Oz and I went out and sat on the flight of steps which lead down from the rear entrance porch.

"Listen," he said after I had explained about the McIvers, "last night when I came home there was a Lincoln car parked at the edge of your grounds. Out at the north end." He waved a bronzed hand. "I didn't think of it when I came over here and hell had broken loose; it never occurred to me. I didn't think of it again till this morning."

"What time?"

"It must have been close to eight—it was about ten after when I got in the house."

"It wasn't ours?" I asked. We have a Lincoln. But Leo had not had the car out after taking Jocelyn to the train.

"No." He passed that by: he would have recognized our car. "There was just the one man." He squinted his eyes against the sun as he tried for recollection. "I remember at the time my impression was that he was waiting for someone. I didn't notice particularly—I'd say, though, he wasn't young.

"Well . . ." He stood up and leaned against the rail. "I'll pass it on for what it's worth. They've probably had a hundred or so such things by now. The police are swamped with the stuff that's offered in a case of this kind."

Here was something that pointed to an outside source, and I seized on it eagerly. In the face

of impossibility I still clung to the idea. I heard
again Holt's harangue that morning to a man I
didn't know.

"Nobody shinnied up any pillars. We've been
over the whole place and there's not a mark. A
white house and painted in the spring . . ." He
made a derisive, hissing sound. "Take a look for
yourself! If anyone got in from outside, he was
let in, that's clear," he asserted in those positive,
jerky tones I had come to dislike so intensely.

But here was Oz's story of a car lurking in a
shadowy place at the edge of our grounds.

"The headlights were turned off," he was saying, and that clinched its importance for me. I
wanted him to be off imparting this new information.

"Call me up, Oz, after you've seen Mr. Bigelow."

But he was in no hurry to leave. "That secretary of Ham's—she's a funny one," he observed.
He took his elbows from the railing and sat down
beside me again. "What do you know about her
anyway?"

"Why, she's been with Ham a long time, of
course."

"I know," he said. "What's she like?"

I considered. What, after all, did we know of
Miss Wycke for all the years she had been a part
of our household?

"She's wrapped up in Ham's work," I said slowly. "All those evenings after her research stuff—that was her own idea, I believe."

"Was Ham in his study when she worked at night?" he asked as if he had been struck by something new.

I tried to think. "Not since his marriage. Not much anyway." I paused; where Ham had spent several of his evenings these last weeks I had learned that morning. But before that, when he was still under Jocelyn's sway? There was the evening he had gone with her at the last moment when it was plain she neither expected nor wanted it. "Decided on mirth and gaiety after all," he announced as he joined her where she waited in the hall for Leo. That sort of thing had not fooled anyone. But it was something not to be noticed; the picture of Ham begging small favors from this girl was not a pleasant sight.

There were the times he had gone at it the other way. "It's not a bad night to stay by the home hearth." The nice smile with the quiet good humor behind it was always wasted on Jocelyn. And she, betraying by her manner that she would be delighted to have him do just that: "I've made this engagement in town, but you stay, Ham." Her suddenly vibrant voice, more than her words, urged it.

What had been Ham's thoughts in those hours of restless waiting for her return? His attempts to make her part of his own circle had been a failure. I have an idea that she was hilariously amusing as she described and caricatured those evenings. I have heard her on the telephone: "I couldn't get through another state dinner tonight, Phil. Suppose you meet me . . ."

As I looked back Ham's bewildered efforts to fit Jocelyn into his life were pathetic in the extreme.

"But, Jocelyn, these people have been asked to dinner. It is your place to be here."

"Tell them I have a professional engagement," she would say carelessly. And that was what he did, then and on other occasions. "Jocelyn expected to be here, but her professional demands . . . something that she could not well avoid . . ."

It was this kind of thing we had been so ineffectual in explaining to the district attorney last night when he was incredulous at our lack of alarm over Jocelyn's failure to put in an appearance.

"Well, probably your psychologist could make something out of it." Oz brought me back to Miss Wycke. "In love with Ham and all that stuff. Repressions."

"Oz!" I said it derisively, but I was assuming some of my mockery. I would have been even less inclined to scoff if I had known the result of the search of her small apartment. For, as it came out later, Miss Wycke had kept every scrap of newspaper stuff relating to Ham, reviews and the like. She had all of his books, autographed, of course. There were several notes, too, mere directions scrawled in his small, all but illegible hand and left, no doubt, on her table in his study. There were also a half-dozen letters written to her from abroad; nothing more than requests for this and that. She had kept them, every one.

"Not a bad-looking woman," Oz offered in mild support of his theory.

And she wasn't. Somewhere in her late thirties, probably, she was tall and wore good-looking clothes of the severely tailored type. She was even rather handsome in a dark, heavy way that belonged somehow to her independence, an aggressive independence which, I vaguely realized, was defense mechanism of a sort.

And then, in one of those swift flashes of memory, I did recall something. A look of intense hatred on Miss Wycke's face. Without Oz's prodding questions I might never have thought of it again; it had happened weeks ago while Ham was still in a state of blind infatuation. I had dropped in to see if he wanted to ride, and was still there when Jocelyn made one of her galvanic swoops on the study.

"Darling, I'm going now," she announced. "Stay here and slave if you will." In a charmingly impetuous little rush she was across the room; a demonstrative farewell which forestalled his quite obvious intention of abandoning all work for the rest of the day.

It was then I had seen it, that one look of deep loathing which Miss Wycke had darted at Jocelyn, standing there, breathlessly lovely, kissing Ham good-by.

Had Miss Wycke seen Jocelyn's demonstration for what it unmistakably was? Or did it go deeper than that? The neurotic jealousy which Oz was suggesting.

"Well, I'll get along." Oz rose but didn't move down the steps. The sun, filtering through the leaves of a sycamore tree, made a moving, lacy pattern of light and shadow on his blond hair and the deep tan of his skin.

"I shouldn't say this, perhaps," he said after a moment of standing with both arms stretched along the rail, "and don't quote me on it"—he grinned—"but I can see only one person in this."

"Who?" I demanded.

"Not yet. I can't disclose anything yet." Another grin that didn't conceal the earnestness beneath the burlesque.

I didn't urge him; he meant Miss Wycke, of course. Oz is never subtle. But there was something oddly embarrassing in this definite singling out, even with the name withheld.

10

When I went inside, Mother came toward me with the same vague air of starting someplace without being quite certain where it was she wished to go.

"Nancy, you might call Leo." She fluttered a slip of paper out to me. "I want him to drive over and get this filled. It's a prescription the doctor left for Katherine, something for the nausea."

I started for the telephone and then decided to go to the garage instead. If Leo was permitted to leave, why shouldn't I have the same privilege? There was a man stationed outside—I saw him now over near the gardens chatting amiably with McAllister—and to my knowledge, no one had left the place except Ham and Brooke, but we had received no orders beyond Mr. Bigelow's little talk of the night before.

"Going out, Miss Sherwin?" Leo inquired surprisedly when I asked for my car.

"I'm going to try it," I told him, and he grinned a quick response, approval of what he chose to

see as a mild triumph over the forces of investigation.

Though it was out of my way, I turned the car
north as I drove out, unmolested, passing the
place where the parked car had stood. Why had it
waited in the shadow, with lights dimmed?

This was my first contact with the outside world
since the crime, and I was not prepared for the
charged excitement my appearance in the drugstore created. It was something I could both see
and feel. With an assumption of ease which I was
far from feeling I handed my prescription slip to
Mr. Hones himself. I had been in and out of that
store for a matter of thirteen years. Now, with the
lurid accounts of a brutal crime spread over the
pages of the newspapers, I automatically became
a subject of intense interest. The clerks and the
three or four customers watched me under a cover
of sudden volubility and quick moving around,
and I saw myself being pointed out so that a new
entrant would not miss me. Already I regretted
having come.

While I waited in a detached position at the
front of the store, I was relieved to see O'Meara
emerge cumbersomely from one of the telephone
booths in the rear.

"Made something of a stir, your arrival," he
said on joining me. This levity of O'Meara's in
the face of what had happened was not jarring.

He was O'Meara, and you expected the levity and took for granted the awareness of tragedy.

He planted an arm on the glass surface of the cosmetic counter, leaning comfortably. "They didn't place me when I made my own entrance," he went on, "but now I can bask in the reflected notoriety. I shouldn't be surprised at movie offers. Certainly a vaudeville engagement." He glanced back toward the rear counter. "What are you waiting for?"

I explained about Katherine and deciding to come myself. "I didn't know it would be like this. I wanted to see if the man would stop me, but I drove right out as usual."

"The same here," he said. "It didn't make any great difference whether I left or not, but I was ready to put up a heavy argument and never had a chance to use it."

There was a pause; quite obviously he was turning something over in his mind. "I'm going over to my place," he announced, almost too carelessly offhand after that moment of consideration. "Not to stay," he added hastily. "I'm not breaking faith, as the saying is, with the district attorney, but I want a bunch of notes I have over there. Why not come along? We'll be back by five or not much after." He looked impatiently toward the prescription counter. "What are they mixing back there?" he demanded.

"I don't know if I should leave," I said doubt-fully. "I might phone and find out, and they would deliver this stuff for Katherine."

"Would they!" His face was expressive of what he thought of the general public's avidity for murder. "A chance to drive right up to the seat of the crime!"

He drew his arm from the counter, stretching and shifting himself into position. "Go on out. Work your car into a quiet spot, and I'll carry the good news to the lucky man to get the assignment, and telephone."

I had been to O'Meara's house only once be-fore, an afternoon when I drove out with Marian. It is a pleasant place, rather detached from the small village, and was their permanent home until Lois got her divorce. Since then he has divided his time between this and an apartment in town. For all his aversion to golf, long energetic walks, the kind of thing that Ham and Marian go in for, he likes digging around the grounds and claims he can't really write anything without alternating it with spells of gardening.

"Better stay outside, Nancy. I won't be a min-ute, and I fancy it's pleasanter. Just at present the help is scarce."

O'Meara's difficulties with his help are well known. He is always being exultant over some new arrangement. "I've got a man and his wife," he'll announce on some chance encounter. "They're perfect." And then, shortly after that—it may be a month, possibly as much as three or four—there will have been changes. "A woman comes in from town. The work is done and I don't have anyone in the way when I don't want her." There are also stretches when there is no one at all, and in its initial stages he is equally enthusiastic about that. "It's the way to live!"

I have an idea that this same uncertainty characterized his life with Lois, for in the years previous to the divorce, I understand, one or the other of them was always leaving with similar abruptness.

O'Meara's minute stretched into ten or more. I left the dusty bench to wander about the sprawling garden, a little unkempt and not very well laid out. He was gone for perhaps half an hour before he came back with a large envelope, crowded to bulkiness, and a portable typewriter.

"Probably won't touch the stuff," he said, dropping them on the grass, "but all this effort of coming out here and hunting for it gives me a fine, industrious feeling." He took a stick and bolstered up a spreading chrysanthemum plant, and stood admiring his patch of marigolds.

"We should be starting back, Frank," I reminded him.

A little reluctantly he brushed his hands together, picked up his envelope and typewriter, and lumbered to the car in the drive.

"If only it hadn't happened," I said out of a not unpleasant silence on the drive back. This time away with O'Meara had made realization of murder doubly difficult of comprehension.

"Go back farther than that," he said quickly. "If only Ham hadn't waited until he was fifty to go off his head. "But"—he lifted his hands from the wheel for an instant, a little gesture of futility—"those things happen. And when they come late, they go hard, I understand."

"Frank, what do you think?" So far I had just sidled up to something that I feared—just what, I didn't quite know—and backed away without facing it.

Beyond our talk in the drugstore we had not touched on the crime these two hours away. My approaches had all been deftly turned off. Nor would he discuss it now. He watched a yellowjacket settle on the upholstery above the small mirror.

"Look at him!" he declaimed dramatically. "There he is being carried miles away from home. The thing worries me; it's something I've brought my mind to bear on any number of times. Shall I push him out or carry him on? The thing is, what am I shoving him back to? Boredom, dull monotony, domestic wrangling? Then again, if I speed on with him, is it high adventure, a casting away of ties that irk and hamper? Or is it loneliness—an awful sense of loss?"

O'Meara could go on this way for hours, as I well knew, and my attempt to look at things squarely was abandoned right there. The problem of the yellowjacket carried us into the village and my own car.

"It's there, then," he exclaimed as we drew up. "I hadn't said a word, just brooded over it in silence, but I had every idea it would be carried off in small sections as souvenirs."

Coming into the house, I had a momentary sensation that nothing was wrong after all. The library door was open once more, and a mingling of voices came from the terrace room. But I had no more than gained my own room when it was brought violently back to me. Irene must have been watching for me, so exactly did her appearance coincide with my arrival.

She had already changed for dinner, but in spite of careful make-up, the studied slickness of her black hair and the good-looking green dress, she looked neither fresh nor rested. Irene looks older than her actual years, I imagine. There's an intensity about her, an air of never relaxing, that gives her face an expression of worn discontent which accents and emphasizes what is only a slight disparity in years between herself and Larry.

I asked her to sit down, but she shut the door and leaned her thin, lithe body against it. "So you and Doctor Jarvis blabbed to the district attorney about Larry!" she said. "Sneaked back down and got his letter!"

I was aghast. Had one or the other of them been peering from the door and watched that second descent of mine? But I was guiltless as far as Larry was concerned.

"No," I told her, controlling my voice as well as I could, "I didn't." And I added, "I didn't know there was a letter until this morning."

She smiled in contemptuous disbelief.

"If anyone thinks Larry had anything to do with killing Jocelyn, they're crazy," she burst out. "He was wild about her!" Anger raised her voice, which had been restrained and cautious. Her shoulders pressed against the door. "He'd been more apt to kill me!"

Her bitterness told better than any protestations of affection of the jealous intensity of her love for the good-looking, indifferent Larry who didn't even trouble to conceal his strayings. For her next words indicated plainly that Jocelyn was not the first, nor would she in all probability be the last.

The explosion came in answer to my question. "Do you think it could have been Jocelyn who came to the door yesterday, Irene? That she went back because she wanted to avoid a . . ." I felt for my word, I didn't want to say "scene."

But she gave me no chance to finish. "And I didn't have anything to do with it either!" she flung out. "Why should I? What good would it do? There'd be someone else."

I felt sorry for her, came nearer to liking her than at any time since she had begun to frequent our house. With this swift glimpse at her kind of seething love that brought her no happiness, only torment, she became less hard and unpleasantly repellent.

"I don't know who it was," she said more calmly. "I thought it was Jocelyn, naturally. Why shouldn't I?" she demanded.

"Perhaps it was," I responded, "and she went back and stepped into the sitting room—"

She gave me a quick, sharp look. "It was the murderer who came to that door," she said. "And maybe someone else saw who it was if I didn't. Only they're all hanging together. Larry and I are outsiders." And with that she jerked the door open and left.

What had she meant by that? Was it a reading of the afternoon papers, the same insidious suggestion of a tight family affair, a family leagued against interlopers from outside? Too emotionally keyed up for the rest and leisurely dressing I had planned, I changed and went down at once.

The lower floor was deserted. Only Thompson was there, adjusting lights, giving little twists to chairs, wiping the film of ash from polished surfaces. The radio was playing softly, a lilting dance

movement that I recognized dully. A sound came
from the upper hall; someone else, moved perhaps
by the same driving restlessness. Larry appeared
at the head of the stairs, and an embarrassed unease kept my eyes on Thompson. The first meeting
after the stormy session of the letter and Irene's
ravings was bound to be difficult.

But I need not have worried. He came down
buoyantly, slap-slapping his hand along the rail, a
sort of rhythmic accompaniment for his feet. Idly
I watched Thompson as he placed a fire screen
with neat precision. Suddenly he wheeled about,
his hands still stretched and curved to the screen's
width, and stared at Larry. It was like watching
someone under a hypnotic spell. He stood immovable and trancelike, his eyes fixed on Larry in his
jaunty descent.

A final arpeggio of little slaps on the newel
post, and Larry swung into a leaping dance step
which brought him down the hall to me. One hand
described a wide parabola in the air so that his
curving fingers pulled out a cigarette case at the
precise moment his feet tapped out an intricately
clever finale.

As if released from some spell, Thompson's arms
dropped, his eyes sought mine for a meaningful
instant before he turned and bent to the screen
once more. These brief moments had been fraught

with some deep significance for Thompson, but I couldn't so abruptly leave Larry to go to him.

"Stick to dancing, I guess," Larry announced audaciously as he snapped the silver case shut. "Off the books for life." An engagingly ingenuous grin gave the final touch to the picture of a gay irresponsibility that could slide easily from the tangled mess which had driven Irene to a state of frenzy.

Not until Brooke, following close on Larry, came down did I seek out Thompson. He was in his pantry and quite evidently expecting me. Mildred was sent on some inconsequential errand before we moved into the dining room. Mindful of impending interruptions, he plunged directly into his telling.

"Miss Sherwin, there's something I think the police should know." His face above the starched white jacket was anxious and disturbed. "Mr. McIver came back downstairs yesterday afternoon. It was while Mrs. Shephard was at the phone."

I waited. Why had he withheld this last night?

He sensed my thought, hurried on to explain. "It just came to me when Mr. McIver ran down, hitting the banister that way. I remembered it then. He came down just like that. I didn't see him—I didn't see him go back—but I remembered it the minute I heard him. I thought the police should know," he said again and bent to the table to rearrange a group of glasses at the place nearest him.

Larry again. This had been Larry's day all right. But I had just left a Larry carefree to complacency. Besides, the very mannerism which had recalled the incident to Thompson seemed to absolve him. No one intent on crime would bang out with every step an announcement of his coming. I half smiled as I watched Thompson's hands move on fussily to the centerpiece of roses and brilliant blue cornflowers; the blithe impudence of Larry had aroused my own protective instincts as surely as it had called forth Irene's tigerlike defense.

Thompson was waiting uneasily; a murder had taken place, but dinner must be served. "Probably it isn't important," I told him. "But Mr. Bigelow—some of them—will be here tomorrow." I conceded reluctantly that the police should be told.

11

That evening we were again gathered in the terrace room. Throughout the day people had been in their own rooms or in little segregated groups here and there on the lower floor, but tonight we were all there in much the same manner of the evening before.

As we drifted in from dinner I found myself with Dr. Jarvis at the far end of the room, away from the others. Thinking it over afterwards, I wondered. Was it by chance, or had he manipulated our detached position? He stood before me as I sat in the deep window.

Like O'Meara, he seemed to be avoiding all discussion of the crime. He was not so deft about it, however. He was too watchfully alert, and his talk of a newly opened supper club had the feel of being dragged in. Suddenly, without warning, he said, "Nancy, have you happened to discover what Mrs. Shephard said to Marian yesterday afternoon?"

It came out almost precisely as Brooke's question at breakfast. I was startled, dismayed. It had changed nothing, of course, but this second notice seemed to sharpen and point up my own fears.

"Like you," he went on, "I noticed it at the time. Though I might not have thought of it again if you hadn't happened to speak of it."

"I don't know," I said, "I've scarcely seen Marian all day." I must have looked my alarmed misgiving, for in a single instant his face changed completely, a swift kaleidoscoping of expression, and he smiled. His smile is attractive, quick and warm, and pleasant in its unexpectedness, for his mouth, closed, has some of the same precision which characterizes his speech.

"It's probably not important. Don't look so upset. It was just—well, I wondered about it. I'll ask her later on. As you say, she's been more or less tied up all day." Absently he picked up a Lowestoft bowl from the table and turned it in his hands. "It all seems to be pretty much up in the air," he said. But he gave the impression of having very decided opinions that he was withholding from a member of the family, and I had not forgotten his aggressive determination of the morning.

"Of course I haven't talked to anyone today," he added, and I understood that he meant the district attorney and his men.

"But you had only just met Jocelyn," I said. That readily explained itself.

He set the bowl carefully down. "As a matter of fact, I had met her. Just met her and that's all. It was more than a year ago, I should say. One of those passing introductions—some after-theater place."

I was surprised, not so much at the meeting, but that this, so far as I knew, was the first mention of it.

He seemed to feel that. "Don't know why I didn't speak of it to Bigelow last night," he said disturbedly, leading the way from our secluded window position.

It was an unsettled, interrupted evening. Ham was in and out; a murmured conference with Marian, another with Brooke. The telephoning that is usual after a death summoned one or another of us at various intervals. I took a call for Marian and stopped beside her to report.

"Mrs. Schwaggerman," I told her, and in the forthright manner that made her seem jubilantly herself for an instant she said, "Ruth? What did she want? She called this morning."

I surprised an odd look on Brooke's face. Overzealous people irritated him.

"Solicitous to a fault, Ruth," he said with a grimace of faint distaste.

Katherine had recovered sufficiently to come down, but looked so badly that it was distressing to see her. As always she had dressed carefully, but the glow and shine were missing. Irene was there too, a pathetic figure, to me at least, slumped and flattened in a deep chair. She kept up an almost constant moistening of her dry lips, drawing them in with her teeth and flicking her tongue against them.

It was Larry who gave the evening its semblance of naturalness. With an utter lack of constraint he moved about, joining easily in the bits of scattered talk. O'Meara, too, was calmly and indolently himself.

We had something to drink again shortly before going up, and once more it was Dr. Jarvis who insisted on it. "And no coffee tonight," he said firmly. "What everyone here needs is a night's sleep, and this will help."

There had been little or no rest the night before, and the day had been an exhausting one. I think it was the first letdown for Marian. Beginning with the long session with the district attorney, the varied demands on her had been unceasing. This was the first time I had seen her unoccupied and at ease.

She still sat with Brooke a little apart from the rest of us, and when Brooke's laugh sounded out, it was pleasant and reassuring as is any normal sound after some shocking event. It came as if he were suddenly amused and had forgotten what was hanging over us. Marian, too, seemed relaxed and free from strain. And yet they were talking of the crime, for I heard Brooke say, "But wait! I get an idea out of it, Marian. It may not lead anywhere, but there might be something—you can see where it could go." The amusedly pleasant laugh again. "Keep it tight until we get a chance to see the D.A. in the morning."

We went up before one. The policemen, who were stationed inside and out, went off duty at twelve. I had observed Teeple giving some sort of regulation report to the new man as they walked through part of the lower floor. This was McKenna's first appearance at the house, and before we went up Mother stopped to explain that Thompson had left a lunch in the kitchen and coffee in readiness. Just a matter of plugging in, but Mother went on in her lengthy, detailed way.

"I'll have it at two and five," he said as he thanked her. "It breaks up the night."

It struck me as I went on up and left Mother talking with McKenna how soon we come to accept the new and startling. Already it seemed quite natural to have that blue-coated figure planted there in our lower hall.

Lying in bed that night, I faced something I had been trying to avoid all day. There had been ten people on this floor, eleven with Miss Wycke, and that the investigation was narrowed to a consideration of those eleven people I was well aware. The evidence of the loosened pane seemed to have been entirely discredited. The idea was preposterous, but more to prove the absurdity of it than with any willingness to accept, I went through them one by one, ruling out only those who could in no way be concerned.

When I had finished, I had only increased my confusion and uncertainty. It was revealing in one way, however. It did show the fantastic lengths to which the mind can go, once having given way and resolved to accept what is contrary to all reason. For I was appalled to find myself recalling small happenings, singling out inconsequent bits of talk, seeing again the glimpsed expression of a face. I even caught myself dwelling on the swift glance Mother and Marian had exchanged after Jocelyn's body was discovered, giving to it the same ridiculous significance, until exhaustion got the better of my crazily distorted thoughts and I went to sleep.

When the shot awakened me I had no real idea what it was nor how long I had been sleeping. I sat up suddenly to a deep stillness. Had it not been a time of stress and fear I might have dismissed it as some extraordinary but not alarming noise from outside.

I scrambled out of bed and without stopping for a negligee opened the door and looked out. No one was in the hall and the smell of coffee was comfortably reassuring. McKenna, probably in the line of duty, had left everything open. Marian's door stood wide, with the light streaming from it, and it was to that patch of light I ran. I believe I had some hazy idea that she had been awakened and was investigating as I was. At that first glance into her room I was frightened, but I didn't sense another tragedy. She was lying on the floor, a dark silk robe over her pajamas, her feet in slippers. My thought was of illness, some sudden attack following on all the strain and excitement.

"Marian!" I called out her name, rushed across the room and bent over her. At the sight of the wound in her head I cried out and turned around to all but stumble into Ham and Brooke, who had followed close on my own steps, Ham in pajamas, Brooke with a navy cloth robe belted around him. He pushed a small leather-bound book into my hands and knelt quickly beside her.

McKenna was there at almost the same time, others crowding after him. McKenna came into the room, revolver drawn and head thrust forward. He had lost no time in his rush up from the pantry, where he had been having the lunch left in readiness for him—with the dining-room and pantry doors propped open, as he explained to Rumsey later.

"What's going on here?" he asked, and with one sweeping glance around bent over Marian. And then he acted swiftly. "A sheet—something," he said, and, still clutching that small volume of Brooke's, I started on a run for the linen closet.

Hamilton, who had been nearer the door than I, careened stumblingly down the hall ahead of me. His stocky figure blocked and impeded me as I reached blindly round his swaying shoulders, struggling to get at the piles of linen. Quietly dependable and bearing himself with a kind of steady dignity throughout the shocking horror of Jocelyn's death, he was now beside himself.

"Ham!" I cried sharply, and as he shifted, turning a haggard, distracted face to me, I snatched something and rushed back.

McKenna was bathing the blood from Marian's face. Quickly, skillfully, without a waste motion, he tore the sheet into strips and bandaged her head. A neat, expert job. As Brooke said afterwards, "He may have been caught downstairs drinking coffee, but those fellows know their first aid all right."

Dr. Jarvis had gone to the upper hall phone at McKenna's command to call a doctor, and here Hamilton had stopped. Bent to the low light, his shaking hand groped through the pages while Jarvis waited, telephone in hand. From my place in the doorway of Marian's room I saw them and ran to supply the number. Dr. Hawley has a place in the same park section; he would not be long, I thought relievedly.

McKenna's next move was to the telephone. His voice came back to us, the clipped tones that were both summons and report. "Through the head— she's still living. . . ." Another phrase or two, and he turned to take stock of us.

"Where's the other man?" he asked sharply. "The one with the white hair?"

In the confusion we had not missed O'Meara. Instinctively we looked toward his room in the north wing. The only closed door, McKenna went to it swiftly, tried the brass knob and pounded decisively; waited an instant and repeated it.

"Open up!" he shouted. After what seemed an endless interval the door opened and O'Meara stepped into the hall. He stood there in green pajamas, his thick white hair in great disorder, looking at us all in dazed astonishment.

"What's up?" he wanted to know and with McKenna came down the hall. Turning incredulously from one to the other of us, he listened to our scattered, incoherent accounts.

It was then that I noted another absence. "Irene—where is she?" I pulled at Larry's arm. He started at my cry, and I could swear to the genuine astonishment of his look as he turned to face me. During all these minutes he had not given a thought to Irene or her safety; he had forgotten her completely.

He stood another instant, his eyes seeking her among huddled, scantily clothed figures, then he started down the hall almost at a run, I after him. The door to their room was open with only the half-light from the hall. Larry pressed the switch, and I felt a sudden sense of relief. It was the natural, the expected thing, to find her sleeping, here in this room in the extreme north wing of the house, but some blind fear had brought me after Larry. I watched as he strode over to the bed where she lay with her face thrust into the pillow. He called her name and shook her. But she was not easily wakened.

"Irene!" He shook her again. She stirred then, and, sliding a hand under her shoulders, he brought her to a sitting position. She blinked dazedly, slowly taking in the fact of my presence as I moved over to the bed.

"What is it?" she asked. Her hands went to her eyes to shield them from the sudden light; or perhaps it was an unconscious gesture to shut out the rush of recollection that waking brought.

As Larry told her what had happened, I expected an emotional outburst, but she listened in a stupefied quiet, as if she were not fully awake even now. Nervous exhaustion? I thought, that and the highballs Dr. Jarvis had insisted on.

"Come on. Snap out of it, Irene," Larry said and half lifted her to her feet. "Here!" He caught up a green negligee that was flung across a chair and waited impatiently while she worked her arms into the sleeves and groped for her mules.

"Come on—we have to get back there," he urged her. I caught the note of worry in his voice; McKenna, the others, would question this delay.

Rumsey had arrived and the doctor was on his way up the stairs when, still dazed and none too steady on her feet, we got her down the hall to the gallery. "Sleeping," Larry said to McKenna. "Slept through it all." McKenna, busy with Rumsey, nodded and made no comment.

Dr. Hawley made his examination, complimenting McKenna on his work. After a brief consultation with Ham he called a New York hospital, the hospital the Shephards have endowed in a small way.

"I can't tell," he said carefully to our frenzied questions. "It all depends on the direction the bullet has taken, just how far it has penetrated." He mentioned hemorrhage, probing for the bullet, added those noncommittally encouraging things.

With the arrival of Rumsey and Slade there was again the examination of windows. In Marian's room first. Her windows look out on the grounds to the south, and one was open half the sash with the screen in place. There is no balcony; if an entrance was made there a ladder must have been used, but flashlights failed to reveal any marks of ladder or other tampering. Besides, Marian's door had been open when I looked out.

The reading light beside her bed was on, and a magazine lay face down on the table. Nothing was disturbed or out of place in the room. "A neat job," Rumsey said, a grudging admiration which did not mitigate the grimness at all.

"Now who got here first?"

Measuring with his eye the distance between the two doors, Rumsey listened to my account of looking out, seeing no one in the dimly lit halls, and going to Marian's lighted room.

Ham had opened his door in time to see me pass in and had followed. Brooke, too, had observed me as I stepped into the gallery.

"I sat reading," he said. "I hadn't gone to bed." And his more orderly appearance in that disheveled crowd bore evidence of this.

Like me, he had not been sure it was a shot, but he had snapped off his light and opened the door quietly to investigate. The halls were empty, and he had stood there listening. When he saw me pass through the gallery he had started after me at once.

"Shephard was just coming in," he finished. "We got there at about the same time."

The doctor and Mother were with Marian until the coming of the ambulance. The rest of us stayed huddled in the hall, talking only in response to rapid questions put by Rumsey and Slade. We were stunned and silent except Irene, who wept with a racking noisiness, saying over and over to Larry, "I wanted to go! I wanted to go! But you made me stay."

"Shut up!" He said it sharply in an effort to quiet her, and then moved deliberately away. Exasperation or that trick of sliding away from disagreeable situations. Both, perhaps. She was still weeping, though less hysterically, when Bigelow and his men arrived.

They listened to Rumsey and Slade and stepped quietly into Marian's room. The doctor was there, and after a brief stay they withdrew to the front gallery opposite Katherine's room. Cooper, I noticed, left them almost directly to come back and stand before Marian's door. Here, oblivious to the confusion around him, he stood, arms folded, pivoting and turning on one heel to let his eyes travel the length of gallery and the halls to both wings, coming back each time for a long, thoughtful look into the opened doorway.

Holt's unpleasant tones broke through from the conference down the gallery, and I forgot Cooper.

"It looks like it," I heard him say. "If Kaufman finds her prints on that gun—and I think he will

. . ." He let that trail off. "The best way out for
her, and I guess she knew it. She was due for an
indictment if anyone was, and she probably knew
that too."

Slowly the words sank in and their meaning
penetrated. They believed Marian had tried to
kill herself. They thought she had been Jocelyn's
killer, and now, in remorse and fear, the hopeless-
ness of the whole situation brought home to her
through a day's investigation and a press that had
missed nothing, their conclusion was that she had
tried to take her own life, and in so doing admitted her guilt.

But Marian. I couldn't, I wouldn't believe it.
She had given no evidence of any self-reproach. I
remembered that moment downstairs a scarce two
hours ago when she had seemed to throw off the
tension of the day and lapse into something that
was close to her normally crisp self.

The revolver was Ham's. He nodded in a sod-
den, half-comprehending wretchedness as it was
held out to him. Propelling himself to action, he
walked across to his room and pulled out the top
drawer of a small carved walnut chest which forms
a bedside stand. The drawer was empty. There was
no surprise; he had not expected to find it. "I've
always kept it there," he said in the same flat tones.
The police themselves could support this; it had

been found there the night Jocelyn was killed, and left undisturbed.

Ham had no idea when it had been taken from his room; he had not looked into the drawer that evening. The implication was that Marian, during the early evening perhaps, had removed and placed it in readiness. There had certainly been no occasion on going up to bed, for Ham was already there when she came up with Brooke a little after the others.

"In good spirits, too, considering everything," Brooke maintained in protest against Holt's statement.

But when the chest was examined for fingerprints none were found. And on the revolver were only the blurred marks that spoke of previous handling by Ham. Marian's prints were not there, and Marian's hands had, of course, been bare of gloves.

Once more began the round of questioning. As before, everyone avowed that he had been in his own room, asleep this time or on the verge of it. Except Brooke, who in pajamas and dressing gown had sat reading.

"So there we were," as Mr. Bigelow said later, "two crimes committed on that floor with ten or more people there each time, and no one in either case had heard or seen anything."

But that was exaggerating a little. There had been the call of "Joss" heard by O'Meara and Miss Wycke in the first instance, along with Irene's story of someone coming to Jocelyn's room and going soundlessly away. The brief evidence in the second case bore a similarity to it other than in its sparseness. For while we were still there in the upper hall, Katherine told of hearing a knock on Marian's door, a light tap.

"I paid no special attention to it," she said. The hand at the breast of her dotted satin negligee trembled noticeably. "I remember thinking that Helen or Nancy had come to the door for something. I was very nearly asleep, without much idea of the time. I know I heard the door unlocked, and I think—I'm not sure"—she spoke slowly, struggling to recall just what she had heard—"that Marian laughed and said something. If I had had any idea of sudden illness or anything like that, the sound reassured me. I was almost asleep," she reminded Mr. Bigelow.

But neither Mother nor I had been to Marian's door. There had been one little gasp from Mother as Katherine spoke our names, and her face held its look of stupid astonishment through the rest of Katherine's recital and the questions which followed.

Katherine insisted that she had heard nothing else, just that half laugh with no reply of any kind in return. "Then there was the shot," she went on. "I should say almost directly after," she answered Cooper's question. "But I don't know, really. I didn't connect the two. I didn't even know it was a shot."

Save for hearing the light knock on Marian's door, the responses from the rest of us were similar, and everyone disclaimed having gone to the door. We had wakened without any realization of what it was that roused us. Only Ham had had an immediate consciousness of a shot. O'Meara had heard nothing until McKenna's peremptory pounding brought him out of a sound sleep.

O'Meara was almost sheepishly apologetic over that serenely deep sleep in the face of a disturbed household. The lazy nonchalance so habitual to him was missing as he explained. He had been completely done out. "Never was so dead for sleep in my life. And I'd had a couple of highballs. Strong ones," he added. He had returned to his room for a bathrobe. Bright patterned and too small, it covered his huge bulk with ludicrous inadequacy as he stood in the center of the stunned, white-faced group.

For all of Katherine's story, the police did not entirely discard their theory of attempted suicide.

"But she couldn't have done it," O'Meara said to me that night when, all thought of sleep abandoned, we had collected downstairs.

"Nancy, Marian no more committed that crime than you or I. And if she didn't, then why the suicide?" He pushed perplexedly at the disorder of his hair. "And why the murder? Neither makes any sense. Why should anyone wish to kill Marian? Unless"—he seemed to be thinking aloud now as much as talking to me—"could she have gone back to that sitting room for something and surprised the murderer—" He stopped quickly.

But I understood. He was arguing that Marian might have gone in and, having seen the murderer, wished to shield him. That, if followed through, opened the way to such frightening possibilities that the bare suggestion overshadowed what had already taken place.

When Hamilton and Brooke, who had driven in after the ambulance, returned from the hospital in the early hours of the morning, they reported that the bullet had lodged in the motor area of the brain, causing a partial paralysis. They had operated at once, and there was a chance for recovery, but just how slight that chance was we did not need to be told.

Ham had himself in hand again. His face was so gray and ravaged that it was painful to see, but a certain solid dependability, which quiets and reassures, wrought its changes in the room. Unconsciously taut muscles relaxed and some of the strain gave way.

"Yes, the doctors seem to think she has a chance. A pretty good chance," he took it upon himself to add as his eyes came to rest understandingly on me.

Throughout his telling he had been quietly matter of fact where Brooke had been feverishly impassioned, pacing about and talking in rapid excitement. In a dull, apathetic way I noted the difference, surprised that Brooke should be so much less controlled than Ham, Brooke who ordinarily displays a sang-froid in all situations. That faintly amused imperturbability is as much a part of him as his ever-ready charm; indeed, I suppose it is a factor in that charm.

It was after five then, and at Ham's suggestion we went to our rooms for two or three hours. "Even if you can't sleep," he urged, "lie down for a bit." I silently agreed, following his glance to Mother, who, since the departure of the ambulance, had sat, weak and dazed, without even her nervous fluttering to relieve the unnatural quiet.

But everyone was reluctant to break away and go upstairs. I don't think it was fright so much as excitement, that overstimulation which any form of violence produces. From now on, however, there was fear, a deep sense of insecurity that Jocelyn's murder had not brought.

It was during the difficult and uneasy breaking up, the slow straggling to the hall, that Hamilton called to me from the terrace room.

"Nancy"—he said it abruptly, his eyes fixed intently on my face—"when that shot woke you, where was your mother? Are you sure she was in her room?"

I stared at him. "Ham, what do you mean? You can't think—" I stopped, gripped in an icy dread.

He was swiftly aghast at what he had done. Until they were out he had not grasped the full import of those questions. Now he was concerned only for me.

"Nancy, stop looking like that!" He pulled me to him, shaking me gently. "I never thought how they sounded. Stupid fool!" Tone and words excoriated himself. "It just came to me as I saw Katherine go out —what she said upstairs, I mean. I spoke without thinking. You understand?" he said anxiously, releasing my shoulders with another little shake.

I managed a smile that minimized and dismissed the incident, but the shock of that question remained with me for days.

12

The papers that morning carried their headline of probable suicide, the inference plain; Marian had killed Jocelyn in a fury of rage that had increased to madness since her arrival home, and then tried to take her own life.

Though the reporters had written their stories, Mr. Bigelow and Cooper never actually believed it suicide past the moment the revolver was shown to bear only Ham's blurred prints. That, coupled with Katherine's story of someone at the door, barred the possibility of a self-inflicted wound as far as they were concerned, even before the discovery of the gloves in the shrubbery beneath the windows.

The flashlight search for ladder marks had failed to reveal them for they had not been merely dropped, but flung far to the right. One was lying close to the base of the house, completely hidden from view, the other had caught on a branch where, tilted rakishly, it just held.

The murderer must have tossed them from Marian's open window before his departure from the room, that was evident. That he had not entered or left by the window, however, was conclusive. The ground, the sill, the side of the house were all examined without avail.

There they were, a pair of men's gloves, natural pigskin, and showing only a brief period of wear.

"They're mine," Dr. Jarvis said, "but how they got there—" He stopped, deciding against postulations. He looked angry rather than surprised, and his square-fingered hands were perfectly steady as he held his lighter to a cigarette and snapped it shut. "They were in the pocket of my coat. Downstairs in that hall cloakroom."

The police went methodically about the business of finding out who had been to the coatroom that evening.

"I know I was," Jarvis was the first to admit, the angry flush all but gone from his face. "O'Meara and I took a turn about the grounds around nine o'clock. I had my coat then. I couldn't be sure the gloves were in the pocket, but I'd say they were—I don't remember missing them."

O'Meara had been there at the same time, of course. Brooke thought that he had gone in too. "Yes, I did," he said, and his deep, cadenced voice lightened as certainty came to him. "I was after cigarettes, but there were none in my coat, and I went on upstairs."

I remembered this, remembered Katherine's languid acceptance of one as he stood beside her, opening the box of his own special brand.

Mother hadn't exactly gone to the closet as she recalled it. "The door was open a little and I stopped to close it." There was something appealing about her fragile elegance as she stood there, trying so earnestly for recollection; Holt's rasping tones lowered a little as he prodded her to continue. "There was a scarf on the floor—Mr. O'Meara's, I think— and I folded it and placed it on top of the drawers just inside the door." It was some time after O'Meara and Jarvis came in, she explained, going into unnecessary details of her passing through the hall on her way back from the telephone.

But this was all more or less futile, for there had been opportunity for any one of us to step to the coatroom unobserved. Teeple, for the most part, had been in the service wing or outside until McKenna came on at twelve.

It was the same when the matter of access to the revolver came up. During the course of the long evening everyone had been upstairs at some time or other, it was shown.

Following close on the discovery of the gloves, questioning was renewed concerning our

movements in the gallery and halls directly after
the shot. But, outside of details that amplified,
nothing was changed or added to those first
accounts.

That morning I resolved to do two things which
had been on my mind since the day before. The
curious conversation between Jocelyn and Marian,
which had gone unnoticed at my first mention of
it, seemed to me of crucial importance—doubly
so since the attack on Marian. I was determined
now on making Mr. Bigelow and his staff see it as
I had, as had Brooke and Jarvis too, for that matter. And after that I knew I must tell of Larry's
return to the lower floor, a return which his own
slapping descent had recalled to Thompson.

Mr. Bigelow was in the library. Until then I
hadn't realized that I had hoped to find Cooper.
Something likable about the tall, rangy figure, a
ready understanding behind the earnest gaze, for
all it could be so disconcerting in its intentness,
made him easier of approach.

I couldn't know it at the time, but Cooper was
in New York, where he had been since the early hours of the morning, examining with characteristic thoroughness certain records of the New
York police.

The incident of Larry's return belowstairs was
more definite, and I began there, feeling uncomfortably like a talebearer as I gave Thompson's

story. "It's probably not important," I finished. "The very fact that he came down so noisily . . ."

Thompson arrived first when they had both been sent for. He completed his account and repeated it step by step as Mr. Bigelow went over it.

"You're sure you didn't hear him go back?"

"No—but I was in and out, to the pantry and back." Though he was so conscientious in his exactness, Thompson seemed to find this involvement of Larry as unpleasant as I did. His unease was almost painful when Larry came in, suspicion and alarm spread over his good-looking face.

"Why didn't you tell us you came back downstairs just previous to Mrs. Shephard's murder?" Mr. Bigelow demanded without any forewarning of explanation.

Larry whitened under the abrupt attack, but his answer came without hesitancy.

"I didn't think of it at the time—then I couldn't see what good it would do to bring it up." He had recovered a little, and, taking in the meaning of our presence there, his look of quick distrust went from Thompson to me.

"Was Mrs. Shephard phoning at the time?"

"No." He shifted his long, slim frame from one foot to the other. "I didn't hear her, anyway."

As to the door of the telephone room, the one which gives on to the hall, he couldn't remember whether it was open or closed. "I didn't notice one way or the other."

"Then Mrs. Shephard might have gone up ahead of you," Mr. Bigelow said slowly, weighing the possibility.

"Well, I don't know. I thought I was out there on the terrace about five minutes. Might have been longer. I wasn't timing myself." He had put on the same belligerent obstinacy of the day before.

Larry might have passed the sitting-room door at the very moment those furious blows were being struck at Jocelyn's head; I went a little sick at the thought.

"What did you come down for?" Mr. Bigelow snapped out of his thoughtful consideration, his eyes under the black brows again coldly uncompromising.

"Cigarettes." Larry shifted again and clamped one hand on a chair back. "I missed them as soon as I was in my room and ran back down and took some from that big silver box there in the hall. I went right back up—it didn't take a minute," he forestalled the next question.

"It's the truth," he said truculently and refused to be swerved under Mr. Bigelow's adroit and varied attack.

The telephone rang in the midst of it. Thompson answered it and announced the call for Mr.

Bigelow, whose question tapered off into a murmured word of apology as he stepped to the telephone room. Larry watched him go, frank relief
on his face, and promptly walked out of the room
after Thompson.

"Oh yes? Yes, Cooper." Mr. Bigelow's careful,
polished tones came to me clearly. "Turn anything
up?" I caught a hint of amusement in his voice,
glimpsed the smile that flicked his mouth for an
instant, as I deliberately watched through the
open door.

Then his face changed swiftly. Surprise, speculation, doubt followed in rapid succession. But
what made the proceeding important for me was
his involuntary pronouncement of a name, three
names, in fact. "What!" he exclaimed, and the
muscles of his face set in excitement. "Parsons!" A
longer pause this time. "And Whitmore—Stuyvesant Hill!"

I recognized the names and was astonished to
hear them now. Men of position and prominence.
In short, men like Parsons, was what I was thinking. Important in the world of finance, I knew
in a vague way. Important socially, too. At least,
their families were.

Yesterday I had been startled enough to hear Parsons' name creeping into the case. But Whitmore
and Stuyvesant Hill—what possible connection

could they have with the horrible events of the last
two days?

Evidently Mr. Bigelow wondered too. Amazement had given place to doubt once more. "Yes
. . . Yes," he repeated with monotonous regularity,
the charged excitement gradually going out of his
voice. "Yes, look into it—follow it through—but
I'm inclined to think . . ."

It went on interminably, but with Mr. Bigelow
in the role of listener I could get little or nothing. He was still at the telephone when Thompson
appeared—our cars would be leaving shortly—so I
left without any mention of the conversation that
seemed to me fraught with some hidden meaning.

Jocelyn's funeral was at eleven from a chapel
in a neighboring town. The crowds about the
place were enormous, though the list made out
by Marian the day before had been limited to our
own family and guests and about forty of Jocelyn's
friends, names supplied by Larry and Irene.

When we drove up, the street was full, and police were finding it difficult to keep an entrance.
There were audible cries of, "There's Shephard!"
And, "There's the girl!" by which they probably
meant me.

I had never thought about Jocelyn's family until the night of the crime, when relatives in Cleve-
land had been reached only after securing the aid
of a special information service. Jocelyn had been

alone, detached, with no hindering ties. But that morning her mother, a married brother and his wife appeared, the mother a pretty woman with something unpleasant and repellent about her. Not even Ham, I think, had been aware of this close relationship.

They were deliberately hostile, and that evening's papers carried stories of a grief-stricken mother, with the innuendoes pointed at us. "They killed her!" she had declared hysterically for the delighted reporters. "They killed my little girl!" And the suggestion of social registerites, unable to tolerate a waif of the stage, was played up in the tabloids despite the fact that Marian was lying in the hospital, gravely wounded.

After the short service I managed with Brooke's aid to get a taxi home while the others went on to the cemetery, a maneuver planned with Mother as we dressed. Someone beside the servants should be in telephone reach of the hospital, we felt.

Driving in, I saw Cooper coming from his car, a young woman with him. He was surprised and, I think, disconcerted on seeing me.

"I didn't expect you people back yet."

I explained, and after a moment's awkward hesitation he introduced the girl with him, fumbling over her name, finally calling her Miss Smith. His eyes met mine, a flash of humor at his own lack of skill.

"I want to place Miss Smith in that front room next the dining room while you people are at lunch. Do you think we could manage it so that no one sees her—or knows she is there?"

"Perhaps," I said, trying to cover my curiosity. "Things are disorganized. . . . You can't be sure, but it might be all right."

The woman herself stood looking from one to the other of us, not joining in the talk at all. Now that I observed her, I saw that she was an extraordinarily beautiful girl. Blonde, with darkened lashes which looked perhaps a little too obvious there in the late September sun. In the same way the smart brown dress and small mink cape seemed to belong to some luncheon place in town.

"Miss Smith could wait in my room," I offered, "and you could bring her down after everyone is in the dining room."

"I don't want her presence here known," he warned me. He spoke privately to the girl, cautioning her not to talk, I decided. As she turned to where I discreetly waited I had a sudden, swift impression. This girl was afraid. What made me aware of it I don't know, for she gave no outward evidences of fright, but it was there, unmistakably.

"Which room was it?" she asked curiously when we had reached the gallery. I pointed out the door of Marian's morning room and then her bedroom.

She didn't ask to see them, though I knew she wished to, but her eyes darted to the open doors of the other rooms before we turned into mine.

I wondered about Miss Smith as she sat in a chintz-covered chair and drew a cigarette case from a stunning handbag. My first glance there in the drive had assured me that she was no reporter or writer of special features, those persistent women who had made Thompson's life unbearable.

She was anxious to talk of the crimes, and avid interest soon got the better of her little attempts at tact. "She was beautiful, wasn't she?" she asked after she had drawn from me the facts of finding Jocelyn's body in the sitting room. "Did she look like that? Really, I mean. Sometimes pictures . . ." She went into a discussion of what modern photography can do for a face. But not for long; it was the murder that fascinated and held her.

"It must be terrible," she observed. "I don't see how you can be so calm and unconcerned about it all."

This to me who was torn with so many emotions that, even now, I can't recall that day after Marian's shooting without a sick, sinking feeling. Fortunately there was little time for this sort of thing.

Thompson came to the door to say that Mr. Cooper wished to see us both downstairs. "He's in the hall." His eyes met mine worriedly, moved on for a covert glance at the girl. All this was telling on Thompson; he looked pathetically tired and old.

Cooper was pulling a chair into position as we went down the stairs. Arrangement for a conversation piece, I thought as he dragged up another one, twisting and shoving it about for the exact placing he wanted.

"Now if you'll sit here . . ." Long fingers reached out to touch the first chair, and he looked at Miss Smith. I saw that she would be immediately visible to anyone entering from the front door or the west entrance at the other end of the hall.

I reminded him of his plan for secrecy.

"Decided on this instead." He brushed it aside without explanation.

"What do we do now?" the girl inquired. Her tone made the words sound flippant, and she leaned with a show of ease against the Venetian red of the upholstery, but once more I caught a fleeting glimpse of smoldering fear.

"We just sit here," he told her. "And talk. Make it natural," he appealed to me, sitting down in a chair by the drawing-room door, a position which gave him a firsthand view of anyone entering from either way.

Now that we were in place, with nothing more to be done, we sat in a constrained silence. The quiet, the shadowy hall, the girl's suppressed

fright, all combined to produce in me an unease
that was more than the discomfort of an unnatural
situation. I looked across at the lovely blonde girl
where she sat clutching the little fur cape on the
arm of her chair, her eyes watching the door uneasily. Who was she? Why had Cooper brought her
here? It was the girl herself who gave me a clue.

"I don't want to do this," she said suddenly,
and was out of her chair. Fear was in her voice and
in her eyes, in the trapped look she sent toward
the stairs. Cooper sprang to his feet and placed
himself in front of her. "It's all right," he assured
her. His hands on her shoulders sought to ease her
down into the chair. "I wouldn't have brought you
here if there was any danger. There isn't. Just sit
down—"

"No." She resisted Cooper's efforts to press her
back in the chair. "I don't want to go through with
it. I can't, I tell you. I'm afraid. Look what she
got—they're burying her now. No. No, I can't,"
she ended in a little cry of terror that filled me
with a cold dread.

I was frightened, bewildered. This girl was
connected with Jocelyn in some way. She feared
a similar fate. But why? Had she known Jocelyn?
Her words to me upstairs a few minutes ago would
seem to indicate that she had never seen her. My
brain reeled dizzily as I tried to fit this girl, a
total   stranger,   into   Jocelyn's   murder.   Almost

unseeingly I watched Cooper's capable handling
of the girl. His tactics were succeeding; she was
seated again and fumbling in her bag for cigarettes.

"There, you're all right now." Cooper stood
ready with a match. "Just jittery . . . the wait."
His tone, that encouraged and commended, struck
the right note. It justified her fit of nerves, approved the recovery. "Sit down, Miss Sherwin."
He turned to me with a coolness that refused to
admit anything unusual, a matter-of-fact manner
that was more calming than any amount of soothing cajoleries.

But now, with the stage set and the cast once
more in readiness, we were without an audience.
Realizing with what difficulty the cars would move
through the jammed streets I had recently left, I
snatched at the interval to carry out my plan of
the early morning.

"While we're waiting," I said to Cooper, "there's
something—I think it might be important." I
glanced at the girl, still sitting too intensely alert
for the indifference at which Cooper was aiming.
How much should I say with her there? "It really
belongs in the library." I looked doubtfully at
Miss Smith. Would it do to leave her alone?

She caught my hesitancy, understood it. "I'm
all right," she said. "I'll stick it."

Stopping only for a look out at the drive, Cooper followed me down the hall to the library. This time I was not disappointed as I told of that encounter, putting forth every effort to make him see Jocelyn's pent-up excitement and Marian's sharp recoil which I had interpreted as unutterable disgust.

He heard me through with a sort of sparkling attention that seemed concentrated in his eyes. The same electric alertness was there as I enacted the scene for him, showing the exact place in the room where the meeting had occurred, turning as Jocelyn had turned when she left to go in answer to the telephone.

"You didn't hear what Mrs. Shephard said? Just a word? Think!" He waited, a motionless, galvanic instant, ready, I felt, to spring forward and shake the words out of me.

But I hadn't—I was only too sure of it—and he relaxed to a kind of exasperated acceptance.

"It fits," he said. "It belongs." The flaming excitement fell away, leaving him spent and exhausted. "If I'd known what I know now"—the words came with a slow jerkiness as his mind went on working—"we might have protected her."

I stood stricken, unable to speak.

"Oh no!" He caught the look on my face—an earlier telling might have saved Marian.

"I didn't mean that." He was concerned for me, and in his rush to make me understand said more than he intended to, I think. "This just confirms something else. And that—I didn't know until after Miss Shephard was wounded. There's no dead certainty about it now," he admitted.

In our complete abandonment we had forgotten the setup waiting in the hall. It was Miss Smith who called out a warning and came hurrying to bring us. Without a word we slid into our places and set our faces and bodies to an appearance of conversational ease that grew a little strained in the minute or two there was still to wait.

I glanced around in brief greeting as they strung in by twos and threes, but for all I could see, they gave Miss Smith no unusual notice, nothing more than the added awareness which shocking and abnormal events had given to each of us. What Cooper got out of it, if anything, I couldn't tell.

Mother and Katherine went directly upstairs. Irene followed them, swiftly and purposefully. The intent to pack and get away was in every turn of her body. She did pause, however, halfway up the stairs for a look at the girl, a sweeping look which missed no details of face or dress.

Brooke went into the terrace room, the others drifting after him, all except Ham, who spoke to Cooper in passing, his eyes on me as I continued to converse softly with Miss Smith. It was an odd time to think of it, when he had just returned from

Jocelyn's funeral, but, for all the horror hanging over us, Ham had become in some indiscernible way more the old Ham. Release was the word I thought of, watching him disappear into the library.

We stayed as we were a few minutes more before Cooper took his departure with Miss Smith. I went with them to the west entrance, hoping for a chance to question him, once the girl had been put into the car, but at the door we ran into Oz, who had just driven in. He waited until they reached the drive and then ran up the steps, a low, knowing whistle in acknowledgment of the blonde girl in Cooper's company.

"I didn't think Cooper had it in him. Who is she? Where does she come in?"

"Smith is the name," I told him, "and I've no idea why she was here."

He screwed up his face exaggeratedly to indicate deep thought. "I've seen her someplace," he said. "I almost have it." And he continued to contort his face by thrusting out his lips to a grotesque pout and half closing his eyes. "I've got it!" He brought his hand up sharply, held it. "She was pointed out to me once. Last summer. It was some roof or other. . . ."

But it didn't come through after all. She had been singled out to him as someone's current favorite, but the name evaded him. "He's important—I'll bank on that." He gave his hand a series of irritated little shakes and brought it down in a gesture of abandonment. "No—I can't get it."

I considered an instant and then told about Miss Smith, stressing that moment when terror had made her forget herself. After all, Cooper had not enjoined me to secrecy.

He heard me out, a quick excitement in his face. "Look—they were tied up together in something."

I repeated that bit of conversation when Miss Smith had asked if Jocelyn was as beautiful as her pictures. "She'd never set eyes on her," I said.

Oz considered that, shook his head disbelievingly. "Nope. They're tied someway. She was just playing up then—following instructions."

That was possible, but, remembering the naivete of the girl's question, I was not convinced.

Oz went over it at length, offering implausible theories, finally admitting that he couldn't explain Miss Smith's connection with the crimes.

"Hear anything about the car?" he asked. This was what he had stopped for. His own interview had elicited nothing in return for his information.

I shook my head. "I'll ask about it if I get a chance," I told him.

He was disappointed, annoyed. "Why don't they do something? Running around with blondes!" He grinned, mildly pleased with the shot. He could stay only a few minutes, and the rest of his time was taken up in worried discussion of Marian.

13

Luncheon was bad, of course, but not as awful as I had anticipated. Perhaps it was the consciousness that this was to be the last of those uncomfortable meals with everyone striving to keep off the topic uppermost in our minds or making efforts to speak of it without restraint. Both were forced and unnatural. Already we had become cautious and experienced, and only O'Meara's questions veered toward the dangerous.

"What is Bigelow doing anyway? Just what line are they taking—anybody know?"

It was this sort of thing that was apt to become awkward if permitted to go its length; with more or less deftness we had learned to steer away from it. Ham, whether by intent or not, now interposed to ask, "Who was that young woman with you in the hall, Nancy?"

It was unexpected, and as I groped for a reply which would not involve me too far, I felt a quickened interest all around me.

"She was here when I came back," I said vaguely.

Hamilton didn't pursue it. A negligent interest in a perfunctory question had been satisfied. But I had not been mistaken in the undercurrent of excitement about the table. It was there, and I wondered, despising myself even as I did so, had they all been as indifferent on their arrival as I had fancied? Had Cooper, after all, gained something from his little staged effect?

Directly after we had left the dining room our guests made their last preparations to depart. They were leaving with the knowledge of Mr. Bigelow and would be within reach, in New York or close to it. There were warm protestations of sympathy during those last minutes, with the baggage clustered in the hall, offers to stay on. But Brooke and O'Meara alone sounded sincere in their suggestions of remaining.

Poised and trained as these people were in meeting varied situations with skill and ease, the very atmosphere in those last moments was charged with a feeling of relief, escape from a place that had become intolerable, even terrifying.

It was soon after their going that Mother utterly collapsed. We were still in the hall speaking of the last word from the hospital; I had called at Brooke's request not long before they left. The report had not differed from the earlier ones, but

Mother chose to see a promise of improvement; just the fact that Marian lived at all, I suppose. She talked on, the incessant, nervous talk which had alarmed me over and over, so overwrought and really ill it made her seem.

"When I go in this afternoon we'll know more," I told her. "As you say, if she's come this far—"

"I'm going too, Nancy!" She said it sharply. "I must see her. I must!"

And when I attempted to dissuade her, urge that she wait until tomorrow, she broke down completely in such a fit of crying that I was frightened and sent for Ethel. Annie came too, and together they got her upstairs and to bed. When Dr. Hawley came, he gave her a sedative and ordered her to stay there. "Shock and exhaustion," he said.

We have known Dr. Hawley for years, though our association is more social than professional, since we have always been a healthy lot. He stayed on now to talk about the whole unbelievable situation, particularly Marian and her condition.

Miss Wycke arrived while we stood in the lower hall. Thompson let her in, and she sat down to wait the moment or two before Dr. Hawley brought his talk to a close and went.

With his departure she rose and came toward me with the same firm, purposeful stride. "Could I speak to you, Miss Sherwin?" she said quickly, ignoring my greeting.

I turned toward the terrace room. I was curious. In all the years she had been a member of our household I had seen little of Miss Wycke beyond the luncheon encounters. Something about Miss Wycke precluded anything else.

With a half look at me for permission she closed the door, and so usual is it for that door to stand open that the room looked oddly hemmed in and strange.

"I didn't know whether to ask for you or your mother," she said, "and then you were right there . . ."

I told her about Mother, steering her to a comfortable chair.

She didn't sit down; she stood, hesitant and undecided for all her solid erectness. "I don't know what to do," she said. "I took the gloves—after Mrs. Shephard was killed—and now I don't know what to do."

If the words had burst out—but they came quietly, almost monotonously, so that it was a full instant before I grasped their import. The gloves which the police had hunted so unceasingly when searching questions had revealed no departures from the place after Leo's trip to the station in the early afternoon.

"But you didn't see her," I said inanely.

"I did." She spoke in the same flat tone. "I saw her before I turned off the bathroom light. I didn't know who it was. I didn't even know what it was. I just saw something. I didn't think about anything like murder—I don't know what I did think. But I went out and turned on the light—that lamp by the big wing chair. And then . . ." She stopped as if she were seeing once more the full horror of it.

"But why didn't you call someone—give an alarm?"

"I don't know." She sat down heavily, as if the weight of misery were too much for her. "I don't know. I backed to the door and started to open it—I had my hand on the knob, I remember that. And then I saw the gloves. I didn't wait or consider. I picked them up and put them in my coat pocket," and as she spoke her hand went to the pocket of her rust-brown jacket.

I listened, neither moving nor speaking as she went on.

"I went downstairs and slipped the gloves in my brief case. I left then." She sat stiffly on the edge of her chair and stared at me painfully.

"Did you destroy them?" And in that minute I think I hoped she had.

She put a hand to the dark lump of her hair and took a breath. "No. I thought of it. When I left the park, I walked toward the village. I had an idea of putting them in a waste can. Away from this section, you know."

I waited, staring fascinatedly at the two burning spots of color in her cheeks.

"And I don't know—something came to me about destroying evidence, and I didn't. I took them home."

"But they searched your apartment, Miss Wycke—" I stopped. Had she known of that search?

"I know." She brushed that by as of small importance now. "They didn't find them." Her voice evinced a certain grim satisfaction. "I dumped the coffee out of a can and put the coffee back on top of them."

Why had Miss Wycke done all this? Coming as it did now, I was filled with a dread sense of misgiving.

"And then this morning, when I read about Miss Shephard, I knew—" She stopped short, leaving me to wonder what it was she knew.

"You have them here?" I asked it fearfully. What would those gloves tell? I wanted to know, and yet I was afraid.

"They're in my bag." She was already opening it. She drew them out, in a plain white envelope now, and handed them to me.

I pulled off the rubber band and, still smelling faintly of coffee, they dropped to my lap. I gave them a single quick look, and then we sat staring at each other over a pair of men's light-colored gloves, hand stitched in brown.

"They're Ham's," I said finally.

She nodded. "One of three pairs he brought from Copenhagen."

Whether it was the result of Oz's talk I don't know, but it struck me as strange that Miss Wycke should know and remember such trivial details. I was forced to ask the inevitable question. "You thought it was Ham?"

But this she would not admit. "I don't know what I thought," she insisted. "Anyone could have taken Mr. Shephard's gloves. They'd want gloves, and they wouldn't want to use their own. And why"—suddenly her voice lost its dogged, monotonous calm, rose without warning to a crescendo of fury—"why should Mr. Shephard be badgered for the murder of—of that little trollop?"

It was over as quickly as it came. The color receded from her face and throat and concentrated in the two hard, bright spots in her cheeks. She sat, shaken and aghast.

"You had better take them over to Mr. Bigelow," I said at last. The suggestion did not startle her; that had been a foregone conclusion since her decision to give up the gloves.

"I just wanted to tell someone in the family first," she said dully.

"I would drive you over, Miss Wycke," I told her, "but I can't very well leave. I'll have Thompson call a taxi—Leo has taken Ham in to the hospital." I talked fast, and in the stir of her leaving we both covered and ignored the indiscretion of her outburst. If I had known how much her coincidental appearance was going to add to Ham's bewildered discomfort that afternoon, I would have held her there at all costs.

For Leo had not driven Ham to the hospital. In the subsequent explanation Thompson told me that, after I had gone upstairs with Mother, one of the men—he was one that had been around—had come for Hamilton, and they had driven away at once.

Not for several days did I learn what actually took place when Ham, his story of the afternoon in New York found to be untrue on at least one important point, was confronted by an implacable district attorney.

A second crime had been committed, the first was still unsolved; there was no deference to their questions now.

Hamilton had not gone directly to his publishers' on Thirty-third Street as he had stated on Thursday night. A terminal cab had driven him straight to a jewelry house on Fifth Avenue, and there he had asked for an appraisal of the narrow diamond and sapphire band, found that night in the pocket of his topcoat.

He insisted that, when he set out that afternoon, it had been his intention to walk as usual. The trip to New York had been a sudden idea. On an impulse he had returned to the house, left Dan and taken the bracelet from Jocelyn's room. Then he had walked to the station, making the three-five train as he had already told them.

Outside of the time spent in the store while he waited for the appraisal, his story did not differ essentially from his earlier telling; the walk up to the Grand Central, the telephone call to Jocelyn.

The bracelet, however, was not of Ham's purchase as he had previously stated, or at least led them to believe. And who had bought it the district attorney's investigators had not been able to discover. The store positively refused the information.

"The rule of our house," the questioner was told courteously but firmly. "And I think you will find it true of any firm of similar standing. We cannot let you have the name of any customer of ours."

They did divulge the fact that it was a recent purchase. They also disclosed that neither Mr. Shephard nor any member of his family had bought the bracelet; the Shephard family were not customers of their house. That was all that could be obtained.

But that was something. Since neither Ham nor Jocelyn had bought the bracelet, the natural conclusion was that it had been a gift from someone outside the family, and Hamilton, faced with these facts, must necessarily change his story and submit to a severe grilling as well.

"Who gave this bracelet to Mrs. Shephard?" he was asked.

"I don't know that," he told them. His brown eyes remained steady. Only an uneasy, nervous shifting of his body indicated his discomposure at the turn the examination had taken.

This they would not accept as the truth, and Ham was questioned interminably on the point. They left it only to return to it again and again, but, beyond a growing weariness, Ham remained firm in his response.

"Mr. Shephard, two crimes—brutal crimes—have been committed. This is not a time to withhold information."

"I'm telling you all I know," Ham insisted. Perspiration stood out on his forehead; his heavy shoulders slumped in exhaustion. "I would not have kept it back in the first place if I had thought it had any bearing on the crime. I don't think it has."

They went farther then. "Isn't it a fact that J. Stanley Parsons gave that bracelet to Mrs. Shephard?" The next was pure hazard at the time. "Didn't Parsons give that bracelet to her in exchange for some letters?"

Ham was suddenly on his feet, the flat of his hand came down on the broad table in front of Mr. Bigelow. "I don't know who gave it to her!" he shouted.

Mr. Bigelow's polished exterior remained un-ruffled. "Sit down, Shephard. No need to get excited."

Disconcerted at the violence into which he had been goaded, Ham dragged a handkerchief across his dripping face and dropped back to the straight discomfort of his chair.

"Why did you have it appraised?" Mr. Bigelow renewed his questioning imperturbably.

"I wished to know how valuable it was."

They glanced at him sharply, but there was no intent of attempting a wisecrack.

"And you found it was worth about two thou-sand dollars." Then suddenly, "Had you had an argument, a disagreement over that bracelet?"

Ham winced noticeably. "Yes," he told them. "Something like that."

"Did you at that time make any effort to find out where it came from?"

"Yes," he admitted, worn down by the repeti-tion of the question.

"And Mrs. Shephard refused to tell you?"

Ham's discomfort at this stage of the examina-tion was painful. "Yes," he said again.

"This argument—what about that?"

He deliberated, their eyes boring into him in the unpleasant silence of the overheated room. "Mrs. Shephard was a woman of the theater world," he told them finally. "I think her acceptance was quite harmless." It came haltingly as he searched out his words. "She didn't look on it as I did, and I attempted to give her my viewpoint. I asked her to return the bracelet."

"And she refused?"

"Temporarily, yes."

That, briefly, is the story of a long, exhausting hour and a half in the district attorney's office. Ham was still there when Miss Wycke made her inopportune appearance with the gloves, waiting in an outer room for her own grilling.

Confronted with the gloves, Ham stared at them for a moment, the black streaks standing out starkly on their beige coloring, and claimed ownership at once.

"Yes, they're mine," he said. "One of three or four pairs I bought in Copenhagen the last time I was over." And in answer to the next question: "I wouldn't be certain, but I should say yes. Or a pair just like them. I have them all in use, I think. But the gloves I wore that afternoon—I left them in the downstairs coatroom. That is, I took my coat off down there, so I must have left the gloves."

"So he says," was Holt's comment on that a few minutes later, when Ham had been allowed to go.

"Yes, I believe his story—in the main," he went on in answer to someone's suggestion that Hamilton's account had borne the stamp of truth. "But I believe there's a whole lot he left out. I think he went home that afternoon worked up to a jealous pitch. Crazy jealous." He paused, turning his red, perspiring face from one to the other of them to let that sink in.

"And when he went upstairs he saw Mrs. Shephard reconnoitering from the door of that room, and McIver disappearing down the hall to his own. And right there he grabbed up that statue and pulled her back. Then, when he saw the wrench, he took that and killed her."

Mr. Bigelow listened, eyes narrowed and thick black brows drawn together. "You would have to presuppose," he pointed out, "that she was silent while Shephard seized her, dragged her into the room and shut the door. That she still makes no outcry when he sees the wrench, drags her over there and exchanges weapons."

"Well, she wouldn't want to yell—not with the house full of people." Holt flung himself about and centered his pugnacious look on Mr. Bigelow. "She didn't have any idea of murder in her mind—remember that."

Mr. Bigelow stroked down the back of his gray hair as he pondered it. "It still seems to me that whoever killed her was in that room, ready and waiting, when she went upstairs."

"The man was in a jealous frenzy." Holt's voice was disagreeably positive. "Crazy jealous," he said again. "Look how quick he went off in here when you mentioned Parsons," he reminded them. "He could have done it with his hand gagging her mouth." And he recalled to them the marks the medical examiner had found on Jocelyn's face.

But though there were a number of things that seemed to build up a fair enough case against Ham, particularly now that the gloves and Miss Wycke's strange appropriation of them linked him directly with the first crime, they took no action against him that afternoon.

All this, of course, I had no way of knowing at the time. As it was, the thought of the summons nagged and disturbed me after Miss Wycke had left. More than his nervousness, Thompson's painful efforts to keep both face and voice unconcerned added to my disquiet. But, I argued with myself, they had to do something, the investigation must go on. The suicide suggestion had satisfied the papers for the duration of the day, but the next issue would renew the clamor for something in the way of progress.

And when it came to that, what had been accomplished? What did they have in the way of tangible evidence? The stained wrench and the unused bronze figure in the case of the first crime, with the addition now of a pair of gloves, one of them showing dark markings from the greasy handle of the wrench. The loosened windowpane had been entirely discountenanced.

Stains? The medical examiner—Dr. Hawley, too, though not in a professional capacity—had stated that the blows which had crushed the skull would not in all probability emit any gush of blood. The blood that had stained clothing and carpet had come from hemorrhages of nose and ears, following the fracture. Nevertheless, the clothes we had worn that afternoon had been examined; sleeves and cuffs had received a special scrutiny.

In the second crime visible exhibits were limited to Ham's revolver and Dr. Jarvis' gloves, plucked out of the shrubbery that morning, soaked with the September dew, the right one bearing slight traces of grease from the revolver.

Could there, I wondered, be more that had been passed over? Were the authorities limited and inefficient in their methods? I remembered a small incident of the morning, when Ham had accosted Mr. Bigelow.

"I was wondering," he said, awkward in his uncertainty, "I don't know just what is usual, but should we, perhaps, call in some outside service? Some special detective to supplement and—well, work along?"

I had realized a little amusedly that Ham, without being aware of it himself, was thinking of the procession of clever investigators who marched through the pages of mystery fiction: those brilliant and erudite men, so faultlessly dressed and superbly nonchalant; the disarmingly unassuming ones who insinuate their subtle deductions with slyly gentle astuteness; the dashing, forthright young chaps—all of whom solved their baffling and intricate problems in such satisfactory ways.

14

I was lonely that night with the complete clearing out of our guests. Mother was sleeping; Ham had not returned, had telephoned merely to say that he would not be home to dinner. There was no mention of his summons to the district attorney's office, and I did not question him.

I was sitting in the library with only Dan for company, Dan who had given no sign of excitement on either tragic occasion, when Thompson came to say that Cooper was there. I was frankly glad to see him when he appeared in the doorway. The night and loneliness had increased my sense of boding horror.

He didn't get immediately to whatever business had brought him, but sat patting Dan, his long thin fingers following the black ticking of the dog's white coat. When he finally left off the run of small remarks, divided between Dan and me, his eyes regarded me speculatively for a moment, as if he considered what he had come to say.

But, oddly enough, when he began to speak, it was about our departed guests rather than the family and affairs of the house, which had been pursued so exhaustively. Katherine Haskell and the three men. The McIvers didn't come in to it. He asked about their incomes, and here I could tell him little beyond the fact that they were all four wealthy; it was easy to take that for granted when you recalled the way they lived.

But the source of the incomes? For the first time I considered that. Dr. Jarvis was an official of an important firm. Brooke and O'Meara led leisured lives. Certainly the sporadic bits of writing that O'Meara did would never yield the income necessary to his way of life; there were the alimony payments to his divorced wife too. Both men had means ample enough for apartments in town, country places and travel whenever they wished. More than that I could not tell Cooper.

There were inquiries as to their personal characteristics and the length of time we had known them. And the difficulty for me lay right there, I think. We had known them so long and so intimately, with the exception of Dr. Jarvis, that it was not easy to sort out certain definite facts which Cooper seemed to want. It is harder, perhaps, to give a clear picture of someone you have known for years than it is of new acquaintances like the McIvers, for instance.

While I was fumbling for something worth
while, I spoke of the drive out to O'Meara's house.

His interest was electric. "O'Meara drove out
to his place Friday?" he asked quickly. "I didn't
know that." He looked at me a shade too steadily,
I thought. In rapid succession he wanted to know
what we had done, how long he had stayed in the
house. Wondering a good deal, I gave him everything I could recall of the half-hour I had waited
in the garden, including O'Meara's reappearance
with typewriter and stuffed envelope.

"Bennett has a place in Westchester—has he
been out there too?"

But I didn't know about that. I felt an unreasoning guilt at this annoyance of Cooper's. "I
doubt it," I told him. "He doesn't spend much
time there. Drives out for occasional week ends or
a few days now and then. It's just a farmhouse," I
went on as Cooper made no comment. His hands
were busy with Dan again, but his direct gaze
never left my face. "Done over rather nicely inside, but the grounds natural and untouched."

And as I spoke, I remembered Brooke in his
frequent and half-humorous assertions that down
there he just went native. I could see Marian listening with amused disbelief in her gray eyes.

"Of course I know you're not nearly the rustic
landowner that you'd like to make out, Brooke,"
she told him on one of those occasions, "but, come

to think of it, I believe it's this Westchester farm of yours that saves you from being the complete aesthete." And then they plunged right in for one of the pieces of cheerful raillery so characteristic of Marian, which Brooke played up to delightfully.

But in a way it was true. For while Brooke was the adaptable, all-round sort, there was at the same time a fastidious perfection about him; his apartment, his clothes, all those small personal possessions gave varied evidence of it; a perfection not the result of costliness alone, but a very real liking for the objects themselves was there. Nothing overdone or feminine, but always beautifully and unobtrusively right. He warmed and expanded to beautiful surroundings wherever he might be.

"I believe my main hold on you," Marian once accused him, "is that I chance to belong to a really good example of the early Georgian house. I just go with the place."

This, however, was idle wandering, and I brought my mind back to Cooper, who had subsided into a brooding speculation as he leaned over the dog.

The spurt of sharp alertness was over; he was leisurely as he reached around to pick up a brief case from the floor beside him. He pulled out some typed sheets, sat fingering them a moment. He looked undecided, even a bit foolish.

"Listen!" He jerked himself out of his abstract-ed reverie. "This may seem unusual, but here's something I want to read to you. It's a conver-sation," he explained inadequately, righting and patting the sheets into exact position. "A conver-sation between a man and a woman," he further enlightened me. "I can't tell where. If I could I'd have the key to the whole situation. Or so I think," he amended with a slight smile. And I detected, or thought I did, signs of disagreement in the ranks of the investigation.

"Well . . ." He twisted about so that he held the pages under the parchment shade of the lamp be-side him, sent a final embarrassed glance my way and bent to read, turning back for one more ex-planatory bit. "This was taken down—written from memory," he said, and determinedly went at it.

"'I like this place.'

"That was the woman," he glanced round to tell me.

"'That's nice. I rather like it myself.'

"'Kiss me!' The woman now, and after a moment of silence, the woman again, laughing a little: 'You don't mean it. You never do—nicely as you do it.'"

I was astonished. Was Cooper going in for the writing of sophisticated fiction? He sensed my startled amusement, acknowledged it with another embarrassed smile, but made no more attempts at illumination.

"The man's laugh then," he read on. "'That's true, perhaps. But this can be enjoyed. Possibly more so, when you're restrained and civilized about it.'

"'You wouldn't want me to stay? Not tonight, of course, but—sometime?'

"'No.' The man laughed again. 'I prefer my moments.'

"'Are you glad I came? I did it designedly, though I was frightfully surprised when I saw your place. And quite genuinely so when I saw the lights.'

"'Then why come? I like it tremendously, you understand. But if you expected darkness—'

"'I just wanted to drive by—and you might be here.'

"'I see. Sentiment. The pure girlish stuff.' The man's laugh again.

"Another man's voice, evidently calling from downstairs: 'Come on, come on! They're mixed and waiting!'

"'Coming!' The woman's voice, much louder now. And then in the same tone as before: 'Kiss me once more.'

"They went downstairs then," Cooper's highly conscious voice continued as he lowered his pages and swung around, "the woman calling out something to the person below. Just what isn't on record.

"That's all," he said, and looked relieved that it was over. "What I want to know—" He was unsure of himself and broke off for a fresh start. "Well, does that talk sound familiar? I don't mean the actual conversation. I know you didn't hear that. But let me put it this way: would you recognize any of the four people we've been discussing? I mean, would that sort of thing be typical of any one of them? Certain words and a way of putting things—does it sound like them?" He was making a desperate effort to get what he wanted.

The whole proceeding had been curious enough, but this allusion to Katherine and the three men left me dumfounded. With my mind whirling, I tried to think. Katherine in the woman's role? I cast that aside straightway. Her demands for attention were all made so subtly that they seemed not to have been. She would never have offered herself.

"It wouldn't be Mrs. Haskell, I'm sure." I said it decisively, almost belligerently.

Cooper fingered his pages without looking at them. I reached out. "If I could just go over it again," I suggested, and after a moment's hesitation he relinquished the sheets and rose to wander about the room.

Observant of the New York Police Department heading, my eye went down the lines. But it was difficult for me. These men who entered into Cooper's questions had, with the exception of Dr. Jarvis, known me since I was eleven. To a certain extent they still retained with me that manner of an adult with a child so that I had little in the way of personal encounters from which to judge.

I tried to put each in turn in the place of the man.

Who but Brooke could parry so easily, giving the woman her pleasant sense of being dangerous and still keeping the situation where he wanted it? But that "Sentiment, the pure girlish stuff"—that could belong to O'Meara. And the brief, clipped "Then why come?"—I could hear Dr. Jarvis saying that, see the precise closing of his lips.

I gave it up. Any one of them might have said those lines, and any one of dozens of other men might have said them too. That was the trouble, I explained to Cooper. "They seem to be the kind of thing any man might say. Any man of that sort."

"What do you mean by 'that sort'?" Cooper stood twirling the big globe that stands in one of the deep windows.

"Well—men who have been around. Experienced, used to that kind of repartee with women." It was not easy to be explicit.

He gave the globe a final spin and came back to me, disappointment in the long lines of his body. "Then you couldn't pick one out and say definitely that it sounds like him?"

"Where was it? When? If you could tell me that . . ."

He took the sheets, stood looking at them a moment and tossed them on the table. His eyes remained on them, an exacerbated look of defeat.

"When? That's easy." He sat down tiredly. "But where? When we know that, we'll have the case." And once more I thought his voice carried reverberations of a previous argument.

Dan was back at his feet the moment he was in his chair, and in the silence, as he sat fussing with the dog's ears, I recalled my promise to Oz.

"That car—the Lincoln car that Oz saw—I've been wondering about it. And Oz was anxious to know . . ." I stopped; he didn't seem to be listening.

"It was Parsons' car," he said abruptly and rose restively for another turn about the room.

"Oh!" The word was a little gasp. "The papers said nothing about it—about whose it was," I managed to say. Nor had they. No mention of Parsons in connection with those two telephone calls either.

"They will. Before this is over," Cooper said, grimness showing in his mouth and chin.

He stopped by the desk, stood sliding a hand along the clear red leather on the flat surface. "Yes, it was Parsons' car," he repeated in his usual quiet tones. He took his hand from the desk and jammed it against his hip. "I think you're discreet or I wouldn't be giving you this."

The picture that I got from Cooper's telling was of the good-looking, middle-aged Parsons sitting, suave and bland, in the district attorney's office, giving his smooth replies to Mr. Bigelow's deferentially courteous questions. First, over the matter of the two telephone calls, and later, concerning the car.

He had been greatly surprised when Mrs. Shephard called. She had said that she wished to see him about something important. Something very urgent, he had gathered, and Mr. Parsons' tone suggested that he was still nonplused by a very unusual proceeding. He had had no business dealing with the family and knew them only slightly in a social way. It was true, yes, he had met Mrs. Shephard. But that was some time ago, and he had not seen her since her marriage.

"And that seems to check," Cooper broke his story to say. "Nothing that we've dug up shows there's been anything since she left for Europe last February."

He had suggested an appointment for the next day, but Mr. Parsons was not sure she had definitely acceded to it. The impression he had gained was of some crisis in money affairs, a need to consult with someone.

They made a lengthy attempt to find out exactly what Jocelyn had said, but that was all, Mr. Parsons told them, just that excited request to see him. The supposition of financial difficulties had been entirely conjecture on his part. But at the close of that first interview the examiners had been inclined to agree with Parsons' idea of a problem involving money. Only momentarily, however, for a close probing of Jocelyn's affairs yielded nothing in support of this.

Mr. Parsons had denied at first that he had been in Crichton Park that evening; this was on his second summons to Mr. Bigelow's office. But when he was confronted with the fact that the patrolman on duty at the south end of the village had identified him as the man who had asked how to get to Crichton Park, he laughed depreciatingly.

"I had hoped to keep that dark," he admitted ingenuously. "I was out there, yes. But when the odd matter of the telephone calls came up, I very much hoped it wouldn't be discovered."

He was still bland and expansive. "I drove out to see Sam Dwyer," he explained readily enough now. "He has a place in the park. I'd been there a time or two before, but not driving myself, and I wasn't sure where you turned off. But driving around—" He broke off. "After all," he demanded, "what harm would a few good readable signs

do out there? They wouldn't ruin the place, would
they?" He grew quite discursive on the point,
almost heatedly so. Only the district attorney's
next question stopped what seemed to be a genuine grievance.

"Your car was parked at the north end of the
Shephard place?"

"Yes." His manner became urbanely good-humored once more after his warm remarks on the
matter of the signs. "As I started to say, I had completely lost my bearings, and when I came to the
Shephard place I recognized it. Sam had pointed it
out once. I remembered the pillars and general layout. I stopped—I was all turned around anyway,"
he reminded them. "As long as I was right there,
it came to me that I might drop in and see what
Mrs. Shephard wanted. I waited a few minutes—I
didn't want to interrupt their dinner—but when I
thought it over, I decided against it. I didn't know
them well enough to call informally, and it was just
an impulse in the first place, of course."

"How long were you there, Mr. Parsons?"

"Oh, five minutes . . . ten . . ."

But Oz had seen him before eight, just about
the time Mr. Parsons claimed to have stopped, and
there was evidence to suggest that the car was still
there a half-hour later. Though there was nothing
positive in the way of identification of either car

or driver, at least two witnesses had observed an automobile there at close to eight-thirty.

When Mr. Bigelow pressed the point, Parsons listened in smiling disbelief, the manner of a man who is familiar with the way extravagant information is volunteered in a murder case of any prominence.

"About five or ten minutes," he said, "and then I oriented myself and drove to Sam Dwyer's."

"And that checks too," Cooper told me. "In a way. Dwyer says he was there. But no servants saw him, and Mrs. Dwyer and her daughters were out. Dwyer answered the door himself."

I had been unable to make anything of the conversation which read like the lines from a smart comedy, but the business of Parsons and the car was more solid. If the police were right in their findings that Jocelyn had not seen Parsons for several months, why had she suddenly tried to reach him that afternoon? And why had Parsons been there in the early evening? Not for a moment did I believe Parsons' explanation. The two incidents were connected, but not in the chance way he would have the authorities understand. What had been said in their short conversation to bring Parsons out that night? I thought of those under-the-breath rumors, wondering if the police were correct in their conclusions of no recent meetings.

That Jocelyn's life these last months had been thoroughly investigated a day's papers showed clearly. "Shephard's Bride Led Gay Life" read one headline. But when you had read beyond the glaring head with its promise of startling disclosure, there was not a great deal after all. It was the usual thing of meeting in pairs or groups at various cocktail bars and smart dancing places.

How did Cooper fit Parsons into the affair? Almost simultaneously with the thought, he snapped out of his pondering silence, leaned forward and fixed me with the steady, spectacled gaze. But sudden observation or sharp question, neither came.

A moment before I had heard Thompson open the door to someone, and now Ham appeared in the library door, Brooke with him. They had run into each other at the hospital, and Brooke had driven back with Ham to stay the night. Though he had left with our other guests that afternoon, Brooke continued to drop in at any and all times and to stick by so generally through all the ensuing days that he still seemed a part of the household.

Both looked at Cooper with sharp interest, as if his presence there might presage some advancement in the tangled case.

"Any progress?" Ham inquired, coming on into the room.

Cooper gave them an outline of the day's events, a day that had included Ham's own appearance in the district attorney's office, though Cooper had not been present and made no reference to it now.

But Ham was paying little attention to Cooper. His tired eyes went to the gaping brief case on the floor, to the official-looking papers strung over the table, wondering about them, I knew, in their relation to me.

Connolly, who was on duty that night, had come to the door and stood waiting to speak to Cooper.

"How were things at the hospital, Ham?" I had held back the question as long as I could, restrained the same fear that gripped me each time I lifted the telephone to call.

He pulled himself out of his brooding weariness so that his answer might carry no unnecessary weight of gloom.

"Not much change, Nancy, but holding her own, I think." He managed to infuse his voice with that note of the commonplace which can bring reassurance more readily than profuse protestations.

Connolly, his word with Cooper finished, lingered, frank sympathy showing on his face. He couldn't resist a further encouragement.

"You can't always tell in those cases," he put in. He had known of a similar case, a young chap

mixed up in some shooting affray, and he proceeded to give a detailed account rather more harrowing than cheering. Grim it might be, doubly so in
its connection to us, but Ham's eye caught mine
for an instant with a gleam of humor at Connolly's
gruesome tale, offered so ingenuously as comfort.

Ham and Brooke went on upstairs where they
had been bound when the sound of Cooper's voice
had drawn them in. Cooper stood staring after
them as if they had somehow added to his worry
and bafflement.

I tried to bring him back to Parsons and the
coincidence of his waiting outside our grounds
the night Jocelyn was killed, but there was little
to add, and the talk dwindled. It had been in my
mind to ask Cooper about the girl he had brought
to the house that morning. Crowded as the day
had been, the puzzle of her connection with Jocelyn had stayed in my mind.

It was then, as I sat considering the best way of
approach, that it happened. A scream tore through
the silence. A woman's scream, prolonged and terrified.

I jumped up to stand frozen, rooted in the horror of it. For a stunned instant we faced each other.
Then Cooper was out of the room and up the stairs
like a shot. I followed, clinging to the rail from
actual need.

Halfway down the hall of the north wing Alma stood, sobbing hysterically. Brooke had her by the arm, shaking her in a frenzied effort to still the uncontrollable weeping.

"Stop it!" he said. "Stop that nonsense!"

Ham was there, and Oz too. I remembered being dimly surprised; I hadn't known that Oz was in the house. Without stopping I ran the other way and, utterly beside myself, pushed open the door of Mother's room. I don't know what I had expected to find, but she was sleeping quietly; she had slept through that hideous shriek. Astonishing, even with the doctor's opiate.

Weak from relief, I backed out noiselessly and made for the group in the hall.

"It was there. I saw it," Alma was saying between rasping sobs.

"She ought to be sent someplace until this is over," Brooke took time to say in a harried undertone.

Cooper was taking charge now. "What did you see, Alma?"

She pointed back along the hall and continued sobbing.

"What did you see?" He said it peremptorily this time. Startled, she tried to pull herself together, unconsciously wriggling free of Brooke's grasp on her arm.

"I heard something—a sort of tapping at the window—and when I turned, it was staring in. A face—with something white."

"Which room?"

"Mr. Bennett's."

Cooper's long stride took him to Brooke's room. With Alma in tow, we followed and looked in as he examined the windows. They were unfastened, and he threw one open, thrusting out his head to look along the balcony which runs the length of the two rooms, Brooke's and the one which had recently been O'Meara's.

"Which window was it?" he said over his shoulder.

"That one." Our eyes followed her pointing hand to the window he had opened, the one nearest O'Meara's room.

He came back and stood looking at Alma perplexedly. With or without cause the girl was frightened.

"Where were you, Mr. Bennett?" he asked, his gaze still on Alma.

But Alma gave Brooke no chance to speak. "He'd gone," she said, "and I went back in."

She had been preparing the room after Thompson's announcement of Brooke's arrival, leaving it for the moments Brooke was there.

"Where were you when she screamed?" Cooper asked, and this time she let Brooke answer.

"Head of the stairs," he said. He was looking puzzled, as if he pondered some phase of the queer occurrence.

"And you, Mr. Shephard?"

"In my bathroom," answered Ham.

Cooper nodded, sending his glance along the gallery on to which Ham's room opens. "What about you?" he said to Oz.

"Down in the terrace room," Oz told him and went on to explain. "Thompson said you were with Nancy. Sounded important, so I went in there to wait."

"How long were you there?"

"Came about nine, didn't I?" He looked at Thompson. "Maybe a few minutes before. I went out on the terrace awhile. I'd only just come back in when she yelled."

"Did you leave the door to the terrace open?"

"Yes, but I was right there." Oz's voice took on a defensive note; he couldn't be expected to close the French windows for a brief turn on the terrace.

"Sure no one came in?"

"Absolutely." He began with all his customary assurance and stopped, not quite so certain. "I was walking up and down—I suppose someone could have slipped in. But I'd have heard them, I think." He pushed a hand through his blond hair.

"Now tell me just what you saw." Cooper swung abruptly back to Alma.

"Just that—that face—with the white over it."

"Here!" He pulled a fresh handkerchief from a breast pocket. "Show me."

She took the handkerchief in hands that shook, folded it to a triangle and hung it over her face just below her reddened, swollen eyes.

"You didn't recognize the part of the face uncovered?"

Her incredulous look at the idea of its being someone known to her was answer enough to that.

"Where were you when Mr. Bennett reached you?"

"I don't know." She swayed weakly, and Ham reached out to guide her a backward step or two. Limp and spent, she dropped to a yellow brocade love seat.

"She ran down the hall," Brooke said. "I met her just about where you found us."

"Did you hear a window open in the next room?" Cooper went to O'Meara's door, turning for her answer.

She shook her head. "It was a tapping sound—a queer tapping"—she shuddered—"and then I saw it."

"I'm going to have a look under those windows," Brooke said from behind me and went toward the stairs. The rest of us stood in the door and watched Cooper raise and lower windows. They worked smoothly, without noise.

I glanced uneasily at Alma huddled on the love seat. Clearly the tapping, the white-shrouded face had suggested something supernatural.

"You didn't just imagine it, Alma? You're nervous. Everyone is." I tried to soothe her.

"It was there," she said. "I saw it. I heard the tapping and then I turned around and saw it." The gasping sobs began anew, but softer now, with little spaces between.

Cooper came out of O'Meara's room. "Where's Bennett?" he asked.

"Went down to have a look outside," Oz told him. Cooper started for the stairs as if that had been his next move anyway and he wasn't too pleased at being superseded.

Alma was given into Annie's charge, and the rest of us trailed after Cooper.

I took time to run down the hall again to Mother's room. Standing beside the bed, with only the sound of her heavy breathing in the room, I found myself looking fixedly at something on the floor. Lying there, as if it had slid from the pillows, lay the large, folded handkerchief which Ethel had bound around her head earlier in the evening. I stared at it an instant longer and then, with unreasoning stealth, picked it up and dropped it in the bathroom hamper.

Brooke was coming in by the rear hall door when I reached the lower floor. "I went out underneath that balcony and took a look around." His eyes sought Cooper. "Connolly's out there now with a flash."

Cooper listened to the report from the library door, brief case in hand, evidently ready to leave as soon as he had made his investigation outside.

"Wouldn't have been someone's idea of a joke, would it?" Oz asked.

"No," I said shortly. That was silly coming from Oz, who knew our household as well as we did. Mildred had gone to the movies, and I could scarcely imagine Ethel or Annie in the role of prankster, even in normal times.

"I think she just went berserk then," Oz said.

"No." Ham was thoughtful. "She was frightened; quite genuinely so, I think. Possibly some noise started her off and then she conjured up the rest. Easily excited, of course."

Cooper, at the door now, waited until Ham was finished.

"Yes, she was frightened," he agreed, a grim incisiveness that I had not heard in his voice before, "and she saw just what she said she saw." He paused deliberately, looking at us steadily. "And I think I know why she saw it."

There was an appalled silence as our eyes followed him through the door, opened and closed so quietly. His words, his manner, his abrupt departure, had left us gasping.

Almost directly his car sounded in the drive; his outside examination, if any, was brief.

Oz broke the uneasy quiet. "Any of the rest of that outfit would have spent half the night asking questions," he said, but doubt mingled with his approval. We all felt, I think, that the occurrence demanded further probing.

Which may have been why Oz suggested going out ourselves; Brooke's reminder that he had already gone over the place didn't stay us.

Connolly was still there and obligingly, with an air of humoring us, held his flash while Oz crawled around the ground and stood eyeing the house. To reach the balcony without a ladder was obviously impossible, and there were no marks of a ladder. I followed Oz's gaze to the huge sycamore tree and smiled. A man might have climbed it, but only a monkey could have gained the balcony from its branches. Brooke was right; there was nothing here.

Back in the house, Oz made straight for the terrace room, where he opened the French windows and stood calculating the possibility of some intruder sliding in while he walked the length of terrace.

"He could have done it," he conceded as he closed and fastened the window. "Get the picture." He wheeled about. "Ham and Bennett are upstairs. Your mother's sound asleep."

"What about Dan?" I asked.

"We'll say it's someone Dan is familiar with. We'll start from there," he decided. "He could have come in through that window—someone that knew his way around, knew the whole place. That floor was practically deserted. Then Ham and Brooke come more or less unexpectedly and surprise whoever it was."

"But what did anyone want in O'Meara's room?" I asked by way of some response to Oz. Cooper's odd attitude toward the incident still engaged me.

"Let's go over that room," he said suddenly.

I needed no persuasion. Cooper's swift certainty might blunt my interest in Oz's efforts, but here was activity, some occupation.

We turned on all the lights and began a systematic pulling out of drawers. They were empty, except for the heavy glazed linings, and these I lifted one by one. Oz, frankly enjoying himself now, slung back the edges of the rug and peered underneath. He went over the desk and all its equipment, raised the chintz-covered cushions of the easy chairs. In the closet he pounced on O'Meara's portable typewriter, but it yielded nothing but the battered machine. I recalled Cooper's quick interest in the expedition that had brought it there, and took a look for the envelope, but O'Meara had taken that.

"Oz," I said suddenly, "why, if he were in this room, would he have had to leave it? Alma wasn't in here. He must have been in Brooke's room, then Alma went in, and he escaped to the balcony. He couldn't get up—but he might have dropped from there. On a pinch."

He had been staring in, I reflected. Was he spying on Brooke?

"I'll call down first," I decided and ran to the stairs.

Brooke answered and then came up to watch amusedly from the doorway.

"He was after something," Oz insisted as the search continued fruitless.

"And this end of the house must have been his aim if he came in from downstairs," Brooke offered, but without much conviction.

"I don't understand it. There doesn't seem to be any sense or purpose to it." Oz abandoned the whole business with a kind of sulky exasperation. Results come quickly with Oz or they don't come at all.

Downstairs, his irritation continued. He paced about; the failure of his attempt to find some explanation for the mysterious intruder bothered him.

As I had before that night, I turned to something more tangible and gave Oz a complete account of the parked car.

"Parsons!" He made a clicking sound with his tongue. His good humor and excitement returned at once.

"Why do you suppose Jocelyn called Parsons?"
I asked. "I mean, there must have been some connection between her calling and his coming out
here that night."

Oz wasted not a second on consideration of
Parsons' version. "My idea is he intended to meet
her there, of course, drive someplace for a talk.
Probably she demanded it over the phone."

"But why?"

"Well, look!" he said suddenly. "Ham was getting fed up with her. That you know."

I did, and more completely than Oz could guess
for all his blunt assertion. I had heard those raised
voices, hers screaming angrily. Besides, there was
the evidence of the engagement book and my own
observation, as well, which revealed a warm interest in Katherine. Whether it had gone beyond the
bounds of pleasant diversion, escape from Jocelyn, I couldn't know.

"Well, suppose he was more fed up than we
suspected," Oz was saying. "Ham's the dignified,
trusting kind—but he did have that bracelet
appraised," he reminded me. "Say he wanted a
divorce and had let her know it." It was plain from
his tone how much he would have liked just that.
Oz's inability to credit Ham's marriage remained
unchanged.

I shook my head disbelievingly, but let him go
on.

"She, we'll say, knows that he has plenty to get it on in the Parsons situation. Naturally she'd want to see Parsons, put him on his guard to cover up. She didn't care anything about Ham, but she knew she was sitting pretty and she was going to hang on. That would explain Parsons hotfooting it out."

It was ingenious, it seemed to fit the circumstances.

Still, why had she called at that particular time? "Why not?" Oz countered when I put the question. "Look!" He became more excited as he built up his case. "I believe we have it. Ham called her. All right. Suppose he had been to see a lawyer that afternoon and just dropped a hint of it in his phone talk."

I remembered Ham's hesitant answers the night he was questioned about his trip to New York; it all fitted. And there I stopped. We had swept along without seeing where it must end. A realization of the pitfall toward which we were heading came to Oz at the same moment, I think, something in my face perhaps. We were dismayed, shaken—more so than we wanted each other to know.

"Why did Marian behave so oddly when Jocelyn spoke to her?" A little wildly I went back to the point that seemed to fit with nothing else.

"You're sure you're not overworking that?" he asked. But he was relieved at this shift in direction. He frowned, squinting his eyes. "It wouldn't take a lot to make Marian give her the glassy look, remember."

This was true, but I had watched that brief exchange as Oz had not. So had Brooke and Dr. Jarvis, whose efforts to be offhand about it had only emphasized for me its importance.

We had been embarrassed, even a little frightened, at finding where our deductions plunged us, but that Oz had dismissed it, pushed it under as I had, came through clearly when he said good night. An unwonted anxiety for my safety.

"Nancy," he turned back to say, an uneasy look at the hall and stairway, "lock your doors when you go up. And keep them locked. There's something damned queer about all this, something we haven't even grazed."

15

I was on the east veranda with Brooke and Ham the next morning, waiting for Leo to bring the car around, when Cooper arrived.

"Now what?" Brooke said as we watched him stop in the drive. "Possibly he's decided that he was a little too neatly expeditious with last night's business. Back to pick up the pieces probably."

The flatly disagreeable tone that matched the words was quite alien to Brooke's ordinarily subtle nuances. Then, as I looked at him standing tiredly against the white column of the porch, his face drawn and sallow, I felt suddenly guilty; he had come out to share our anxiety and distress, and had been let in for another harrowing experience.

Cooper, too, as he came up the steps, bore the signs of a sleepless night. In fact, I doubted that he had been to bed at all, so rumpled was he in appearance, with eyes slightly bloodshot.

"You're just leaving?" He looked from us to Leo, drawing up with the car.

"We're going in to the hospital," Ham told him. "But if you want to see me . . ." And then, taking in the hollow weariness of Cooper's face: "How about breakfast? Go in and have some."

Cooper refused mechanically. "I hate to hold you up," he said. "I want to see Miss Sherwin. I won't be twenty minutes," he added, already across the porch and holding the door for me.

Mildred was at work in the terrace room so we went along the hall to the library, which seemed destined to be the center of inquiry.

He wasted no time on explanations. "I have a list of names here. I want to go through them with you." The penciled list was in his hand.

I sat down, opening the jacket of my gray suit.

"Jane Patterson." The name shot out like an old-fashioned roll call, and irresistibly I was reminded of O'Meara's academic comparison.

"What about her?" I gaped at him stupidly.

"Is she good-looking, reasonably young?" Cooper wanted to know.

"Yes, she's nice-looking," I began a little dazedly. "She's big and matronly. And no, not young. She has grown children."

I watched Cooper draw a line through her name. "Leslie Frink?"

"I never heard of her."

"All right. What about this one? Mary Ellen Gilchrist? Mrs. Clarence, that is."

"I know her, yes. Not well—just met her a time or two." I didn't wait for his impatient prodding. "She's good-looking—stunning, really. Gives smart parties—that sort of thing." I watched his pencil put some mark beside the name. "Where did you get the names?" I asked. Why any names? How did these women fit in? was what I wanted to know.

"Mrs. Eugene McGibbon—how about her?" And then, as if he resented the second's interruption: "That one—most of these—are from a dinner list of not so long ago. I know all this sounds foolish," he took time to add, "but if I can eliminate some of these names it's going to save time. And since last night, we need to save time." His brisk haste seemed oddly at variance with the grave warning.

But there was no time to dwell on the reference to the night before. He was repeating the name.

"She's in Europe, I think. I seem to remember hearing or seeing something about her sailing. She's good-looking. Not pretty, perhaps, but—"

"Style, clothes, all that?" Cooper hurried me along.

"Yes," I agreed.

He frowned, put a check by the name and continued down the list, crossing off all the solid matrons, putting an occasional question mark. When he reached the end more than half the names were left clear for whatever he meant to do with them.

But that didn't finish it. "Now I want you to give me some more—women that Bennett, Jarvis and O'Meara go around with."

Cooper gave no sign that he saw what was in back of my staring amazement. "Think, Miss Sherwin. It's important." The same earnest impatience.

But no names came readily to mind. "I don't know, really," I told him. "They each have their own particular sets, of course, besides their connection with us. They travel, they go a lot. They know so many people—I couldn't know them all. There's Joan Barlow." Her name came to me, I suppose, because she had called that morning to ask about Marian. In the end I had managed to increase his list by seven or eight names.

"Here's one." He stood abruptly. "She wouldn't see me yesterday—I tried twice—and she's one I think might be worth while. I'd like to have you call her up, ask her to see me."

"But I scarcely know her," I protested. This was true; she had been with O'Meara once when he dropped in; other than that I had never seen her.

"That's all right." He had the number ready, and I could do nothing but go to the telephone.

She was in and came to the phone without delay. Curiosity, if nothing else, would have managed that.

"Nancy!" Her voice was pitched to the right proportions of sympathy and astonishment. "We're all

so appallingly shocked and sorry about it all." This
had to go its length while Cooper seethed in the
doorway. She would see Mr. Cooper, of course. She
hadn't understood. What did he want? She couldn't
quite keep the burning curiosity from her voice.

"I don't know that," I told her carefully. "He
just asked me to call."

It was over finally. "She'll see you." I turned to
Cooper.

But there was no jubilant response. "Yes," he
said as we left the telephone room, "and then I
won't be sure of anything. Women like that—
they're too clever to give themselves away. Some
you can tell in an instant, of course, and the thing
is closed as far as they are concerned."

But what he could or could not get from these
women whose social poise veiled their reactions
from him I didn't find out.

"You've been fine, Miss Sherwin," he thanked
me. "And you won't discuss it, I know." He paused,
irresolute about the next. "It's important that you
shouldn't." He went slowly, choosing his words.
"Someone, some woman, is in a bad spot."

Last night I would have chilled in horror. But
the sun was streaming in, there was the spread
of grounds, brilliant in the morning light, and
Cooper himself, whose everyday appearance be-
lied melodrama. The whole thing seemed unreal,
too fantastic for belief.

I spent a good part of the day at the hospital. At intervals I made visits to Marian's room and then tiptoed out to return to the small waiting room halfway down the corridor. Nothing that I could do, no faintest hope of her knowing me, but I couldn't leave.

I knew how much the police had banked on an interlude of consciousness from Marian, with the possibility of a statement which would clear things. But as time went on the hope dimmed.

Waiting in the rose-draped reception room, I wondered about Cooper. Could I have known how relentlessly he was driving himself to cover his list with all possible speed, that interview of the morning would have leaped into greater importance for me. I was to discover later that he traveled almost unceasingly through the ensuing days, using planes wherever possible. He made a trip to Chicago, another to a small Virginia town, and contrived to see numbers of people in New York and its suburban sections.

At one I went out for lunch and on to Katherine's for a short call. Ham had evidently had the same idea of breaking the dreary monotony of the day. He was there and looking more comfortably relaxed than I had seen him since the ease of our own household had been shattered.

He went shortly, and I was shocked to find myself watching intently through the moments of his departure. I saw, or fancied that I saw, a look of warm understanding pass between them. My vague disturbance at this evidence of a natural solicitude for each other in a trying time brought home to me more clearly than all else the abnormal state of my own mind.

Katherine was beautifully and faultlessly dressed as always, but she too bore signs of the painful strain. It showed itself in a nervous unease utterly unlike her habitual poise, a poise that was almost languorous in its quiet.

"That young man in the case, the tall dark one—Cooper?" She was uncertain of the name. "He was here this morning," she said. Her voice told me that she was wondering how far she should go.

I understood. Cooper had gone to Katherine, a far better source for what he wanted than I was, I had to admit. He had admonished her to the same silence, hence her careful approach.

"It was curious," she went on, edging her way.

"He asked for names?" I hazarded, my eyes on her as she sat pulling at the folds of her long hostess gown, noting how well she suited her lovely Empire drawing room.

So, going warily, disclosing only what was known to the other, we discussed the interviews.

"It was all so curious," she said again. "Those names—why does he want them?" She seemed disturbed and unhappy.

I could understand; my own contribution to Cooper's list had made me feel meanly uncomfortable.

"If some woman"—her fine eyes watched me closely—if I didn't react rightly she would slur into something else—"if someone is in actual danger, then why don't they protect her and have done with it?" she finished in a burst of nervous energy.

But I didn't know, and when she saw that my knowledge of the odd affair didn't exceed her own, she left it. The rest of my stay was taken up with other things; Marian, of course, Mother's illness. And here her quick, probing questions, a kind of alert intensity as she waited for my answers, seemed out of all reason to its importance. It annoyed me in some unaccountable way, but I dismissed it as merely another example of my distorted viewpoint.

16

There was little in the way of developments for the next two days. Following a telephone request from Mr. Bigelow, I drove over to the district attorney's office for what proved to be a lengthy but, so far as I could see, not very fruitful session. The questioning covered events of before and after the crime, possibly a gathering up of all loose ends. As they continued, attacking from so many angles, I gained the impression that they were at the end of their resources; this was a final drive for some new clue which would provide an opening.

The McIvers entered into it, particularly Larry's intimacy with Jocelyn. This wound up to merge with my return to the library the night Jocelyn was murdered. Did they think Larry had gone back as I had? That seemed unlikely. Certainly after thrusting me into the telephone room he would not have gone without his letter, unless something had frightened him away. But the sub-

sequent unlocking of the door disproved that, I
thought. Besides, I couldn't conceive the gay, ir-
responsible Larry as the person who had created
that hour of terror.

Mr. Bigelow moved on to Ham, working out a
picture of dissension and jealousy from the bracelet incident more incriminating than the facts war-
ranted. I waited with bated breath for Katherine's
name. It came, but, ignoring Mr. Bigelow's pointed insinuations, I stressed a family friendship of
years' standing, refusing to admit anything else,
even when his carefully maintained poise gave way
to open irritation.

On leaving the place, I ran straight into Larry
McIver on his way up the courthouse steps.

"You too?" he said and grinned as if there were
something humorous in a summons from Mr. Bigelow. "Anything new?" he wanted to know and,
without waiting for an answer, asked about Marian. I warmed to him for this. Selfish and incon-
siderate of Irene he assuredly was, but something
about Larry made it more the careless thought-
lessness of an indulged child than callous indifference. Did Marian have a chance? he asked. Had
she been conscious at all? He waited anxiously on
my answers, looking genuinely disturbed and unhappy. "I liked her," he said. "A live old girl." He
went back to his first query then. "What's happening—if anything?"

There wasn't much I could tell him, and after a rehashing of what he already knew, he went on up the steps. If he dreaded the approaching interview, he gave no sign of it.

On the drive home my worry and apprehension welled up. The careful inquiry into Ham's renewed interest in Katherine disturbed me. What had been a faint inner perturbation, scarcely admitted, had been increased to a deep, growing fear which would not be dismissed.

The afternoon was unbearable. In desperation I sat playing solitaire, my fingers moving the cards, my mind going over the morning in the district attorney's office, when Thompson came to the door to say that Mrs. McIver wished to see me.

She was in the room before I could gather up the cards. With scarcely any greeting she plunged into the reason for her visit. "I left a dress when I went the other day. I didn't miss it until yesterday when I wanted to wear the thing—so I thought I'd run out and pick it up."

She talked fast. This was a speech she had prepared, and now she rattled it off in a hurried, pat manner that was somehow pathetic.

I was surprised. We are scrupulous in our prompt sending on of clothing, toilet articles or bits of jewelry that certain people seem, invariably, to leave behind, and there had been no mention of a dress from either Alma or Mildred.

"Alma said nothing about it," I told her. "But things have been upset, of course," I added and rang for Thompson.

A dress? Thompson looked mildly surprised and went to summon Alma.

Irene sat down then, but she couldn't relax, and I saw that her hands were shaking as she lit a cigarette. Once away from our house, I should have supposed that she would have thrown off the painful intensity of those first two days, but her face with its tight, drawn skin, and the feverish glitter of her eyes told their own story. Sherry, I decided, instead of tea, and waited for Alma to relay the order to Thompson.

"There wasn't anything in the closet," Alma insisted when she came. The room had been gone over just as usual, just as the others had. She was on guard as she had been since the night of Jocelyn's murder; if we suspected her of taking anything, the alert, wary manner said.

"Go over the closet again to make certain," I said by way of dismissal and turned to Irene.

"You couldn't have mislaid it yourself? Sometimes, on missing something, your mind flies to a conclusion, and you're so sure that you can't see it any other place."

There was no quick recognition of a common human frailty. She crushed out her cigarette and reached for the packet in her bag.

"What are they doing?" she asked. "The police, I mean." With the cigarette to aid her, she made almost too much of the business of indifference.

This was why she had come; the dress had been a pretext to give a reason for her call. As her eyes watched me warily, even hungrily, I remembered that since their departure they had been outside the range of events. Still, Larry had been in the district attorney's office only that morning.

"Have they any idea who did it?" She was licking her lips, the incessant moistening I had noticed on other occasions. "Have they found out anything new?"

"No," I told her honestly enough, "I don't believe they have." I couldn't tell her about Cooper's activities. For that matter, I knew too little about them myself to make them sound relevant.

"They had Larry at the D.A.'s office this morning," she offered, and I felt her watching narrowly for my reaction.

"Yes, I saw him a moment," I returned. "I was there too."

"You were!" She seemed to be uplifted for a moment with something like relief. But only for an instant. "Did they ask about Larry?" she demanded, and with the question all assumption of casualness fell away from her.

"They asked about everything," I answered noncommittally. I was restive under the fixity of

her gaze. Why had she come? What did she want
to know?

"I can't stand it!" She was out of her chair. "I
have to know. If they have anything on Larry—"

"It's natural to question everyone." I tried to
soothe her. Too well I knew the signs. She would
be shrieking hysterically in another moment.

"Larry told them everything he knew right
while he was here. Why did they take Larry over
there today—when I was there yesterday?"

"You were?" I asked and plunged anew into my
assurances that it was all to be expected. Anyone
who had been present when the crimes were committed . . .

"I hate that Bigelow," she broke in. "He looks
like a movie heavy—and talks like one too."

I smiled. It was apt, in a way. The well-shaped
head of gray hair and the spectacular black brows,
the suave voice and manner which had irritated Irene. It sounded like mere pettishness, but,
though she had dropped back to her chair, she was
twisting and clenching her hands in her lap.

"They've been asking about the time she was
kidnaped. Good Lord! Do they think Larry did
that too?"

"But you knew her then and we didn't," I came
in quickly, still bent on keeping her within bounds.
"They might have thought that she had told you

something at the time, something that would lead somewhere. That's the way they work."

She ignored this and went back to Mr. Bigelow.

"He asks things and says things—they don't sound like anything—and then, without knowing it, you've said something—"

"I know; it's his job." I watched her twisting hands uneasily, wondering what she had been trapped into saying. I didn't have long to wait.

"What if Larry did give me those sleeping tablets!" Her voice was climbing now. Intent on what she was about to say, I made no effort to break in with calming platitudes. "What if we didn't speak of it at the time? I needed them. I often take them. They were right in my bag. Larry knew I wouldn't sleep and gave me a couple."

So that was it. The night Marian was shot and Irene had been aroused with difficulty. It had been more than exhaustion and two stiff highballs which had made her sleep like that. And Larry had given them to her. It was a bad point for Larry, I saw that. I wanted to ask if he had urged them on her, been insistent, but the sight of her bleak misery made me hold my tongue.

My sympathy was short-lived, however. "Why should we be the ones to be hounded?" She was out of her chair again, a leaping motion that brought her against my table and sent cards flying to the floor. Instinctively I braced myself against the ranting anger of her voice. "Larry didn't do it! Larry didn't kill Jocelyn! Larry didn't go to Miss Shephard's room! He owed Joss money—they harp on that. He was jealous!" Scorn sought to rout her fright. "Who would he be jealous of? Parsons?"

"Stop it!" I said. "Don't go on like that, Irene."

"And what about him?" She moved closer so that she was standing over me. "But he has money, he's your kind."

So she was back on that strain; it seemed to be an obsession with her.

"We didn't want her out of the way. It was you people that were anxious to be rid of her. And it was Hamilton Shephard's revolver, wasn't it? And you—you'd have been out on your ear if she hadn't been wiped out."

This heterogeneous jumble of newspaper high points, a clutching at anything and everything, told of days of ceaseless brooding, sleepless nights of turning it over and over in her mind. But I had had all I could stand. Unstable at best, she was beyond all reason now.

"You'd better go." I broke through her strident raving, a repetition of the last enormity, with Mother dragged in this time, and crossed the room to summon Thompson. "Here!" I seized the sherry, poured a full glass and stood over her while she gulped it down. She stood in a dazed sort of wretchedness while I ordered the car, and there was no word spoken as she followed me to the hall to wait for Leo.

"Drive her right into town," I said to Leo. Outrageous as she had been, I realized she was in no condition to be dumped at the station to wait for a train.

I was limp when I came back into the house and got myself upstairs. Her very lack of control had lessened the power of her words, but the scene had left me shaking. She had been alarmed over being caught on the vital point of the sleeping tablets, and Larry's scathing disgust—easy to imagine that—must have heightened its importance for her. A craving to talk and unburden herself had brought her out, that and a need to vindicate Larry. But Larry had not been weighed down by the affair, neither that morning nor in those first days. It was Irene on whom it all seemed to prey to a point where she seemed not quite sane. Why? Was this abnormal solicitude for Larry a cloak to hide her own fears? Irene had waited that afternoon in Jocelyn's room when someone had come to the door. What if it had been Jocelyn, and, wishing to avoid a scene with Irene, she had retreated to the sitting room? Had Irene followed, snatching up the statuette as she passed through the gallery? But Irene had been sleeping soundly on the night Marian was shot. Could that have been a blind, and the sleeping-tablet incident a conjured-up attempt to protect herself under Mr. Bigelow's fire? She was jealous of Jocelyn, giving her the motive which, so far as I could see, Larry lacked.

But where did that leave Cooper and his pursuit of some unknown woman? As O'Meara had said, he was no fool; he must know what he was doing. Twist it about as I would, I couldn't fit that search of Cooper's into my case against Irene. Nervous hysteria alone must account for her behavior. And there I left it, meaning to bring it up the next time I saw Cooper.

But I saw Cooper only once during this time and then only in passing. For on that particular night he went straight to Ham's study and was there more than an hour. He didn't read the sheets of smart conversation, as I could tell on talking to Ham afterwards. But he did go into the subject of incomes, inquiring about the standing of these people in the early days of acquaintanceship with the family, seeking reliable sources of their present financial rating.

Ham was rather more astonished than perturbed, was inclined to view it as some wild shot, prompted by desperation.

"They don't seem to have a great deal." This quite without censure. The case was too inexplicable for ordinary methods.

I told about my visit to Mr. Bigelow's office that day when the old ground had been gone over, step by step.

He nodded; this was what he had just been saying.

"They brought up all that business—the bracelet, you and Jocelyn. They rather dragged Katherine in too." I smiled; I would insert my warning without its seeming a warning.

He was not greatly shocked. As long as the crimes remained unsolved they would stop at nothing. He had already accepted that.

He began a slow pacing past the open shelves of books.

"That bracelet—having it appraised—that was a mistake. Outside of all this"—he waved a vague hand —"it could do no good. Jocelyn . . ." He stopped and stood plucking absently at the wool damask hangings.

I stirred uneasily at the imminence of some disclosure.

"Jocelyn . . ." He paused again, choosing his words with care. "Her standards and values were so totally different from ours that argument only made the situation that much worse. A divorce would have had to come. I had already realized that." He said it so quietly that it was a full instant before the words sank in.

"The whole situation—well, it was one of those things." He dropped the red drapery and spread both hands. Now that it was over, comprehension failed him. In that one sentence he had managed to convey his own lack of understanding for suddenly going off his head, as O'Meara had put it.

A divorce! My mind went dizzily back to Oz's neat explanation for Parsons' stay at the edge of our grounds. "But you hadn't—you hadn't done anything about it?"

"Oh no. No." He caught nothing but the surprise as his eyes met mine in the steady gaze that somehow belonged to his substantial stockiness. "No." He sat down tiredly. "I've thought about that. If something had precipitated it earlier, she might have been away, she might have lived."

My brain was whirling. I thought of Mr. Bigelow's insinuating thrusts which had left me with a boding fear. And Ham—what would he do under a similar inquisition? Would he give away that inevitable divorce? Perhaps he had already done so, with the same grave sincerity, which would be no shield against their skilled maneuvers. Try as I would, I could not throw it off; it stayed and clung through a troubled, wakeful night.

O'Meara came out late the next afternoon and, finding that I would be quite alone, stayed on for dinner. Ham was in New York, and Mother, after her first frantic insistence that she must go in to see Marian, had settled into a despondent apathy, refusing to leave her room, though Dr. Hawley urged a gradual return to normal activities.

Brooke and Jarvis came in the evening, driving out after dinner in town, a meeting to discuss and compare notes on the case, I decided.

Beyond concerned inquiries for Marian, they were insistently cheerful. I was already dwelling too heavily on the past dreadful events, was their attitude, and they were bent on diverting me.

When Frank, suddenly, without warning, started in on one of the newer phases of the case, I was caught completely off my guard. He was on a sofa where, by degrees, he had worked himself into a position of sprawling comfort.

"I have it!" He half pulled himself up. "Millie. Millie Couch. Girl I met last summer. Nice girl, quite pretty too. You give that one to the bright young man from the district attorney's office, Nancy."

I felt myself blushing hotly. How had they found out? Katherine, perhaps. But she had been so warily cautious with me that I had been sure of a discretion equal to my own.

Brooke stood laughing down at O'Meara, and at my discomfiture. "Never mind, Nancy."

"Then there's that girl that spoke to me in the post office last week," O'Meara went right on. "Not pretty. Not spectacularly pretty, but quite

an air to her. Elan, you know—that sort of thing.
Right up Cooper's street. A lot of swish and style.
I don't know her name, but she can be looked up.
This investigation seems to have plenty of time
for things like that. Chase the pretty girls—let
the murderer lie where he will."

"Oh, don't!" I said. I was frightfully uncomfortable. I felt like a traitor.

"You did but your duty, Nancy. I bear you no
ill will." He hauled himself up so that he sat on
the edge of the couch, grinned at me cheerfully.
"That's not what concerns me. I'm just trying to
bring my list up to compare with Bennett's. I don't
aspire to anything like what Jarvis must have from
all I hear."

Jarvis managed a smile, but it was not greatly
amused. Whether he was annoyed on my account
or his own, I could not tell.

"What's Cooper want with all our women?"
O'Meara was demanding querulously. "Lookers
like he has. That blonde he brought right here to
the house. And yet he has to muscle in on us. Jarvis there"—he remained imperturbable to Jarvis'
faint exasperation—"and Brooke—they can stand
it, perhaps. But with me it's different. I've worked
hard for what I've got. I've paid my taxes. I've
been an upright citizen . . ." He went off into a
line of irrelevant nonsense which gave me time to
collect myself.

He drew himself up cumbersomely and stood, making an ineffectual jab or two at his white hair now in disarray from wallowing on the sofa.

"I shall always remember this as the case of the thousand beautiful women. But no joking, where do all these women come in? Cooper's no fool. And Bigelow must give it his approval. Now just where do they come in?

"You understand, Nancy"—he changed back to his light tone—"we aren't asking you to betray your great trust, but if you could just give us a hint . . ."

"I don't know, Frank," I said. "I honestly don't." Which was true enough in its way. I didn't mention the curious piece of dialogue—Katherine had not seen that—or Cooper's anxiety for some unidentified woman, though, in the light of what they already knew, it seemed silly not to.

I had been awkward and at a loss under O'Meara's ragging that, carried on in a light vein as it was, accomplished his purpose. But it did this for me. For almost the first time since my appearance in the district attorney's office I relaxed the nagging fears which both the examination and Ham's own revelations had aroused. Moreover, this business of the women, incomprehensible as it was, seemed to be leading away from ourselves. But this lightening of mood was dispelled when Ham came.

"Ham!" I cried out at first sight of him. His face was drawn, gray with exhaustion. "Marian—"

He glanced up quickly, alive to the alarm in my voice. "No—there's no great change."

But I sensed a change in Ham. It went beyond weariness, so completely dejected and under the weight of some new pressure he seemed. I wondered if he had again been summoned for questioning—he had been absent since breakfast—but he volunteered nothing, and I didn't ask. At his own suggestion we went up almost directly. I worried through another restless night, but in the morning he was gravely himself once more. Perhaps it had only been fatigue after all. That and the added apprehension which night brings to periods of stress.

17

Marian died late that afternoon. From the first we had been given scant encouragement, and certainly I had been prepared since my arrival at the hospital in the morning. Nonetheless, it came as a shocking blow.

Not until she was gone did I realize how completely I was counting on recovery, increasingly difficult as it had grown to read hope into the reports. It would have meant a solution to the crimes, of course. But to us it meant so much more than that. Marian, under whose brusque humor the whole house came to life. Working back to something that resembled the old pleasant ease was now impossible.

That was Tuesday, and the funeral was from our house on Thursday; just a week since Jocelyn had been killed and our lives thrown into a nightmare of anguished unreality.

For the duration of those three days I gave scarcely a thought to the problems of the

investigation. Cooper was there once at least. He
stopped me as I came into the hall with Oz, but
only to speak of Marian, an earnest expression of
sympathy that was somehow exactly right. I liked
Cooper. Holt grated in whatever he did or said,
and Mr. Bigelow, for all his careful courtesy, put
me immediately on the defensive. With Cooper I
could be natural and at ease.

I was wandering listlessly about the grounds in
the afternoon the day following the funeral, when
O'Meara drove in. He waved and called out and
came along the garden path, giving an eye to the
brilliant fall coloring that McAllister always con-
trives. I was gratified at this visit; O'Meara, whose
sardonic amiability remained unchanged through
everything, would be a good person to see.

His first questions, when he came up to me,
were understanding inquiries. Marian's death had
been a keen loss to O'Meara. They had gotten on
well, cronies who baited each other with unflag-
ging vigor.

"Nothing new, I suppose?" he said next.

"Nothing," I told him. I was low and dispir-
ited. This dreary inactivity was more difficult to
endure than the turbulence of the earlier days.

"Well!" he said, and his voice changed, became
abruptly cheerful, as if he suddenly recalled his
role; he had not driven over to add to our gloom.
"This will interest you. You people aren't the

only ones to come in for the heavy investigating. They've gone over my apartment with a fine-tooth comb. No search-warrant stuff, put it as a request.

"Wait!" He raised a hand to hold back my exclamation of surprise. "You haven't heard the half of it yet. They've done the same by my country estate."

"Your what, Frank?" I asked. This is the sort of thing O'Meara expects and all but waits for. It came now from habit, though it lacked the spirit which belongs to that kind of interchange.

"My country estate," he repeated firmly. "But wait—there's more. They tramped over my broad acres, my petunias and marigolds, my fine row of dahlias—you saw them the other day," he reminded me with exaggerated pride. "My well-kept lawns—"

I smiled at that too. Not by the wildest stretch of the imagination could O'Meara's lawn be called well kept.

"They wrote on my typewriters," he went on, "poked over my house. And—I wouldn't swear they took it, but it's gone—my address book. A collection of years."

I quickened at his mention of the typewriters. "You have a typewriter here, Frank," I told him.

"That still here? Remind me to take it when I go." He smiled. "That's one they missed. I can't make any sense to it, but there it is. I seem to be under heavy suspicion." His eyes made a sweep of the grounds, the gardens, the great old trees showing the first signs of turning. "Just a criminal returning to the old scene," he said.

I remembered Cooper's interest in that afternoon trip to O'Meara's place. For a moment I thought of telling Frank—it was the natural thing to do—but something held me back.

"Under heavy suspicion," he repeated. "And so is Brooke. Jarvis, too, for all I know. I tried to get hold of him, but his secretary said he was out of town. I saw Brooke, though. But from what I can make out, they didn't go at his place in quite the wholehearted way they did mine. Not on the same broad, sweeping scale," he assured me. "Or it may just have affected me more. I'm probably the home type who suffers when his castle is invaded."

But for all his ranting nonsense, something that was disturbance came through and showed plainly. His mouth and chin had a grimness, now that he was still.

"It's odd," I said.

"Damned odd," he agreed.

We tried to make something of it as we walked to the house, O'Meara holding carefully to his jocose lightness. We went in by the rear entrance just as Thompson was opening the east door opposite, which was how we happened to receive the Schwaggermans. Meeting there in the hall as we did, anything else would have been impossible.

Numbers of people had called in the last days. I don't mean those curiosity seekers who, under the guise of merest acquaintance, flocked morbidly to a house where crime and violence had taken place; Thompson disposed of these in short order. But the people who know us well came after Marian's death. Some acknowledgment of the hideous mess into which we had been plunged was called for, and those moments of strained, unnatural talk were unpleasantly in my mind as we ran into the Schwaggermans.

Today was less difficult, however. True, the same phrases rolled out familiarly, the kind of thing that tragedy and death seem to demand. But Paul Schwaggerman's calm acceptance of the situation, without that air of going carefully and ignoring what couldn't be ignored, made a difference.

Already I had come to shrink from a feeling of being people apart, people to be handled with subtle skill, conscious all the while of the wondering uncertainty behind the vigilant tact. Paul, with his frank inquiries and candid comments, came as a distinct relief.

"Lord, all this is terrible for you people." He paused to call out a greeting to Brooke, who had just arrived. Like O'Meara, he had driven out to

see us through a bad day. "An awful mess when
the law and press gang up on you." In spite of
the newspapers, it was plain that Paul had a fixed
belief in some skilled criminal gang, something
obscurely connected with Jocelyn's theater experience or the kidnaping which the papers, digging
from old files, had gone into thoroughly, when
every venomous drop had been wrung from the
family side of the case.

"They'll get them," he assured Ham. "Sooner
or later someone cracks and gives the show away.

"Ruth had a narrow squeak the other night," he
said as we settled in the terrace room.

I was glad of the shift in his talk. Mother was
there, and decidedly better since Marian's death
had roused her to a resumption of her daily round,
but any discussion of the crimes brought back all
her nervous fluttering.

"Oh, Paul, don't tell that again," Ruth protested
from across the room. But her dissent was charming, with no rebuke in it for Paul. And therein lies
her cleverness, I imagine. For Ruth is undeniably
clever. With not much in the way of means, they
manage to train with a smartly gay crowd whose
goings and comings are sure of comment in the
social columns. And this is undoubtedly due to
clever manipulation on Ruth's part, though they
are an engaging enough pair on their own merits.

"Wednesday night it was," Paul went right on. "She'd been to a party—Clark's place in Pelham—and was driving herself home."

Ruth looked annoyed—that tolerant, amused annoyance which men like Paul can provoke.

"You tell things so badly, Paul," she cut in. "If these people must have the tale it might as well be as painless as possible. Anyway, it's my story.

"It was like this," she told us. "I drove in and shut off the motor. Nobody believes me," she hastily forestalled interruption from Paul, "but I know I did. That's the funny part of it. And then, when I got out, I fell over something—Tommy's little cart it turned out to be. And the next thing I remember is waking up in the drive with Paul and a doctor and a couple of curious neighbors."

"Don't forget the curious neighbors saved your life, darling," Paul put it. "That monoxide doesn't take long."

"But I never shut the door." She ignored him and appealed to us. "Why on earth would I want to shut the door?"

"It blew shut," he told her in the manner of a man who has covered the ground before. "That door does, if it isn't swung completely back."

"Well, I'll grant you the door then," she said, "but I'm certain about the ignition." She was being brightly argumentative, but something that was genuine disturbance crept in.

"Remember it was three o'clock or darned near it."

Paul's tone implied that anyone returning from a late party couldn't be held to account for inaccuracies. "Probably that door banging shut that woke the Donaldsons."

"Just what happened? Did you knock yourself out when you fell?" O'Meara asked her.

"I did get a nasty crack." Her fingers went to a spot just beneath her tiny hat. "I suppose it was the cart," she went on ruminatively. "Something tripped me, of course. And yet"—here was a point that continued to annoy her—"I don't remember seeing it when I drove in. The cart, I mean. I've tried to place it there and I can't."

And then I think it came to her that this might not be just the conversation for a house which had had its full share of calamitous events in the last week. It may have been Brooke's aloof detachment or the quizzical humor on O'Meara's face. She laughed a little embarrassedly; no one was going to believe her, and since she wasn't too sure herself, she would drop it.

But Paul, who had the reverse idea of diverting us and taking our minds off our own troubles, wasn't so easily turned aside. "It was a close call for Ruth, all right." He picked it up again.

"How's the lake, Paul?" Brooke interposed.

"I'm going up there tomorrow," he answered Brooke. "Tom Jewett and I. Come on up." He

glanced around, quite obviously ready with one
of those sweeping invitations which men like Paul
are always passing out, when something brought
it home to him that this was hardly the time to
suggest a riotous week end.

"I suppose, though, you're all sticking around
until this is cleared up," he said soberly. Again I
warmed to him for the unhesitant allusion that
came without dexterous hedging.

"I might run in on you at that—if it's a good
day," O'Meara said. "Make it up there in a couple of hours, can't you? Not counting that stretch
into the lake," he added.

"That's a fine old corduroy road," Paul defended the roadway which ran into what was evidently
something rather complete in the way of rustic
cabins. "My grand-paw put that road in to get out
his wood." O'Meara had tapped one of his favorite
topics, and he went on to enthusiastic support of
his road, the near-by village and the locality in
general, before he turned cordially to Brooke.

In the end, I noticed, they got away with
Brooke keeping himself clear of any entangle-
ments. Brooke would never be trapped into an
acceptance not altogether to his liking. And a stag
party, dependent on their own slapdash cooking,
was something to be avoided. But skillfully—no
hint of repugnance ever crept into the smooth
ease of Brooke's refusals.

18

Ham was arrested the next afternoon. Coming unexpectedly and without warning, it was a blow almost as terrific in its impact as the actual crimes
themselves. There had been his summons to the
district attorney's office, a second one which I
had only surmised at the time, and my own questioning which had showed the direction they were
taking, all of which had deepened my disquiet.
But it had been an undefined, half-admitted fear;
that this could happen I had never conceived.

Brooke had stayed the night and was still there.
Oz, free for the afternoon, had come in directly after lunch, so we were all four in the library
when it happened.

I didn't see the serving of the warrant. Thompson appeared and Hamilton was called out. A moment or two later Brooke was sent for, and when
he returned shortly with his announcement, Ham
had already departed in a police car. He would
be held for a magistrate's hearing the following

morning, and it was almost a foregone conclusion that the magistrate's hearing would result in his being held for the grand jury.

Oz raged and stormed in indignation. "The fools! The damned fools!" he burst out. He paced around, kicking at the folding ladder in passing. "What have they got on him?" he demanded.

No one attempted a response. I was too stunned for speech, and Brooke went immediately to get in telephone communication with Ham's lawyers in New York. After that he stood, uncertain and considering. "I'll go over," he said. "I doubt if anything can be done—we'll have to wait and see what comes of this hearing in the morning—but I'll see. There might be something."

He dissuaded Oz, who would have gone along. "Better stay with Nancy," he advised. "I'll go right into New York from there." He looked at me. "If there's anything I'll call you at once."

I was surprised. He had been on the point of leaving when the arrest took place, but he had stayed by us so steadily through it all that I should have supposed this would keep him here.

"That car ought to carry weight and impress somebody, if anything can," Oz said as he turned disconsolately from the window. "Bennett himself, when it comes to that," he grudgingly conceded the distinction of Brooke's manner and appearance.

"But what have they got on Ham?" he asked again. It was more than indignation. He has a warm liking for Ham, had been a devoted admirer of Marian's. Her caustic run of comment and his own lively patter had hit it off well together.

He recounted and listed the points which the papers had emphasized and that our own dogged discussions had weighed and put aside.

"Someone called Jocelyn into that sitting room, and it wasn't Ham. That we know. The idea that it could have been McIver, and Ham saw him disappear into his own room, is a lot of hooey, I tell you." He strode about the room, his light hair rumpled and his face knotted up in bewildered rage.

"That bracelet end of it," he flung around to me, "they're all wrong on that." He cast aside with scorn the insane jealousy which the newspapers had played up.

"They're crazy! Plain crazy!" And, taking up his angry pacing again, he went through the damaging list. The gloves that Miss Wycke had taken only to return at an untimely moment; Ham's room in close proximity to Marian's; his revolver beside her; the fact that Marian's murder was, apparently, a crime to conceal a crime, and who else would she wish to protect? Witheringly he brought each point up and as witheringly dismissed it. Katherine's name was carefully left out. And Ham's mention of a divorce—I had not told that even to Oz.

"I tell you there's something to all this they haven't touched," he declared resolutely. "There's something damned queer about it."

I agreed despairingly. And all those women. What about them? I wondered.

"It's here, I admit." At a loss Oz stared around the room as if he would wrest a solution from the old house within whose walls the crimes had happened. "But who? And why? That setter . . ." He eyed Dan in annoyance. Why hadn't he raised a disturbance and taken the responsibility for the murders beyond the range of our household?

Dan, sensing the attention, went to him, and for the first time Oz stopped his furious pacing and dropped into a chair. "It doesn't make sense," he said wearily and leaned forward to play with Dan's black ears.

But he was up almost at once. "Look," he said, "I'm going over there."

I didn't argue or try to keep him. Probably there was nothing to be done as Brooke had said, but driving over at breakneck speed would at least relieve Oz.

I went upstairs slowly, wondering how I would break this last blow to Mother.

"Has Brooke gone?" She turned from her mirror as I went in. "I meant to get down." She chatted along, putting on the slight touches of make-up she allows herself. Mother would dress carefully if the world fell in pieces around her.

The incidental talk after what had taken place sounded discordant and far away.

"What did you think of that story of Ruth's?" Mother doesn't quite approve of Ruth.

"Well, Ruth likes things dramatic." The words came mechanically. I might wait and tell her in the morning, see what came of the hearing.

"Dramatic! Anything to make a good story. She was probably intoxicated. And what was that husband of hers thinking about, letting her drive home by herself? At that time of night!"

"Paul can't sleep half the day. And with Ruth it's practically every night, I suppose." I defended Paul automatically. Why had they arrested Ham? What new evidence could they have?

"Why, she might have been killed. And that little boy of hers . . ." Mother went on in the same disparaging vein.

But I wasn't listening. Something had suddenly been released in my brain. Killed. I heard Cooper: "Some woman is in a bad spot." That was what he had said as he worked down his list of names.

"It's just Paul's thinking she's so cute," Mother was saying. "She's always having some kind of an experience."

She was. I knew that. Absurd exchanges with taxicab drivers. Amusing encounters in unexpected places, which she undoubtedly furbished up a little for a riotous telling. I grasped at it; I was conjuring up danger where none existed. But it was odd; her uncertainty on all the points in question had been real, and the vivacious manner had not concealed her perturbation. Even if I made myself ridiculous, I knew that I had to reach Cooper.

And Ruth Schwaggerman's name had been on the list. What about that? Amusing, I had said, and attractive. And he had crossed off only the stodgy matrons, the young women with neither looks nor individuality.

Downstairs, I asked for Cooper, only to be informed that he was out of town. I thought of Mr. Bigelow, or even Holt, but gave up the idea. What would I say? What could I say? The whole thing was so nebulous that I scarcely knew how to give my fears words. If I could have seen them, I might have managed it, but over the telephone it was impossible. I left a message for Cooper finally: I was going to the Schwaggerman place. And I added enough so that he would know why, senseless as it must have sounded to the person taking it down.

The idea of calling Ruth had been straightway abandoned. I couldn't very well tell her that her life was in danger, not without something more tangible in the way of explanation. I had to see her.

I had never been to the Schwaggermans', but once in the village, not much more than an hour's drive from our own, I found the street after inquiring at a police booth. The low, altogether charming white house, the leaf-strewn lawn, the basket with a rake lying beside it, were so comfortably everyday in appearance that the fantastic nature of my visit was suddenly emphasized.

I felt altogether absurd as I stood on the porch. A child cried out shrilly at my ring, and running footsteps sounded—the Tommy of the little wagon. If I could have retreated then, I believe I would have done so. But a maid was opening the door.

"Mrs. Schwaggerman isn't home," she said in answer to my inquiry.

"Could you tell me where she is? It's important." And at this announcement of her absence it became so once more.

The woman hesitated. "She was called away. Mr. Schwaggerman was hurt, and they phoned for her to come right away."

"Mr. Schwaggerman hurt!" I strained closer. "Mr. Schwaggerman, did you say?"

She was a little taken aback at the intensity of my questions.

"Yes," she told me, "he was up at his lake place, and there was some kind of an accident. She's only been gone a few minutes," she added.

A hunting accident. It could have been a hunting accident, I told myself.

"Do you know who called her?" I asked. "Mr. Jewett?" Paul had mentioned a Mr. Jewett yesterday.

But no, it wasn't Mr. Jewett, she said. "I know him. This was a stranger. A kind of funny high voice it was." She paused a little surprisedly; this had just come to her, a fact that had been obscured in the confusion following the call.

"He just said there'd been an accident and to tell Mrs. Schwaggerman to come up right away. He didn't wait for Mrs. Schwaggerman to come to the phone." She sounded argumentative. I understood. Ruth had been annoyed at that, and the maid now sought to justify herself.

"He rang right off, so I just gave her the message, and she's gone."

"She didn't call them back?"

She smiled at that. "Mr. Schwaggerman won't have a phone in the cabin, and the village is a couple of miles away."

There was nothing more to be found out. I made some conventionally reassuring remark and ran back down the front walk. With Marian's car—on some impulse I had asked Leo to give it to me instead of my own—I stood a good chance of overtaking her even with what must have been a good fifteen-minute start.

The Schwaggerman camp was unknown to me, but the village, as I knew, lay on a main route. We had passed through it numbers of times.

I drove north, watching the road ahead for Ruth's car. There were moments when the whole proceeding seemed grotesquely unreal. Ham was arrested and locked up, Mother was alone, and here I was, rushing madly toward a country village on the chance that Cooper's prediction of danger for some unknown woman was connected with Ruth Schwaggerman's half-facetious story of yesterday afternoon.

But there were oddities that could not be argued away. If Paul had been in a serious accident, why hadn't they taken him to a hospital? Why hadn't they been more explicit and told Ruth where to find them in that case? Possibly, however, it was only a slight injury, and the telephoning had been delegated to some passing native who had garbled the message.

Even with the week-end traffic of a clear fall day, I made good time, and when I reached the long, straggling village, there was still the half-light of dusk. The combined post office and general store was easily recognizable as the locale of some of Paul's tales, and it was here I stopped.

Inside, the place had the same effect as the Schwaggerman house. A typical country store, empty now, save for a small girl getting a loaf of bread from the young chap, in sole charge, as far as I could see.

I stayed near the door to keep my eyes on the road.

"Star Lake? Schwaggerman's place?" the boy repeated after me. "Right there at the corner is where you turn off." He stood with me on the stone steps and pointed down the way I had come. "See where that car is turning?" he asked.

I watched it. It was darker now, but I was sure it was not the Schwaggerman car. It might be the murderer.

And then, standing there in the quiet village street, with the grocer's boy giving me detailed directions, the farfetched nature of it all rushed over me again. But wasn't that what I expected? Why I was here? I shivered a little as we stood beside the car.

"You didn't happen to see Mrs. Schwaggerman drive through earlier?" I asked. "You know the Schwaggermans?"

"Oh, sure." But no, he hadn't seen her. "Schwaggerman went up this morning, though—he and another man. They stopped and got some stuff. She wasn't along. I carried it out to the car. There was just the two men. Some car you got there," he said.

"You haven't seen them? You haven't heard from them since?" I don't know why I was reluctant to ask outright about an accident.

He hadn't, and he would know. Everyone knows things like that in a small town. Besides, Paul's family had hailed from this section. Where I had been doubting and only half convinced, I was suddenly afraid.

"I wonder . . . you couldn't drive out with me?" I was startled at the fear in my own voice.

"Wish I could, but there's no one here right now. But you can't miss it." He repeated the last part of his directions. "Just remember when you get to the top of the hill, there's about a mile to the outlet. That's where the road goes in to the lake—just this side the outlet at your left. You could miss it in the dark if you weren't on the lookout."

I shivered again. The dark had come suddenly. Another car was rounding the corner, and it was no longer possible to see who it was.

The boy opened the door for me, waited while I turned, and waved me on my way.

The houses with the lights in the kitchens were left all too quickly. I met one car rattling toward the village, otherwise the road was deserted.

Suppose no one was there. This was Paul's lake and his the sole cabin on it, as I knew. And what did I expect to find when I reached it? If the telephone message were false, a means of drawing Ruth someplace, what assurance had I that the cabin itself was the spot? Had what I feared—and

just what that was I didn't admit—already taken
place miles back? But how could it on a state road
constantly traveled, with seclusion a matter of
chance?

The mile stretch, which began at the top of the
hill, was dark, with woodland on both sides of the
road. I watched for the turn in to the lake—easy
to miss as the boy had said. It was grass-grown
between the tracks and so narrow that two cars
could never pass. Driving at a crawl, I thought
of O'Meara for the first time, wondered if he had
really had any intention of coming up.

The darkness, the trees pressing close, leaves
blowing as they do before a rain, the slow, cautious going, all intensified my sense of foreboding
danger; I was in a state of jitters bordering on
panic. I had no idea how far in the cottage lay.
Again came the thought of finding it empty and
in darkness. Gone beyond speculation now, it was
something dread and real that might have to be
faced.

When the pile of planks rose up in front of me,
my first thought was that I had somehow missed
the way.

There, with the headlights full on it, was a barrier of carelessly tossed wood. I peered into the
darkness for lights, strained my ears to hear men
talking or calling to each other. But it was deadly

quiet; just the slapping sound of the water and the wind stirring in the trees. Alive as I was to some threatened danger, it was ominous, terrifying.

And then, just off the road at my left, so close that I could not bolster my courage with reminders of woodland noises, I heard someone moving, heard the crackling sound of steps on brush and dry leaves. There were three of them. I heard them unmistakably above the low hum of the engine. Someone was there, standing motionless now, someone unseen and menacing.

How I got myself out of the car in the horror of that ominous silence I don't know. In the full glare of the lights I went toward the obstruction in the center of the road, and, not knowing if a house lay beyond or what I might find if a house was there, I went around it and started down the road. I began to run then, blindly, stumblingly. I fell once and scrambled up without any consciousness of a torn and bleeding knee. My mouth was dry, my breath came in hard, painful gasps.

When I saw the light I wanted to call out, but no sound came. I heard a voice, a man's deep laugh, and stumbled around the porch, up the steps and burst in.

Paul was there, and a man I didn't know. They were sitting with legs outstretched to a great roaring fire. There was a moment of stupefied surprise before they got themselves out of their chairs.

"Nancy Sherwin!" It was all Paul could manage. In any event my appearance there that night would have been astounding, but now, white and terrified, and disheveled from my fall, I was something that couldn't be credited.

"Nancy! What is it? What's happened? Do you want Frank?"

O'Meara was there, then. "You're all right, you're not hurt," I said stupidly.

"What!" Plainly he thought I was crazy. "What is it, Nancy?" He steadied me with an arm over my shoulders. "What's the matter, girl?" His voice sought to soothe and calm.

"Ruth—where's Ruth?" I said.

He looked at the other man helplessly. "Ruth's home. She didn't come up." He said it slowly and patiently as to a child.

"But she did—that's it—she left before I did." My eyes went around the big shadowy room, up the well of the rustic stairway. "She started," I said again. "Oh, where is she?"

"Now listen, Nancy—let's begin at the beginning. Where did you see Ruth?"

"I didn't see her," I said, and saw their hopeless, despairing glances at each other. "I went over there, but she had gone. There was a telephone call—they said you were hurt." I couldn't take time to explain fully. "We must do something," I said. "Something's wrong!"

And then, as if my words were the cue, a shot sounded out. Another followed in close succession.

The two men looked at each other a horrified instant. A shot there in the hunting season was not extraordinary, I suppose, but coming as a climax to my incoherent ravings, the effect was hair raising.

Paul dived out of the door, and Jewett, stopping to pull a flash from under a pile of coats, followed. Once more I was running over the uneven, rutted road.

Around the barrier of piled wood, I saw that another car had come in and halted directly behind my own. Paul was looking in the rear, feeling the floor and seat.

"She's not here," he said. "It's our car. . . ."

We stood on the wet grass-tufted road, the trees crowding close, staring at each other.

"What's that?" Jewett said sharply.

On the other side of the road, farther away, and moving without the guarded slowness now, someone was making his way through the dry undergrowth.

"Ruth!" Paul shouted, "Ruth!" and plunged into the wood. His own crashing body and repeated cries obscured those other sounds receding off in the direction of the outlet. Jewett started on a run down the road, a saner course if they hoped to overtake that figure hurrying through the thick woodland.

Left alone, I waited fearfully in the lighted space between my car and the wood, stacked there, evidently, to halt Ruth. She must have driven in and climbed out to investigate as I had. Where was she? Had a third car come in and backed its way out? But there were the steps I had heard; there had been no car then.

I heard someone coming from the direction of the house and stepped quickly into the shadow. There was a deep mumbled cursing as feet stumbled over a rock, then a querulous, "Hey—where are you?"

O'Meara. I had completely forgotten him. He came on into the light and stood surveying the cars and the obstruction of wood. His ear caught the sound as I stepped out, and he swung around, gaping at me in amazement.

"Nancy!" He leaped heavily across the roadway and seized my arm. "What are you doing here?"

I began to explain, a more rational telling this time, breaking off when the lights of another car appeared down the dark, narrow road. It came on slowly to a stop, and Cooper got out. With O'Meara following, I hurried to meet him.

"I got your message," he said, taking in the two cars and the barrier of wood. His keen glance went on to O'Meara, swept back to Jewett, who had come down the road and rejoined us.

Without waiting for questions I gave him the main points of the story quickly.

"Where was this noise you heard?" His eyes went from my car to the trees opposite. He had placed it almost exactly; the steps had been just off the road, ahead of the car.

"How long was it between the shots and your getting here?" he asked Jewett.

"Not more than three or four minutes. Schwaggerman was here first."

"You were all in the house when you heard the shots?"

"No. O'Meara had gone out," Jewett told him.

"Where were you?" Cooper's head, his whole body, was poised to a tense alertness, a need for haste.

"I had walked down to the shore," O'Meara said. "I was there when—"

"Then you got here." Cooper turned to Jewett, and O'Meara's explanation was left hanging,

Jewett told about finding the Schwaggerman car and someone crashing his way through the woods toward the main road. "A car started up and went toward the village," he said, "just before I got down to the outlet. I went on, but I couldn't see it."

Cooper went over to the edge of the road, a little in front of Ruth's car. "Get in, someone, and then get out and walk toward Miss Sherwin's car."

I was nearest and went through what must have been Ruth's movements on her arrival.

"All right!" Cooper called when I had reached the stretch of light. He crossed back and examined the ground near me, working over to the ditch and into the trees that edged the road. The marks of her little spiked heels showed clearly in the soft earth of the gully, but as Jewett and I followed into the wood, his flash revealed only the leaf-matted ground where no tracks were visible.

We were back on the road when Cooper reappeared.

"The shots were probably fired from about where I was standing." We followed his glance to the position he had taken when I walked into the light before Ruth's car. "She must have dodged in there." His eyes went to the trees on the other side. "Wounded, no doubt, she could have gone a considerable distance before she fell." He stopped. Paul was running down the road. Pausing an instant at the third car, he came on. "Is she here?" he called out before he reached us, panting and wild eyed.

Cooper went over what he had just been saying. "Wait!" he said as Paul would have flung into the forest again. "This may not be easy. It's thick in there—and in the dark . . ." He eyed the narrow road. "One of these cars had better get turned around and go back to that village. We'll need some men. There's a lot of ground to cover, and we've got to hurry. She wasn't killed outright." He half turned to the ditch where he had found the small heelprints. "If she's wounded and dropped someplace, there's no time to lose."

He started for the piled wood, pulled himself up short and swung around. "This man you were following"—he looked at the two men—"could he have been carrying Mrs. Schwaggerman? He must have been hurrying," he reminded them, "and through that thicket . . ."

They agreed that it would have been all but impossible. "He was making time—I never got near him," Paul said. Still breathing heavily, he sprang after Cooper and Jewett, and the wood was quickly tossed out of the way. It took but a few minutes more to drive the cars into the clearing and make the turn.

"I'll go," Paul said. "I know who to get."

The other three lost no time breaking into the trees at the right. I went after them, halting as Cooper turned back to say, "You'd better stay here, Miss Sherwin."

I had far rather have gone than remained on that lonely stretch of road, hemmed in by the black trees, but they were insistent, and, fearful of delaying or hindering them, I didn't protest.

I could hear their voices when I had walked back to my car and climbed in to wait. It seemed an incredibly long time before Paul was back from town with the men, but it was just under an hour by the clock on the dash. I was out of the car at the first sound of their voices, but they had disappeared into the woods before I reached them. There were loud shouts back and forth and then a silence, a conclave to map out the search, I decided.

It was another hour before I heard O'Meara calling to me.

"Nancy," he said when I had run to meet him, "this may go on all night." He was puffing noisily. Heavy as he is and unaccustomed to physical exertion, the two-hour search had already exhausted him. "Why don't you go over to the house and go to bed?"

"I think I had better go home," I told him. There had been time and plenty for anxious worry; I had left with no explanation, and only Leo knew of my going.

"And you didn't telephone?" O'Meara said when he had heard me. "Good heavens! They're probably all crazy by now."

But when he had helped me get my car on the road, he was doubtful about my going alone. "I'll go out to the village with you and find something to bring me back."

I wouldn't hear to it. "I'll be all right," I insisted. "If only they'll find her before it's too late." I was ready to drive off when something came to me. "Frank, did you know about Ham's arrest?" I asked him.

"What!" he shouted and looked as if he thought my senses had entirely left me.

"This afternoon—just before I came away." I gave him the meager facts hurriedly.

He listened, stunned and unbelieving, plied me with excited questions, though there was no more to tell. "So I'd better get back," I said superfluously, and left with his promise to call the minute he was in range of a telephone.

Why that mention of telephoning didn't prompt me to stop someplace and get in touch with our house I don't know, but, drawn on by an urgent need to get there quickly, I drove straight through and was home in less than two hours.

Brooke was there and, ahead of Thompson, had the door open before I could get out of the car. Ethel and Annie had waited up too. They had been alarmed to a point where they were absolutely frantic—I saw that as I came in. Mother, as I learned later, had called Brooke and O'Meara repeatedly, finally reaching Brooke at his apartment.

"Where have you been, Nancy?" For once Brooke's imperturbable calm was entirely missing. He was excited and beside himself.

"The Schwaggerman camp," I said, and before I could go on he broke out.

"It's an odd time for you to go off on a party, but at least you might have telephoned. Your mother's in bad shape," he said, blunt in his shaking excitement. "The doctor's been here—she's sleeping now. Opiate."

The telephone rang. "Oz, probably," he said and went to answer it, unheeding my rush of explanation. "He's been tearing around the country with the police, trying to trace you."

It was Oz. "She's here; she just came." Brooke's voice, unnatural in its loud shortness, came back to us. A pause, and then with weary disgust: "Up at the Schwaggerman camp."

He came back, and I got the story out, a choppy, broken telling, interrupted by Brooke's quick questions and Annie's alarmed exclaiming.

Oz tore in, and I went through it again. "And they can't find her," I finished, taking the sherry Thompson had brought me. He alone in that wild, disorganized group was anxiously taking in my shattered state.

"Then you don't know whether she's alive or not?" Brooke asked.

"No. But she couldn't have been killed—not right away." I repeated Cooper's line of reasoning.

"She could have hit her head—been knocked out," Oz put in. "A rock."

"There were two shots," I reminded him. "She must have been wounded."

"You shouldn't have gone up there," he burst out. "When you got out of the car, it was just a chance—" He stopped at Brooke's warning look.

"How could this Mrs. Schwaggerman be tied up with the affair here?" he asked instead.

"I don't know." They knew as well as I did that Cooper had been looking up various women.

"Where was O'Meara if he wasn't with the rest of you?"

"He'd gone down to the beach," I told them. "Walking around and smoking. He didn't think anything about the shots, just noticed them and thought nothing of it there in the woods." This I did know: that fleeing figure had not been O'Meara's, for he had appeared from the other direction a very few minutes after we had heard the sounds of someone going toward the open road.

"How did he act?" Oz asked none too subtly.

"Surprised, of course." I said it sharply. That astonishment of O'Meara's on finding me there had been real. I was certain of it.

Brooke and Oz hung over me while I had dinner on a tray, going through it all, point by point.

At one o'clock, when there was still no call, I left reluctantly to go up to bed. Oz went with me to the gallery.

"Nancy, I can't get over it—up there alone in that Godforsaken place. A wonder you weren't killed when you stepped out of the car." He was unstrung and made no attempt to conceal it as he had downstairs. "Promise me you won't pull any more wild stunts like that," he said as he let me go. "Now you've got to get some sleep. We're waiting—we'll let you know the minute anything comes through."

The call came between two and three, but it was such distressing news that I was not awakened to hear it.

19

I was down early the next morning after a night more awful than any I had yet put in. Far too overwrought for sleep, the experience at the Schwaggerman place went through my mind, over and over. And mingled with that were thoughts of Ham, the indictment which would follow his appearance before the grand jury, the sensational trial.

Early as it was, Brooke was down and gave me the news.

"She was dead when they found her. Cooper called, not O'Meara. She'd been shot once. Died before they got to her.

"And now"—he shook his head and turned away as I began asking where they had found her, if they thought she might have lived had they reached her sooner—"let's not talk about it anymore this morning. Cooper didn't give me much anyway."

He was right, I suppose. Going over it all could do no good. And Brooke, though he was calmly himself after his mad distraction of the night, looked so unutterably dragged out that I said no more. But the thought of Ruth, lying wounded and uncared for, was not to be dismissed.

"What time is it? We have to do something about Ham now," he said nervously.

"What happened yesterday?" I asked. "When you saw Mr. Bigelow?"

There was a moment before he answered. "I didn't see anyone," he said evasively. "Nothing I could do." There was a faint touch of irritation in his voice, which I put down to worry and a sleepless night.

Ham himself telephoned before ten. He was hurried and brief and not at all certain what had brought about his prompt release. The magistrate's hearing, I gathered, had been turned into a routine affair, with Ham's dismissal the unquestioned outcome. He said something about new evidence, but he was vague; he didn't really know.

Ham's arrival followed close on his telephone call. He was still confused as to why they had allowed him to go. To our excited inquiries he could add nothing beyond an uncertain suggestion of new and important evidence. That, in some strange way, it connected with the shooting of Mrs. Schwaggerman I was sure.

"They didn't say what they had? You didn't hear anything more?" Brooke asked, a sharpness to his tone which spoke of all we had been through in the past hours; Ham's arrest had been a needless, shattering blow.

But Ham was perplexed as we were, and reluctantly we allowed him to go upstairs for a bath and a change of clothes.

"Now what on earth could they have?" Brooke pondered as we turned back to the terrace room.

I stood staring out on the grounds; a thin rain was drenching the chairs on the terrace. Ham was back, and the relief was almost overwhelming. But once we had taken in and accepted that, there still remained the agonizing fact that Marian was gone; Jocelyn and Mrs. Schwaggerman had been killed; all the intolerable notoriety and the unsettled, ominous feeling of uncertainty hung over us.

It was a vast help to have Brooke there. "You'll come often, won't you, Brooke? This won't make any difference?"

He caught at the suggestion in my words, a suggestion that we had become pariahs, people apart.

"Stop that, Nancy!" he said sharply. "You must shake yourself out of this. You have to go on, you know. None of it is your fault, and you have your own life. Frightful as this has been, you have to put it behind you."

I turned surprisedly; I was so accustomed to Brooke's unvarying, pleasant ease, his actual unwillingness to exert himself to heated discussion, that the warmth of his remonstrance was unexpected.

"How can we," I asked drearily, "when it isn't even cleared up?"

"I know." He accepted that without making any useless protestations. "And perhaps it won't be. There are cases like that. The most I'm hoping for now is that they won't make another of these half-baked arrests. To satisfy the newspaper public."

"But, Brooke, someone committed those murders."

"Yes," he said, and then added: "Nancy, I'm not sure—but it may be better—if we don't know."

I was astonished. Then Brooke, like Dr. Jarvis—and Katherine, too, I felt sure—believed the crimes did not go beyond our own family. I got hints of it on every side. What did they mean? Did they know themselves? I thought of Ham's frenzied question the night Marian was shot: "Nancy, are you sure your mother was in her room?"

Did they think that Mother and Marian had connived to kill Jocelyn? That Marian in remorse and revulsion of feeling had threatened exposure, and Mother in a half-crazed condition had shot her?

"Nancy, your mother . . ." Brooke paused, and the hideous feeling in all its completeness took possession of me. It was so strong that it was a physical weakness, and I felt my legs giving way beneath me.

But when he went on, it was to suggest that we go someplace as speedily as possible, which meant, I suppose when the authorities would permit. "Your mother is badly to pieces," he said. "I have a couple of good spots in mind—we can go into it later."

I hated the idea. Outcasts. Under suspicion. I saw ourselves dodging from place to place, trying always to avoid those curious, revolting stares which we had already had occasion to feel on the day of Jocelyn's funeral.

"No"—I said it decidedly—"I'm not going away, Brooke. Not even if the thing was cleared up, I wouldn't. To go away now and then come back—we would find this house, this whole place, intolerable. I'm going to stay, whatever happens. And certainly there's no leaving till it's settled."

He smiled suddenly. "You look like your mother, but you might be Marian saying that. The same indomitable facing of things. The most difficult way always. Just out of sheer self-discipline, I think."

Mother came in, and he related for her this example of what he called my iron will. But I was right, I thought. Stay and work things out there. The same urge, probably, that takes an aviator up almost immediately after a crash from which he has miraculously escaped.

While I stood there feeling warmly grateful to Brooke for keeping Mother occupied and diverted,

I saw a car drive up and park well within the grounds. I recognized Connolly out of the four policemen who moved across the lawn. Two of them took positions within my view, the others passed out of sight as they went toward the rear.

A second car drove in, and I spoke to Brooke. He joined me at the window, Mother following, though I had tried to speak without rousing her notice. Three men got out. Cooper, Holt and a man I had seen at the house but did not know by name. A fourth man stayed at the wheel.

"What's the idea of the cavalcade?" Brooke shot a swift look at me.

I didn't try to answer. There was something ominous in that procession of three men as they passed by the window, up the steps and across the porch.

They rang, and Thompson let them in. I heard their voices in the hall, then they were at the door, in the room.

I was frightened as I had not yet been frightened, a quick perception that there was something different about this visitation. These men had not come to examine the murder rooms or to renew their interminable questioning. They were decisive, certain, authoritative. They did not stop for any amenities of greeting. Straight across the room they came, steadily, inexorably.

Holt flipped a paper wide and thrust it before Brooke's eyes. "Well, Bennett!" Expertly he jerked

Brooke's hands into position and snapped on handcuffs.

It had all happened so quickly that I had taken it in only in flashes: the incredulous astonishment on Brooke's face as the warrant was produced; the beautifully tailored gray sleeves pushed back from his wrists; the implacable look on the faces of each of those three men.

"Just what is the meaning of this?" Brooke's voice after that astounding moment of the hand-cuffs was more startling than noisy protestations could possibly have been. A deadly quiet. "If you will explain—"

"You can do the explaining later on," Holt said. "And you have a whole lot of it to do. Here and in New York besides."

As they led Brooke from the room Cooper detached himself from the others and came to me. "I can't stop," he said, "but I wanted to tell you— Mrs. Schwaggerman is all right. She's wound-ed, but it's not serious. The shock and exposure were the worst of it. She'll come out of it in good shape." With a little pat on my shoulder he hur-ried off. I stared after him, too stunned to utter a single word.

That was all. Without further words Brooke was taken from the house, with a brief stop in the hall, an order for Thompson to produce his hat and overcoat.

Dazedly I followed, watched them drape the coat around his shoulders, clap the hat down on his head. I waited for Brooke to speak, some scathing reminder of police bungling, the need of a victim, but he didn't glance or turn my way. His face, drained of all color, was shocking in its fixity. In dread apprehension my eyes followed them down the wet steps and over to the parked car. With Brooke between Cooper and Holt, and the third man in front, they moved down the long drive and turned into the road.

Thompson closed the door and, white-faced and trembling, we faced each other without speaking. Frenziedly my mind flew back to O'Meara's story of the search, the assertion that they had gone over Brooke's place at the same time. I remembered Cooper's unaccountable questions about the three men, the women whose strange entrance into the case had culminated in some way in the shooting of Ruth Schwaggerman.

Mother was standing in the doorway of the terrace room. "Brooke," she said, and there was horror in her face and voice. She was shaking; shock and terror had completely unnerved her.

"It's a mistake, of course," I said. "They'll bring him back. Someone has had a brain storm." But I had no conviction in my own words.

"Jocelyn—and Marian. Brooke couldn't do that. Brooke couldn't kill Marian. And Mrs. Schwaggerman . . ."

"Ruth is all right, Mother." I told her what Cooper had said and steadied her to a chair, motioning for Thompson, who had not stirred since closing the door. The whole thing had taken less than ten minutes; the swiftness with which it moved had made it impossible to call Ham, and now, unheeding Mother's state of collapse, I flew down the hall to the stairs.

20

Brooke's arrest had taken place at eleven. Hamilton, on hearing my half-demented account, had driven off with the idea of seeing Mr. Bigelow. It was useless and futile, but it seemed the thing to do at the time.

Mother had been taken upstairs, and without even a pretense of luncheon I set myself to wait for Ham's return. Of what lay behind Brooke's arrest I had no knowledge. Feverishly I once more went through all those oddly disconnected happenings which had seemed extraneous and alien at the time: the questions about the three men who had been our guests; the visit of the strange Miss Smith; and, finally, Cooper's effort to trace some unknown woman. All these were remote and unrelated so far as I could see, but somehow they fitted in and belonged.

The late editions of the afternoon papers would have the story, but my anxiety and excitement were at such a pitch that waiting for the newspapers to interpret an event which I had actually witnessed seemed impossible.

I heard Cooper when he came, and rushed to the hall, thinking it was Ham.

"I had to go through this way," he said, "and thought I'd run into the park and let you have the story.

"Well, we have our man," he said as he followed me down to the library.

Not Brooke. It couldn't be Brooke. I waited, every nerve protesting against what I already knew was the truth.

"Yes, it's Bennett all right." He sat down and looked at me with a kind of sparkling intensity. "I've thought so since the day after Miss Shephard was shot. But—what did we have?"

Then it was true. Brooke had killed Jocelyn. But why? And granting that, unbelievable as it was, I could not conceive of Brooke's shooting Marian. And Ruth—had Brooke done that too?

"Mrs. Schwaggerman—" I started to ask him.

"I'm sorry about that." He leaned forward in earnest regret. "It was almost morning when we got her out, and I had to see Bigelow—the warrant and all the rest of it. She was unconscious when we found her—I couldn't talk to her until this morning. So when Bennett answered your phone last night I decided to do it that way."

There were a hundred things I wanted to ask, but I couldn't: there was too much, and I was too dazed. One fact had penetrated, however. Brooke must have set about the Schwaggerman business the moment he left our house yesterday afternoon. He had not gone to the district attorney's office; he had made no attempt to aid Ham. That accounted for his evasion of a few hours ago, an evasion which I had ascribed to distress and defeat.

"Yes, it was Bennett"—Cooper settled back again—"and I've had my ideas from the second day. But my thinking so and something to take before a jury—that was something else again."

But why? my mind kept asking. Brooke had never seen Jocelyn until that afternoon in the library. I said it to Cooper, got it out gaspingly: "He had never seen Jocelyn."

Cooper didn't take that up for the moment. Methodical, orderly as always, he went back to give me in their proper sequence the various steps which had culminated in Brooke's arrest.

"In the first place the murder of Mrs. Shephard was obviously committed suddenly, without planning."

I nodded. I had heard this and read it. Over and over again.

"Done suddenly that way meant one of two things in all probability. Either someone was in a

white heat of rage or she held some dangerous information which made it necessary to put her out
of the way before she had a chance to use it.

"We stuck too long on the first," he admitted.
"But it looked funny. Here was Marian Shephard
and your mother, both worked up to some kind of
fury—or so it seemed. And in a way their anger
had reached a pitch that very day."

This too I had heard before. He sensed my impatience but held to his step-by-step procedure.

"Well, there was that. And then take Hamilton
Shephard. From things we had turned up it looked
as if he had reason and plenty for jealousy. And
what people won't do when they're jealous . . ."
He let that go. "I staved off that arrest as long as
I could," he added.

"But as I say, the situation right here in the
house looked bad and we wasted time. It was her
telephone call to Parsons that gave us our first
step in the right direction. Parsons was mixed up
in it someway, but it didn't break right. We dug up
plenty that showed he knew Jocelyn King a whole
lot better than he was willing to admit, but there
hadn't been anything since she married Shephard.
And then that affair of the bracelet came up, and
they were all off on Shephard.

"But—and here we are." He smiled—he had not
missed my impatience. "Take it easy, Miss Sherwin. Mrs. Shephard's murder was a crime to cover

up a crime. To cover up a whole series of crimes, in fact.

"Jocelyn King disappeared for several days last November. The sixteenth, to be exact. That was before you knew her, of course. She was playing in her show at the time, and the papers made quite a bit of it for a few days, and then it all died down. Anyone that was interested and had followed it probably put it down to a publicity stunt and nothing more." He caught my look. "You did yourselves."

We had. Jocelyn and publicity had gone together. I thought of O'Meara's words in the library that afternoon: "Ran the show another six weeks."

"Naturally we didn't pass over the kidnaping," he went on. "The abduction took place in New York, and we got what there was in the New York records. Which wasn't much.

"But once we were off on that, it looked as if it was due to flatten out before it started. There were four people here that day who had never seen Mrs. Shephard before. But look at them!" he demanded. "Wealthy, not one thing on record against any one of them. Prominent socially. Just the fact that they were friends of your people gave them stability.

"We dropped Mrs. Haskell almost immediately. Nothing pointed her way. But the three men—all with plenty now, but ten or a dozen years ago none of them had a great deal except O'Meara. The other two were young men on good salaries, but nothing big. Jarvis looked all right. He's worked up with his firm and is an important official. And right about there Jarvis was eliminated anyway. Plenty of things that let him out, but one's enough. On one of the dates in question—you'll hear about them later—he was in South America. But except for one thing the night of Miss Shephard's shooting—you'll get that later too—certain things pointed to O'Meara as well as Bennett. His trip out to that place the day after Jocelyn King's murder looked funny too. Evidently he wanted the stuff, though."

I nodded in agreement. Frank keeps no systematic hours for work as Ham does; he lets it pile up and hang over him, a constant irritant to all his leisure.

"And Bennett's income was understandable. A young man in New York has all sorts of breaks in a social way. Especially with the looks and manner Bennett has. And social opportunities sometimes mean market tips, things like that, in a big way. Or they did a few years ago. Looking into Bennett's affairs as much as we could—and mind you, we didn't have anything that would warrant an audit—they looked all right enough. Bennett was good." He stopped, caught by a sudden thought.

"Taking out that pane of glass—that wasn't so bright, come to think of it."

That night in the library. There had been no time to connect Brooke with that. From his room in the north wing he could easily have observed Connolly on a remote part of the grounds, calculating the length of his stay to the time it would take to smoke a cigar. But why remove the pane of glass after the crime was committed? Why remove it at all?

"No, that wasn't so good," Cooper said again. "He hoped to lead the trail away from the house, of course. He had already had time to see how Miss Shephard—Mr. Shephard too—was being dragged into it. He didn't want that to happen."

Marian. Even Ham had thought she might have killed Jocelyn. I saw that now. It explained the oddness of his manner toward her, it gave meaning to his deep concern on finding that Miss Wycke had been in the bathroom when the murder was taking place. Jarvis and Katherine had believed it too; and when Marian was shot they had had some idea of Marian and Mother working together. A dozen scattered happenings, bits of talk, bore it out.

"Well, let's leave that there." Cooper's excitement increased. "It was probably one of the cleverest things in the way of extortion that's ever been pulled. Not this one alone. It was a system, a rack-et."

I fastened on one word. Brooke and the word "racket" did not belong together.

"This was just one of a series," Cooper went on. "There are two others on record. But we believe there were more. Five, six, a dozen—no one knows. It was clever. It was perfect." He amended that with a slight smile. "Almost perfect."

"The thing lay in knowing his victims. And by victims now, I mean the men who paid the ransoms. Men like J. Stanley Parsons. Yes," he responded to my quickened interest, "that's how he comes into the picture.

"Well, let's get on. He picked his men. Not just wealthy men. That wasn't enough. Besides that they had to be prominent socially or politically. Or both. Men that had made the mistake of getting themselves involved with some girl. What he played on was their fear of publicity. Disgrace and the social ostracizing of their families—sons in school and college, debutante daughters.

"It was good." Cooper's voice held a certain awed admiration. "There wasn't a hole in it. He took the girl and sent his one letter. And that's all there was—one letter. And that letter was all right too." He pulled from an inside pocket a single sheet, unfolded it and dropped it in my lap. "Read it. It's just a copy, of course, with the names omitted."

I have abducted Miss — — and am hold-ing her for ransom. She will be freed as soon as you have paid fifty thousand dol-lars for her release.

I shall send no further letters; there will be no telephone calls. You will re-ceive no other communications of any kind.

At the appointed time have the mon-ey in the place named, and Miss — will be released, unharmed. She is being well cared for, but there must necessarily be a mental torture which I cannot altogeth-er prevent. That is one reason I am de-manding the ransom in so short a time.

In the event that the money is not paid Miss — will be put to death pain-lessly, quite unaware of what is about to happen to her. Her body will be placed where it will be discovered promptly. I need scarcely point out that you will be drawn into the subsequent investigation, an investigation which will disclose the facts of your association with Miss — to the public.

My advice is, do not in any way confer with the police. Simply place your money in the spot designated, and the matter is closed without publicity of any kind.

Neither will there be any recurrence of the episode. With the payment of the ransom the matter is finished and closed for all time. Once more, I urgently suggest that you keep the affair entirely to yourself. Think this over carefully before you take anyone into your confidence.

There followed details about the money and its placing; a concluding sentence whose quiet finality left no room for doubt.

"Do you see?" Cooper asked when I had finished. "You believe it. It's intelligent and there's something conclusive about it that rings true. There're going to be no more letters, no other communications, and you know it. The money is placed where he asks—"

He broke off. "That's smart too. In the three cases we have any data on, the money was placed right on his own route; not too near, but where he would be apt to be.

"And there we seem to have his system. Everything on the surface is perfectly natural. The girl is kept in his own house, a place that he visits often. As you know, he went down there frequently, sometimes with help, sometimes without. And he was keen enough to go without servants occasionally when he didn't have any business afoot.

"That's another thing," he paused to tell me. "O'Meara had the same sort of layout in lots of ways. But let's stick with Bennett. The people in the neighborhood knew him and liked him. He was never observed doing anything unusual or out of the way. And, as we have reason to know after going over his places, there was nothing around that didn't belong there. My guess is that as soon as he wrote his one letter on the typewriter, the typewriter was dumped every time in the ocean or some other safe place.

"The girls—the three we know about—when they got loose, talked and talked plenty until somebody silenced them. Then they were like clams; they didn't remember anything. But in looking up these girls' records, the New York police found there was a man—and a big man too—in the background every time. But he wasn't admitting anything about a ransom.

"The first one did look like publicity stuff. Then another one cropped up, and the stories checked. These girls didn't know each other, remember, but there were certain things that linked the cases. They were all kept for short periods of time, five days at the longest. There were similarities in the abduction and treatment. And that's interesting. The girls were kept drugged pretty much of the time between periods for feeding and so on. He evidently gave them hypodermics of phenobarbital. It's harmless and a shot will keep them sleeping heavily for about four hours. All reported a voice pitched very high—

"Try it, Miss Sherwin!" Cooper stopped suddenly to say. And then he repeated his own words with his voice pitched several degrees higher than its ordinary tone. "You see?" he said enthusiastically. "It absolutely changes the quality and tone. No chance whatever for identification." He seemed fascinated with it and tried it on various phrases.

"The abduction was slick. I'll give you Jocelyn King's, but all three were pretty much alike. Her show was running at the time, and shortly before her usual hour for leaving, the garage is called and told that she won't want her car that evening.

"Then she gets a call—the garage speaking, presumably—and she is told that her regular chauffeur has just had an accident. They are sending another car and man right away. She comes out of her apartment house, and as she steps into the car a pad of chloroform is placed over her mouth and fastened behind. Adhesive strap probably. Wouldn't take a second if it was all prepared, of course. She is put in, and he drives away.

"She has no idea how long or how far they drive, and when she comes to, her eyes are closed with adhesive. The situation is explained to her; she is told she has nothing to fear. Bennett seems to have made a real effort to allay their mental anguish. He realized that was the worst and told them so, explained that they wouldn't be there long, but must remain blindfolded. Bound too, except for feeding and using a bathroom that adjoined. And incidentally, the layout of that bathroom is about the only definite thing we had till last night.

"So there he was, down there as usual, just his regular routine. Not the kind of place that would be suspected, everything aboveboard," Cooper reminded me again. "Not a thing that would be noticed or questioned.

"But in the end, it was that very appearance of the natural and all right, his strict maintaining of it, that gave him away. On one of the nights when he was holding Jocelyn King, two people, a man and a woman, stopped there for about a couple of hours. And on that night Jocelyn King heard a conversation carried on in the hall outside her door, heard Bennett speaking in his own voice."

The sheets of dialogue that read like a French farce.

"And right there is where he overplayed his part of everything normal. He went too far. When those two people drove in he was just as usual, just the way they expected to find him. He visited the locked room soon after he let them in. Jocelyn

King was awake and heard him, but gave no sign that she was conscious. He left her and returned to his friends.

"Bennett's stuff was darned near perfect, but not quite. The police—the New York police, that was—decided that what happened was this. Those Luer syringes—if the bulb is pressed too hard, sometimes the air pressure inside forces the needle off, or it slips a little—isn't air tight, and a person gets maybe half the regular shot. That's evidently what happened with Bennett. Jocelyn King had waked up and come to, when she was due to sleep another two hours at least. There's a cumulative effect to the stuff besides, and he was probably counting on that too.

"She heard him go out and lock the door. And then, before he could go downstairs, apparently, the woman came up, presumably on her way to the bathroom. And it was there in the upper hall that they carried on the conversation which Jocelyn King heard clearly and gave to the police later as nearly as she could recall it. She didn't realize at the time, I believe, that it was the same person talking. But her statement to us was that she would recognize that voice if she heard it again, the voice and the laugh both. She was lying there in a highly sensitized state. Blindfolded, everything else shut out, she was receptive, of course, to the conversation outside her door. And Bennett's voice is one you'd remember—there's something about it. It's deep and there's something else . . ." Cooper felt around for words to describe an arresting quality in Brooke's voice, a combination of perfect speech and resonance of tone, which baffled him. He gave it up and went on.

"Well, that was the third case of its kind, and they went after it hard. They came down on Parsons and got nowhere. He absolutely denied any knowledge of it, knew nothing about a ransom. If you know Parsons . . ."

Parsons' bland suavity was left to my imagination.

"They looked up certain things that connected him with Jocelyn King, but he admitted nothing. They didn't stop there, though. In fact, they never stopped. But what did they have? Not a thing, not even the letter in that case. Only one of the three ever opened up when they tried to link him to the ransom, and he produced the letter and the serial numbers of the notes. But that came to nothing.

"Jocelyn King was the only one to hear Bennett's natural voice, and the police have had her listen to any number of voices in the last year, the voices of the educated sort of crook. There was never any wavering or doubt—she remembered that voice and laugh. She remembered it when she walked into this library and heard Bennett talking."

"To me," I exclaimed involuntarily. He had been talking about Oz, pretending to be jealous.

Cooper nodded a quick agreement. When he went on some of the excitement of disclosure had worked itself out of his voice.

"When Jocelyn King spoke to Miss Shephard that day she undoubtedly told her that Bennett was her kidnaper. And Miss Shephard, I believe, took it as a wild piece of raving on the part of her sister-in-law, the kind of unbalanced, extravagant thing she expected from her. Remember, she put just about as much credence in it as she would if Jocelyn King had suddenly proclaimed you an international spy."

That was easy for me. Even now, with Cooper's words piling up to a damning completeness, I could not visualize Brooke as a kidnaper and murderer. And later, when Jocelyn had been killed, it was doubtful if Marian had connected the two events. Shock and excitement had driven it from her mind until I asked about it that night. She had started to answer, then it must have come to her that it was not the sort of thing that outsiders would grasp in the right way. But the next evening, the first time there had been any letdown for her, she had mentioned it, brought it up as some curious coincidence, very likely. And Brooke—easy to imagine, first his quick amusement, and then, in his striving for the normal and natural, his seizing on the significance of the abduction idea; the suggestion that there might be something in that, absurd as Jocelyn's assertion was, and they would take it to Bigelow in the morning. Dimly words and laugh that confirmed it all came back to me. "It may not lead anywhere," Brooke had said, "but you can see where it could go."

Cooper's words met my thoughts. "That dovetails all right with the snatches of conversation that you, and Bennett himself, for that matter, gave us afterwards. More of the perfectly natural stuff, you see.

"Bennett must have realized almost instantly that Jocelyn King recognized him, and when she went over to Miss Shephard he probably had a pretty fair idea of what she said. If he needed any further proof he got it when he stood on the landing and listened while she got Parsons on the phone.

"He may have done some thinking. Should he let her make her accusation and act precisely as he would be expected to act? He could have made a good job of that. But it was dangerous, and I doubt if he wasted any time considering it. Besides, he didn't know what Jocelyn King had on him, was amazed, of course, that she had anything at all. He must have planned her murder while he stood talking in that pleasant, classy way of his that hour after she came in."

Even the investigators had come under the spell
of Brooke's compelling charm.

"He knew the house, he knew Mr. Shephard
would not be there until later. But when he went
to her room and found Mrs. McIver there he had
nothing to do but retreat. Then it must have
been that the possibility of the sitting room came
to him, and he stepped inside with his weapon,
and—well, the rest of it is clear. You have only to
put it together.

"I began to get ideas after the attack on Miss
Shephard. Not only did that eliminate Miss Shephard herself, but I could see only two people
after that: Brooke Bennett and Hamilton Shephard. One of those two was in the room, covered
by the opened door, when you went in and bent
over Miss Shephard.

"The way I reconstruct the second crime—when
he came up with Miss Shephard a little after the
rest of you, he got into his pajamas and dressing
gown, but he didn't go to bed. He didn't sit reading his book either. When he was sure McKenna
was in the kitchen he went to her room. This is
only a guess, but he may have told her that he had
a big idea on the very angle of the case they had
been discussing and he had to let her have it on
the spot. She started back into the room, and he
closed the door, stepped over to her, fired his shot

and chucked the gloves out the open window. I don't get the gloves—probably a sudden impulse as he stripped them off."

I saw it all. He had flung the gloves away and without a waste motion opened the door and stood behind it. He had planned it to a second, counting on the moments of startled listening, the getting out of bed, the walk to the room. Ham and I were the ones he had expected to arrive first, and he had followed Ham as he came over to me. The book had been thrust into my hands before he knelt beside Marian.

"Bennett knew we were on to the kidnaping end of it, of course," Cooper was going on. "He had to when we went through his places. But he had it closer than that. Alma's screaming . . ." He paused, eyes on my face, waiting for me to grasp the connection.

I nodded uncertainly; it was Cooper's own attitude that night which had stayed in my mind.

The fixed, spectacled gaze of Cooper's dark eyes relaxed. "He saw the papers there on the table when he came in—probably got the New York Police heading. Then when he went upstairs he stepped out on that balcony and got the shriek from Alma that cleared this floor. It might not work, but he was going to have a try at it, and he knew the sort she is. In the excitement he runs

downstairs, has a look at the record of that conversation and goes on outside. After that he knew
he had to get Mrs. Schwaggerman.

"And I did too, only I didn't know who she was."
He passed a hand over his forehead and down the
back of his head, a tired motion that spoke of his
desperate efforts to trace the unknown woman.

"The murders were smooth and, like the kid-
nappings, everything looked right. Nothing on
him, nothing in his room, his act perfect afterwards. But"—and Cooper smiled for almost the
first time—"I imagine he did have a bad time
when he heard Miss Wycke had been in that bathroom—until he got her account later on.

"But though I suspected it after Miss Shephard
was shot, what proof did we have? We went over
both his places, and the result was nothing. Not
a thing to give the show away. Not a fingerprint
that didn't belong there, and we didn't miss any
places.

"We got hold of one of the other known victims
and took her down to Bennett's place, but about
the only thing we got out of that was the layout of
the bathroom. That she remembered and was sure
of. Sounds and that sort of thing—she wasn't too
much help there. It's not the same time of year,
and that makes a difference. And, like the others,
she was kept drugged most of the time. She was

the one I brought around that day after the funeral to listen to the voices. But that didn't work out. She had heard only the high-pitched version and not much of that—he didn't talk beyond what was necessary. And all told, there wasn't enough to take before a jury. We'd be laughed out of court.

"The one thing left was to locate the woman who had carried on that conversation with Bennett the night she dropped in there with some man, her husband or someone else. We didn't know. And right there we were up against it. Even if we got the woman, that conversation wasn't anything she was going to admit—if the wrong person went to the chair for it." Cooper looked to me for assent, and I pulled myself together to agree that this was so.

"And after Bennett had seen that record, I knew we had to hurry." His voice changed abruptly. "I saw Mrs. Schwaggerman, you know. But, like the others, she was sitting tight. You can't blame her. To be mixed up in a case that's had the publicity this one has means a lot of unpleasant notoriety for anyone connected with it, no matter how innocently.

"Then Bennett made his first attempt to knock her out, just enough to make it look like an accidental death by monoxide. Remember, I didn't know about that," he put in. "May have been that which brought her around to your place that day.

She got enough from me to make her curious. And when Schwaggerman mentioned going up to his lake place Bennett saw his chance."

The best chance in the world, I saw that. A private road, closed in by the woods on both sides, and Ruth's arrival timed for darkness. Only my own appearance there had defeated him in the completion of his purpose. One of the shots had wounded her, and then, before he could get to her, Paul and Jewett had come. No wonder he had been distraught until Cooper's call came through last night.

"Your going up there just as you did—that was fine, Miss Sherwin. But when you stepped out . . ." He stopped and looked at me much as Oz had done.

"But it broke the case. We've got her statement—she was in the house on the night in question and carried on that conversation upstairs with Bennett." Cooper sat back and looked at me for a moment, saying nothing. Then he went on filling in and rounding out the points which my dazed questions and comments reopened.

When he finally pulled himself from the deep chair and stood, there was great weariness in the motion, but it was a satisfied weariness. "I was due home to get caught up on my sleep when I stopped off here," he said. "The sleep I've had in the last forty-eight hours wouldn't make a good

nap. You look as if you could do with some yourself, Miss Sherwin."

But he was loath to leave it there. "Except for
that one slip," he said with measured emphasis, "a
slip that made Bennett hang himself with his own
system, we wouldn't have him. As I said before, he
was darned near perfect."

Perfect. The word belonged to Brooke. He
had worshiped perfection. His surroundings in
all their beautiful ease. Traveling, accomplished
always without hurry or discomfort, wherever a
fancy of the moment might take him. The fault-
less rightness of each possession, down to a white
jade goddess, a new acquisition he had been telling me about at almost the moment of Ham's
arrest. Perfection—Brooke had gone after it tena-
ciously, gained it in everything. Except for that
one slip, which Cooper was still dwelling on, he
had achieved it even in crime.

COACHWHIP PUBLICATIONS

CoachwhipBooks.com

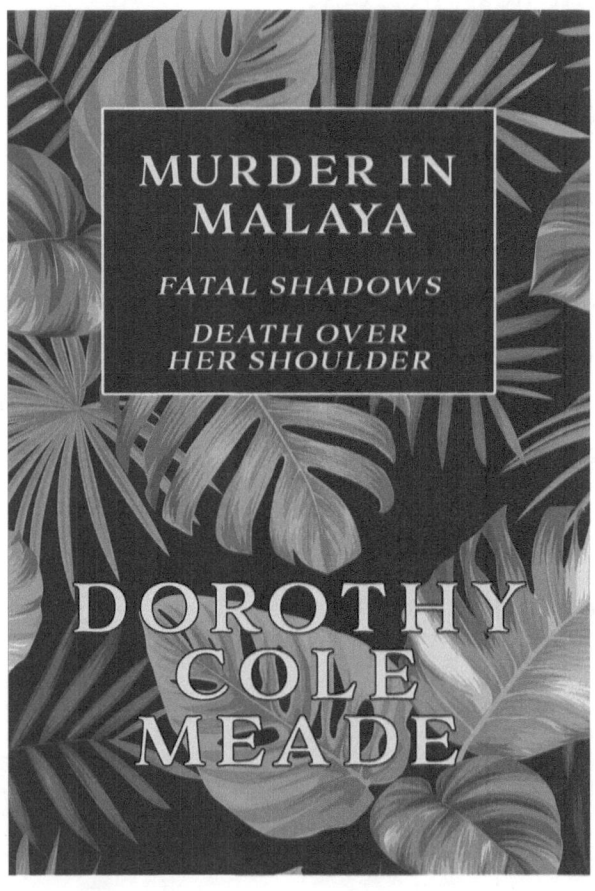

MURDER IN
MALAYA

FATAL SHADOWS

*DEATH OVER
HER SHOULDER*

DOROTHY
COLE
MEADE

COACHWHIP PUBLICATIONS
CoachwhipBooks.com

DEATH
ON THE CAMPUS

ADDISON
SIMMONS

COACHWHIP PUBLICATIONS
CoachwhipBooks.com

VIRGINIA RATH

DEATH AT
DAYTON'S FOLLY

COACHWHIP PUBLICATIONS
COACHWHIPBOOKS.COM

MURDER ON
THE DAY OF
JUDGMENT

VIRGINIA RATH

COACHWHIP PUBLICATIONS
CoachwhipBooks.com

THE
SARA ELIZABETH
MASON
MYSTERIES

MURDER RENTS A ROOM

⟫⟩⟩ ⟪⟨⟨

THE CRIMSON FEATHER

COACHWHIP PUBLICATIONS
COACHWHIPBOOKS.COM

COACHWHIP PUBLICATIONS
CoachwhipBooks.com

MURDER A LA MODE

ELEANORE KELLY SELLARS

CLASSIC RED BADGE PRIZE MYSTERY

MURDER
IN TEXAS

Ada E. Lingo

"The story of a big-time murder in a small town, with the atmosphere of a hard-boiled newspaper office, a background of 'hot oil' and sudden gushers, and the intensity of a Texas heat wave."

www.ingramcontent.com/pod-product-compliance
Lightning Source LLC
Chambersburg PA
CBHW032227010726
47494CB00002B/383